THE *fortunate* SON

AIMEE NICOLE WALKER

THE
fortunate
SON

chapter
ONE

Tires crunching on gravel pulled Ivan's attention away from building a beehive. His newest queen was due to arrive next weekend, and he wanted to be sure her castle was good enough to suit Her Royal Highness. Happy bees produced unrivaled liquid gold, and the many awards and ribbons Redemption Ridge had won validated his logic. His ambitious goals were within his grasp, and the newest hive should see him across the finish line. Ivan's competitive streak had been present since birth, but he would've laughed himself silly if someone had told him he'd someday be more passionate about making honey than playing football. But it was true as hell. Nothing made him happier than researching better ways to keep his bees safe and make the hives sustainable while producing the highest quality honey.

Fuck, I need a life, and I need to get laid. Probably the same damn thing, but he'd settle for one at the moment.

With one last glance at the hive, Ivan headed out of the barn to greet Kieran and Finley. Word had cycled through the ranch that Kieran's auto-theft conviction had been overturned. Ivan was eager to help them celebrate, though he had to plaster a grumpy expression on his face so Kieran didn't realize he'd won Ivan's favor. He enjoyed keeping Kieran on his toes to ensure the guy treated Finley with the respect he deserved. He'd once had a major crush on Finley, the blond horse trainer who stole everyone's hearts upon introduction. Ivan had thought his adoration was love once, but it only took seeing Kieran and Finley together to fully understand that he hadn't stood a snowball's chance in hell. Those two were made for one another, and Ivan loved Finley like a dear friend. The realization hadn't eased the loneliness gripping Ivan's heart, but getting over the disappointment was easier knowing his friend was so happy.

A glance to the right revealed a somber-looking gray sedan with government plates instead of Finley's truck. Ivan quickly recognized the car belonged to Cash's FBI buddy, Agent Nick Scott. Well, Special Agent in Charge now, whatever the hell that meant. Ivan had never cared for the slick guy, but Cash trusted him. If he were honest, he suspected his mentor's feelings ran deeper than friendship, but it wasn't Ivan's place to poke his nose into Cash's business. He owed everything to Cash Sweeney, and prying felt disloyal, a trait no one would ever associate with Ivan Gallagher. He kept his gait nice and steady as he crossed the yard toward the gathered group, noting Cash wasn't among them.

From his periphery, Ivan saw the driver's side door open, and he turned his head just enough to confirm the visitor was Nick Scott. But something was off about the man. Ivan continued forward but glanced in Nick's direction again. His posture was less erect and more slouched. He didn't quite remind Ivan of a scolded dog, but there was a rounded hunch in Nick's shoulders that wasn't usually present. Was this an official visit? Cash could've invited him to the cookout since he'd helped to bring down the auto-theft ring, which had spawned Kieran's exoneration. But no. Nick's demeanor was off for a friendly visit.

The fed ducked down and looked back inside the car, diverting Ivan's attention there too. Sunlight glinted off the windshield so he couldn't see who was sitting in the passenger seat, but it felt like the person's interest centered on Ivan. Maybe his imagination was working overtime, but he'd swear he felt the weight of the person's stare. Nick's lips moved, but Ivan couldn't hear what he said until he barked out something that sounded like, "Rory!"

Ivan reached the edge of the gathering under the tent and turned his full attention to the sedan. The passenger door swung open, and a man of medium height stepped out of the vehicle. He had dark hair, a trimmed beard, tan skin, and light eyes zeroed in on Ivan. So it hadn't been his imagination. The stranger, Rory perhaps, curved his lips into a sly smile as they continued to stare at one another. Ivan hadn't fabricated the man's interest before, and there was no mistaking it now.

Something responded deep in his belly, an ignored urge unfurling and awakening. The stranger was stunning, and he fucking knew it. Five months had passed since the last time Ivan had used his Grindr app, and it was starting to take a toll on his body. Thankfully, he had business meetings in Denver in a week, and he'd get ample opportunity to find a hookup. He imagined spotting someone like this guy at a bar or night club and walking over to introduce himself. Ivan could buy him a drink, lead him to a dark corner, and tell the sexy stranger what he wanted to do with his pretty mouth, among other things. They could leave together without finishing their drinks and head some place close. Ivan would keep every dirty promise he'd made in the dark. And if it was as good as Ivan pictured in his brain, they would start from the top and do it all over again at least one more time before parting ways.

But that side of Ivan only existed in his fantasies. He would find a horny guy looking for a hookup on the app, bend him over, and fuck out his frustration until they were both spent. Then he'd dress and leave. The encounter wouldn't vanquish Ivan's loneliness, but it would smooth the edges until the ache became too great to ignore once again. Kind of like the need now pulsing below his belt and gathering steam the longer he stared at the beautiful stranger who'd just arrived at the ranch.

Look away, idiot. This isn't a bar, and your crew is watching.

The reminder should've been enough to make Ivan look away, but he continued staring into mesmerizing blue eyes that enticed him to be the brave man in his fantasies. A quick glance at Agent Scott revealed a man who looked on the edge of losing his cool with his sidekick. The entire situation was puzzling. "Who the hell is that?" Ivan thought he'd asked in his head until Dylan, his best friend and the ranch's K9 trainer, chuckled and slapped him on the shoulder.

Ivan had been too entranced by the dark-haired stranger and the evocative fantasy he'd imagined to even notice Dylan had moved to stand beside him. When Ivan stepped out of the barn, his buddy was flipping something on the grill while chatting with Harry, the ranch's domestic goddess, Finley's older sister, and the object of Dylan's desire.

"I was about to ask you the same thing," Dylan said, giving Ivan an exaggerated once-over. "I hardly recognized you." He lifted his hand and messed up Ivan's freshly styled hair. "You said you were getting a haircut at lunch. You said nothing about going for a new look. The fade looks nice and tight and so does your chin bush. I like it."

Ivan stepped away and used his fingers to fix the strands Dylan messed up. He resisted running his hands over his shorter beard. He'd asked Danielle to tidy it, but she'd shorn a few inches off the length. Ivan's sideburns and cheek lines looked sharp enough to cut glass. He'd asked her to shake things up and had given her free rein, and he'd loved the results. Ivan had left the barbershop feeling great about himself, but Dylan's comments made him feel self-conscious and maybe a little foolish. Who had he been trying to impress? "Then stop finger-fucking it," he groused. "Let me have nice hair for a few hours." There was no way in hell he'd ever get it to look this good again. "Danielle used a round brush and a blow dryer to style the swoop on the top. I can't replicate that."

Dylan rolled his eyes. "*Can't* really isn't a word in your vocabulary."

"I just said it."

Unfazed, Dylan said, "You could learn to style your hair like that if you wanted to, but you don't, so you won't."

Ivan appreciated the vote of confidence, but it looked like too much trouble. Not only would he have to dry and style the top simultaneously, he'd have to put a product in it to finish the look. Danielle had sent him home with a jar of something that looked like painter's putty, but he didn't intend to use it. "It would require a lot of wrist action."

Dylan snorted and leaned closer. "And you're saving up your strength for other things."

Ivan chuckled and elbowed his friend. "Shut up, man."

"I get it," Dylan said. He darted a glance in Harry's direction and released a forlorn sigh that made Ivan's heart hurt. "Trust me, I do. I'm just saying you could totally pull this hairstyle off. Great look by the way."

"Thanks," Ivan said, suddenly feeling shy.

He looked back toward the newcomers and discovered the dark-haired man was still staring at him, but then again, he'd already known it. Ivan couldn't recall another time he'd been so aware of another person, let alone a perfect stranger. A dark flush stained the man's cheeks. Was it hunger? Shame? A darted glance between Dylan and Ivan and he understood, though he couldn't explain how. This guy, Rory, was jealous of their interaction or at least irritated by it. *Possessive.* He'd misread Dylan's familiarity as something more intimate, but he couldn't be more wrong. What right did this interloper have to feel possessive about Ivan? And why the hell did he want to cross the divide between them and clear the air?

Ivan took an involuntary step back. Then another. He willed his feet to still, to not surrender his ground. The stranger took two steps forward and ran into Agent Scott's forearm when he swung it up in front of him like a crossing gate. When Rory turned to argue with the federal agent, it broke their eye contact, and Ivan felt like someone had lifted a weight off his chest. The two men looked as if they were about to throw fists when Cash exited the house and approached them at a fast pace.

"This is getting very interesting," Dylan said. "There's something kind of familiar about the guy with Agent Scott, but I can't place him." He narrowed his eyes and pursed his lips as he studied them. "If I didn't know better, I'd say these guys argue like family. Only an older brother would block you from introducing yourself—ass first—to the sexy dude you've been eye-fucking for ten minutes."

Had they really stood there that long? "Hardy har har," Ivan said dryly. "For someone so astute, how is it you haven't noticed the woman you've been pining over for years returns your feelings?"

"Bullshit," Dylan said, though he cast a glance in Harry's direction. The stunning redhead was talking to her mother and stepfather, Hope and Gary Newton.

"Dude, she's made your favorite dishes for the past ten dinners in a row," Ivan replied. Then he turned his attention back to the gathering across the driveway in time to see Cash approach the duo. The rancher stopped and assessed Nick with a puzzled expression on his face before closing the distance and hugging his friend. Cash had noticed there wasn't something quite right about Nick Scott too.

"The way to a man's heart is through his stomach, I hear," Ivan said. *Not that anyone made that kind of effort for him.* His best friend made a noncommittal noise he barely registered when Cash hugged Rory instead of shaking his hand. The smile on Cash's face indicated Rory was someone his mentor knew well and liked a lot. Agent Scott's expression was unreadable except for his tightly clinched jaw as he too watched the interaction. Something unfamiliar and unwelcome gripped Ivan's heart with icy tentacles. Did his eyes burn with the same intensity Rory's had when he'd assumed things about his relationship with Dylan?

Surely not. Dylan's deep guffaw said surely yes. *Son of a bitch.* The quicker these guys left, the sooner he could get on with his day and put this incident behind him. But Cash gestured for Nick and Rory to follow him inside the large ranch house, and Ivan got a gut feeling the trouble was just getting started. Cash and Nick led the way, chatting like usual, leaving the troublemaker to follow behind at a leisurely pace. Nothing in his gait showed distress or concern. His posture, demeanor, and stride screamed troublemaking brat as did the cute little five-finger waggle he sent in Ivan's direction.

"Dude wants in your pants," Dylan said.

Ivan turned away from the sexy distraction to glare at his friend. "What's wrong with you?"

"Me?" Dylan asked in disbelief. "What's wrong with you? I could distract everyone so you could give your future friend a private tour and—" His words died at Ivan's glare. "Just helping my buddy out. It's been *months* since you went away for a weekend to *recharge*."

"I'm well aware of how long it's been. Maybe you should worry about yourself." A light blush stole across Dylan's cheeks, and Ivan studied his friend closer. The longer he stared, the pinker Dylan's cheeks got. "Wait a minute." He darted a glance toward Harry, who was blissfully unaware of his scrutiny. "Are you telling me what I think you're telling me?"

Dylan cleared his throat and darted a nervous glance in Harry's direction. "I'm not *telling* you anything."

"Which says everything I need to know." Guys talked about their conquests until they met someone special. Then they clammed up and apparently blushed like a virgin at a strip club. He wouldn't pry, even if he was dying to. Ivan placed a hand on Dylan's shoulder and said, "I'm happy for you." He couldn't keep his smirk from spreading into a wolfish smile. "And now the nightly ode to Dylan makes sense."

His friend's face went from blushing pink to beet red, and he hastily excused himself to check on the grill. "Shut up," he snarled when Ivan waggled his brows.

Dylan and Harry, huh? *Finally*. It had been more than a year in the making, and he couldn't understand what had taken them so long. He watched his friend pass Harry and her parents and caught the way his hand brushed against the small of her back and how she leaned into his touch. The sigh that escaped Ivan's lips sounded just as pitiful as the one Dylan had released earlier. That gave Ivan pause. Why had his friend sounded like a lovesick puppy? The answer came swiftly. Dylan wanted to tell the world Harry was his, but one of them—or maybe both—had decided it wasn't the right time yet.

Ivan's cell phone vibrated in his pocket before he could give the pair more thought. He retrieved it and saw the text was from Cash, requesting Ivan's presence in his office. He groaned, then tapped out a quick response to let the boss know he was on his way. Ivan returned his phone to his pocket and headed toward the house. Apparently, the business with Agent Scott and his guest involved Ivan or at least the ranch. Cash looked surprised to see Nick and Rory, so this had to be something else. But what? Witness protection? Nah. That type of arrangement would've come from a US Marshal, and they wouldn't stash a witness among convicted felons—reformed or not.

"Hey," Dylan called out as Ivan passed by. "You get called in there?"

"Yeah. Cash didn't say why."

Dylan pursed his lips. "New guy?"

"Don't think so. He didn't mention anything about a new recruit to me earlier, and all the cabins are full." Whatever was going on in Cash's office spelled big trouble.

"Keep me posted," Dylan said.

"Will do."

Dread tightened Ivan's body with each step he took closer to the house. He was wound like a coiled spring when he entered the grandiose foyer with the huge wrought iron chandelier hanging overhead. Familiar laughter echoed from down the hall, and Ivan headed toward the sound. Clearly, Cash wasn't distressed about the subject of Nick's visit. His office was on the other side of the home, so he had to navigate the long corridor that led to the rear of the house. He turned left once he reached the great room and kitchen area, then slammed to a stop. They had left Rory to his own devices in the kitchen, and he was rummaging through a bowl of fruit on the counter.

Rory leaned against the counter with the same lackadaisical negligence as he walked, like he didn't have a care in the entire world. It felt like a weird thing to think. Was he now judging people by the way they walked and leaned against a counter? Irritation prickled Ivan's skin and made the hair on his arms stand at attention. Yeah, that's what he was going with. Irritation, not desire. Once again, Ivan's feet seemingly moved of their own volition, leading him closer to the kitchen and not the hallway that would take him to Cash's office.

Ivan had known Rory's eyes were light, but he wasn't prepared for the exact shade of blue. He couldn't even put a name to the color. Icy didn't seem right. That would be cold, and Rory's irises burned with an intensity that stole his breath. Realistically, Ivan knew this man couldn't see through him or read his mind, but Rory's penetrating stare still made him want to wipe his thoughts clean and maybe squirm a little. Ivan Gallagher didn't squirm for anyone, especially not the stranger who languidly brought an apple to his smirking lips. Rory had tousled hair that looked like he'd just gotten out of bed, but Ivan suspected it took a lot of effort to achieve the style. Ivan would bet Rory had some of the painter's putty stuff Danielle had given him earlier. Rory's beard looked trendy and soft unlike his fuller "chin bush" as Dylan called it. Ivan would also lay money that this guy took a lot of time and care to keep his beard looking that way. Probably used beard oil and shit. The dark bristles drew Ivan's gaze to Rory's lush mouth. There was so much he could do to and with those soft-looking pink lips. He watched, transfixed, as they parted to reveal pearly white teeth. Rory tore away a chunk of apple with a loud crunch.

Lips wet with juice moved slowly as Rory chewed, never taking his gaze away from Ivan's. It felt like they communicated nothing and everything in their silent stare-down. What the hell was happening, and why had Ivan taken two more steps toward the man? The urge to palm Rory's neck and lick the juice from his lips was enough to stop him in his tracks. Maybe his expression gave away his intentions because the minx before him made a big production of sticking the tip of his tongue out and swiping it over his lips. He was temptation personified; the snake in the Garden of Eden.

Ivan's chest expanded and grew tight as his earlier thoughts returned. If they'd been at a bar, club, or even a sandwich shop, he would make the move that Rory's daring gaze encouraged. This wasn't any of those places, and Ivan didn't have the luxury of bringing them both to the pinnacle of pleasure before walking away. This was his home and workplace, and he kept his business clean. That had been the primary reason he'd never told Finley how he'd felt about him. It was a damn good thing too because it would've gotten horribly messy.

"That bad, huh?" Rory asked. His voice was cultured and slow.

"The worst."

Rory smiled as he lifted the apple to his lips again. He paused before taking a bite. "Gird your loins because you haven't seen any-thing yet."

The remark didn't sound threatening; it was more like a carnal challenge Ivan didn't want to resist. Cash appeared seemingly out of nowhere before he could take another step or utter a response.

"There you are." Cash's tone was too bright for Ivan's liking, and he turned toward his boss. "I see you've met Rory."

"No, we haven't been introduced," Ivan told him.

"Well, let me fix that," Cash said, gesturing to the stranger in the kitchen. "Rory Snyder, this is my foreman, Ivan Gallagher."

Turning around, it shocked Ivan to see Rory was standing im-mediately in front of him. He hadn't known the guy could move so fast, but then again, he knew nothing about him. *Except that he was trouble.* He'd bet his next paycheck on it. Ivan extended his hand to-ward Rory because his good manners required him to reciprocate the gesture. Rory kept his apple in his left hand and wrapped the fingers of his right around Ivan's. Electricity sparked between them, and Ivan would've recoiled if Rory hadn't tightened his grip.

"Ivan," Rory purred. "The perfect name for a conqueror."

Ivan politely tried to free his hand to stop the heat from expand-ing beyond his arm. The last thing he needed was a raging hard-on in Cash's kitchen. But Rory held firm, even sidled closer as he raked a sa-lacious gaze over Ivan's body.

"Not a conqueror." Ivan's voice was as low as usual but with added gravel to give it texture. He cleared his throat, tugged his hand free, and unwittingly closed his fingers around his palm to hold on to the sensation a little longer.

Rory's pale blue eyes didn't miss a thing, and his gaze lingered on Ivan's fist until Ivan unfurled his fingers. "Pity," Rory replied. "I'd love to draw you a map to a region that could use a good pillaging."

Cash laughed, and Ivan nearly choked on his saliva as delicious images formed in his mind. If this little minx wasn't on the ranch, he'd take him up on the invitation shimmering in his eyes and rolling off his tongue. "Just a foreman," Ivan said, hoping to vanquish the spell Rory Snyder had cast on him.

"I don't think you're *just* anything," Rory said. "I think you could be everything."

Had anyone ever looked at him with so much hunger and possession? Was it genuine or some weird power trip? Approaching footsteps reached Ivan's ears, but he couldn't tear his gaze away from Rory's. What was this man's game?

"What's taking so long?" Nick asked as he joined them in the kitchen.

"Your brother is trying to seduce my foreman," Cash replied. "I think he might be succeeding."

Ivan heard the humor in his mentor's voice and wanted to dispute the claim. He just couldn't get anything to move on his body except his pounding heart and his hardening dick. If this tableau was a scene from a rom-com, the viewer would hear a record scratch as the hero realized what he heard and jerked back to reality. Ivan nearly gave himself whiplash turning to look at Nick and Cash.

"Brother?" he asked before darting a curious glance between Nick and Rory. He couldn't find a shred of similarity between the two men.

"Half brother," Nick offered as an explanation. Rory's visage darkened, and Ivan realized he didn't like that distinction. The air was suddenly heavier with new tension. "Same mother, different fathers."

"Ah," Ivan said as if that explained it all. It didn't clear up anything. "And you need me here to settle a family dispute?" He'd hoped to inject a little humor into the situation.

"Not exactly," Cash said.

Nick glanced at his watch and scowled. "Mind if we finish this in your office? I need to get back on the road soon."

I, not we. Nick Scott planned to leave Rory at the ranch, but why? There was only one way to find out. Ivan gestured to the hallway. "Lead the way." Nick pivoted and headed back the way he'd come, and Cash quickly followed. Ivan stepped forward but stopped when Rory didn't fall in beside or behind him. The cockiness he'd witnessed before was gone, and a haughty aloofness had taken its place. Ivan quirked a brow. "You're not coming?"

Rory's nostrils flared as life sparked in his eyes once more. "Not yet and preferably not alone."

Ivan shook his head and forced his feet to move. He didn't breathe easily again until he'd put a good fifteen feet between himself and temptation. The relief dissipated as soon as Nick said, "I take it you didn't recognize Rory."

The comment seemed innocuous enough, but it raised the hackles on the back of Ivan's neck. "Should I have?"

"He has a very popular channel on YouTube where he travels the world to explore conservation, cultural preservation, and farming sustainability. I'd love to admit I know what the hell I just said, but I honestly don't have a clue."

Cash chuckled, and Ivan glared. He was familiar with YouTube, of course, but he didn't realize there was much demand for the kind of content Nick mentioned. He thought it was mostly true crime, makeup tutorials, and jackasses pulling pranks and stunts. Ivan ignored the curiosity Nick had sparked and focused on getting to the bottom of the meeting. "And he wants to feature Redemption Ridge?"

"Well, that wasn't the initial reason we came to the ranch," Nick replied.

"But I decided to capitalize on the unique opportunities Rory brings," Cash added.

Ivan shifted his gaze between them, feeling like Nick and Cash were tag teaming him. He might look like a hulking ogre, but he was a nice guy with sharp business acumen. What were they trying to hide with their dog and pony show?

"Let's start with the real reason why you brought Rory to the ranch," Ivan said.

Nick's countenance changed before his eyes. Where before he looked a little haggard, now he looked scared. What the fuck was going on?

"Rory Snyder is the only son of Charles Snyder, candidate for governor," Cash said.

Ivan got a sinking feeling in his stomach. There'd been a lot of talk about the man's run for office. He was embroiled in a hotly

contested primary run for his party. Neither Charles nor his main opponent would be Ivan's first or even fifth choice for governor, so he
hadn't paid much attention to the controversy. He'd shaken his head
over the headlines and moved on, but it seemed the billionaire candidate's troubles were about to become Ivan's. "Fuck," he groaned.

"Rory's personal life has become weaponized against Charles. I
guess they figure Rory is fair game since he's a successful influencer
and a public figure in his own right. Every day brings a more salacious headline than the one before with Rory's private life at the center. Someone with inside knowledge has fed these stories to the press,
who then exaggerate and sensationalize the details that get them more
clicks and views. None of them give a fuck about the toll this has
taken on my brother or the danger it's put him in. Charles's team is
in charge of finding the leaks and neutralizing them. I'm in charge of
keeping Rory safe." At Ivan's frown, Nick rolled his eyes. "I said neu-
tralize, not extinguish."

"Rory was accosted last night after leaving a restaurant," Cash
said gently. "A belligerent man shouted homophobic slurs at him.
When Rory didn't immediately back down, the guy took a swing at
him. He's scrappier than he might seem and avoided getting hit, but
the confrontation shifted from the sidewalks to the streets when the
man aggressively pursued Rory in his car. He ended up running a red
light and narrowly missed getting T-boned to get away from the assailant. Charles convinced Rory to file an official report with the po-
lice so it could be investigated as a hate crime. In the meantime, I need
to tuck my brother away someplace no one will look for him. The
media frenzy is getting out of hand. Charles had to deploy a decoy to
pull the vultures away long enough for me to squirrel Rory away. He
also planted a false story that Rory was heading to South America to
work with sustainable coffee growers. So I brought my brother to the
person I trust most in this world." Nick glanced at Cash, who gave
him the dopey smile he reserved for his best friend.

Ivan was completely sympathetic to Rory's situation, but he suspected there was more to the story. "Why can't Rory stay with you or
a friend?"

"Rory doesn't know who he can trust right now, aside from the people in this room." Ivan wanted to point out that Rory didn't know him and therefore couldn't trust Ivan would have his best interest at heart. But Nick knew damn well that Ivan wouldn't be there if Cash didn't trust him, so he extended his faith to those living on the ranch by proxy. Nick took a deep breath and said, "And Rory can't stay with me because I'm heading to DC for meetings, followed by a teaching stint at Quantico. I'll be gone for a few months."

Cash's steely blue gaze darkened with concern. "When were you going to tell me that part?"

"I'm telling you now," Nick replied.

Cash sighed heavily as he turned his attention to Ivan, and he could tell by the determination in Cash's expression that he'd made up his mind. "I'm not asking your permission. Rory is staying here with us." He looked at his friend. "Though I would've done so without you cashing in your last remaining favor."

Nick smiled and said, "I have a feeling I'm going to owe you quite a few by the time this situation is resolved."

The many reasons this wouldn't work burst across Ivan's mind like fireworks on Independence Day, and he spat them out of his mouth as soon as they occurred to him. The thoughts were random and didn't discharge in any particular order. "We don't have any room. This is a working ranch, not witness protection. Spring is the busiest season for us. I don't have patience for spoiled brats unless they're my cats. The ranch doesn't need to get embroiled in political madness." Each objection came out in rapid succession like gunfire. *Pop, pop, pop, pop, pop.* Cash just grinned with each new grievance while his bestie looked bored.

"Seems to me you could use another set of hands if the ranch is so busy this time of year," Nick added. "Cash mentioned the ranch is transitioning toward sustainable practices under your guidance. Seems to me you and Rory have that in common. He might be able to offer some insight from his travels."

"The cabins are all full, but Rory could use one of my guest bedrooms."

"No," Nick said a little too harshly. Ivan bit back a smile because it was obvious to him Nick didn't want the sassy minx staying under Cash's roof. He'd always suspected the men had deeper feelings for each other. They were either ignorant of the shared attraction or had chosen to ignore it. Nick cleared his throat and ran his finger under his shirt collar. "I had a long talk with Rory on the way here. He knows this isn't a vacation, and I want you to work him like you would anyone else employed on the ranch. To keep Rory completely off the grid, he can't access his bank accounts or credit cards. I've given him some money, but he'll need to earn his keep on the ranch. I think he's looking forward to the challenge."

Ivan knew better than to judge a book by its cover, but he doubted Rory was eager to get his hands dirty. The threat of a media storm surrounding the ranch sent him spiraling back through time to a point in his life he never wanted to relive. The mere thought stole his breath and dulled his hearing from the rush of blood in his veins.

That is until Cash said, "There's a spare bedroom at the old homestead. It's a bit cramped but serviceable."

Ivan fought off a shiver. Sharing a house with that walking, talking temptation? Not a good idea.

A smug smile crept across the fed's face. "Just what he needs." He met Ivan's gaze head-on. "Rory could benefit from someone riding his ass when he gets out of line. I think you're the man for the job."

Ivan nearly choked on his own saliva as Nick's words took on a different sort of connotation. Cash must've read his mind because his lips twitched as he fought off a smile. Ivan ignored him and addressed Nick with a glib, "No pressure."

Cash had already made his decision without Ivan's input, and trying to change his mind would be a colossal waste of time and energy. Cash owed Nick some kind of favor, and Nick was settling the score…at Ivan's expense.

All Ivan could think about was the way his skin tingled when he and Rory had touched and the sensation that Rory could see his deepest yearnings by just staring into his eyes. Ivan needed to make a last-ditch effort to avoid a catastrophe, but it came out louder than he'd intended. "This is bullshit, Cash. Why does you paying up a favor become my problem?"

His mentor stroked two fingers over his salt-and-pepper beard while trying to find the words to appease Ivan. He might as well save his breath. Nothing he could say would make this okay...until it did. "Rory needs us, Ivan. If you could view him through an objective lens, you'd see it too. You've always trusted my judgment, though you have questioned it occasionally." Cash quirked a brow, daring him to challenge the claim. They both knew Ivan couldn't and wouldn't, so the rancher chuckled and continued. "Have I been wrong about any of the people I've taken a chance on?"

The conversation reminded Ivan of the gentle scoldings his father had doled out to his young sons. His ears heated now as they'd done then. God, he missed the man so much. "No, sir."

"Trust me now, Ivan. Please."

He owed Cash Sweeney everything. They'd met through the agriculture program at Arrowhead Correctional Institute. Ivan had been a bitter man, believing he'd been forsaken by those he loved and trusted. He didn't want to like Cash because he reminded Ivan of the large commercial conglomerates that were buying up all the smaller family farms. Cash had proved him wrong with his unwavering patience. The mentoring hadn't stopped once Ivan left jail and joined the ranch, and Ivan owed everything to the man. And just maybe this favor would settle a little of the debt he owed Cash.

"Fine, but I'm not happy about it," he said, then turned to Nick. "And now you owe me. Big time."

Nick stared him down and didn't acknowledge Ivan's ludicrous claim with so much as a raised brow. Ivan stomped out of the office without another word. What the hell was he supposed to do with an entitled rich brat when he had a ranch to run? A replay of dirty images scrolled through his mind. *Ride his ass, indeed.* Ivan corralled his wayward thoughts by the time he reached the kitchen.

Rory was still in the same spot and still working on the same apple, though it looked like he'd taken a few more bites. Kieran was in the kitchen too, and it appeared that Ivan had interrupted a conversation. He was too keyed up to acknowledge Kieran or even congratulate him on his exoneration. Rory's expression was inscrutable as if he'd braced for the worst, and Ivan took Cash's suggestion and really looked at him. It was hard to get past his handsome face and apathetic facade to find the vulnerability the man hid. When Ivan did, it only irritated him more because he didn't want to feel anything for Rory but annoyance.

"You," Ivan barked as he jabbed a finger in Rory's direction. "Come now." He realized his mistake the instant Rory waggled his brows and actually purred in the kitchen.

"Yes, Daddy," he simpered.

Heat engulfed Ivan's body. He wanted to claim it was from fury, but he couldn't form the lie, even for his own benefit, so he spun around and stomped out of the room.

chapter TWO

THE BIG MOUNTAIN OF MUSCLE DOTH PROTEST TOO LOUDLY, EVEN if it was presented as stomping away from the conversation. Rory wasn't really into the whole daddy thing, but it was sure fun as hell to rile people up. His brother had cringed when he'd applied the label to Cash when the silver fox had headed in their direction, but Rory suspected Ivan's reaction had nothing to do with disgust. The guy reminded him of a Viking with his broad shoulders, narrow waist, and thick thighs. He wore his auburn hair in a fade with closely shorn sides and longer strands on top. The Viking's beard was a darker red, and Rory wanted to know what the rest of his body hair looked like. He'd bet the hunk was furry in all the right places too. Christ, the man was even sexier up close. Amber eyes the color of expensive whiskey assessed him in a way that made Rory feel vulnerable. He couldn't have that and decided to regain the upper hand with outrageous flirting.

Ivan. His name, build, and dark scowl belonged to a conqueror as he'd said, but his soft voice belonged to someone gentler like a scholar. Would his touch be rough and firm or soft and teasing? A Viking-sexual such as he could hope for both. Fascinated by the dichotomy, Rory was eager to follow the man who held his fate at the ranch in the palm of his enormous hand, but first he turned his attention to the dark-haired hottie who'd entered the kitchen in time to overhear Ivan shouting his displeasure about having Rory foisted on him to settle a debt between Cash and Nick.

Dark brown eyes had studied Rory with unabashed curiosity. "Who are you?"

"I'm the favor."

Before they could get further into their introductions, Ivan stormed into the kitchen and barked orders for Rory to come on demand. Hell, he'd been sporting a semi since his gaze snagged on Ivan the Ripped, so he probably wouldn't require much stimulation to comply. The dark-haired hottie in the kitchen introduced himself as Kieran once they were alone again and shook his hand.

"I'm Rory."

"Don't worry about Ivan. His bark is worse than his bite."

Rory smiled for the first time since Nick had bid him to stay in the kitchen and let the grown-ups talk. Maybe he hadn't uttered those exact words, but his tone had implied it, and Rory would still be pissed if not for the opportunity to get to know Ivan better. "Let's hope not," he said. "See you around, Kieran."

Rory ambled in the direction Ivan had gone, not bothering to hasten his steps. The sexy ginger would be hard to miss. He pushed open the front door and nearly walked into a gorgeous blond guy with green eyes. Christ. Were they all gorgeous on the ranch? This guy looked like a model with his square jaw and sharp cheekbones.

"Oh, hello," the man said in a soft Southern drawl. "I was looking for Kieran."

Rory noticed Ivan's long strides had created an enormous gap between them, so he didn't stop to introduce himself. "In the kitchen," he tossed over his shoulder.

"Thank you."

Rory lifted his hand to wave and continued his slow and steady gait. Ivan headed into the original homestead, so he detoured to Nick's car. Rory wanted to grab his bag and guitar before his brother could speed off with his stuff or toss it onto the driveway in his haste to leave his little brother behind. The bag felt awfully light for an indefinite stay, and he wished he'd asked more questions before he packed. Nick had stormed into his condo that morning and demanded he pack a bag in thirty minutes, and Rory had been too rattled after the previous night's close call to ask much. He'd pulled down his Louis Vuitton weekender bag and shoved a week's worth of clothes inside along with a shaving kit packed with personal hygiene products and his skin care and beard regimen. Looking as pretty as he did wasn't cheap or easy. He'd added his laptop, recording equipment, and grabbed his prize possession—his granddaddy's guitar. He'd been meaning to relearn how to play it, and hanging out on a ranch seemed like the perfect setting.

Rory felt the attention of everyone gathered under the tent as he continued toward the smaller home. He was used to the scrutiny and didn't let it ruffle his feathers. Rory would allow them to do a lot worse than stare if they shared whatever food was putting out the delicious aroma tickling his senses. He briefly debated heading toward the tent to introduce himself and curry favor with the grill master but followed his dick instead of his stomach.

When he reached the old house, Rory wondered if he should knock first or open the door. Ivan, though sexy, wasn't the least bit hospitable or welcoming, so he let himself inside the residence. His Viking stood in the center of a tidy if outdated but comfortable-looking living room. The place screamed bachelor pad with the mismatched brown furniture, but the couch facing the fireplace looked like a fabulous place to curl up and read a book. Ivan had struck a power pose with hands on hips, chest out, and shoulders back as he waited for Rory's full attention. *Not a conqueror, my ass.* Three cats sat at his feet, staring up at him like he was the next coming of Christ, and Rory understood their worship.

"Who are your little darlings?"

Ivan looked at the cats, who all chorused a pleading *meow*. "It's not dinnertime," he told them. The felines replied with a protest and all rose on their hind legs to place their front paws on his legs. "Spoiled brats." Ivan leaned down and scratched a tabby cat behind its ears. "This is Scruffy." He moved to the butterscotch-colored cat next and smoothed his hand over its back. "This is Candy." Aptly named. Ivan leaned down and picked up a small black and white cat. "And this man is Tux." He scratched the little guy under his chin before gently setting him back down. He opened the arm rest of a brown recliner, pulled out a pouch of treats, and doled out a few to each of the cats. Christ, could this man get any more delicious? Once they were occupied and the treats stowed once more, Ivan turned his attention back to Rory. "We need to get something straight."

"Yes," Rory agreed. He dropped his Louis Vuitton on a corduroy club chair and gently set his guitar case down on the rustic woven area rug. "What do I call you if conqueror and Daddy aren't permissible options?" The big man's cheeks turned red again but not quite dark enough to signal an impending stroke. He probably should've eased up on the guy, but high emotion tended to entice his inner brat to the surface. Rory's stress eased a little more with each reaction he evoked from this yummy man. "I've started thinking of you as Ivan the Ripped." Rory quirked a brow to encourage a response but only received a scowl in return. *God, who knew that could be so sexy?* "Okay, that's a no. How about sir?"

"No," the big man growled. "Just call me Ivan."

"Mr. Gallagher if I'm nasty?"

Ivan didn't show if he recognized the Janet Jackson reference. Maybe he wasn't as obsessed with the '80s radio station on Pandora as Rory was. His mama had loved the era and always played music while working in the kitchen. Ivan pivoted and walked away, not offering an explanation or even a simple *kiss my ass*. He disappeared down a hallway between the kitchen and the staircase to the second story. "Come."

Ivan's soft voice gained some grit and gruff when irritated, and it was so sexy Rory pressed the palm of his hand to his lengthening dick. "Easy boy. We'll replay that when we're alone later."

Rory inhaled deeply and sauntered after Ivan. The big man was easy to find since there was only one room with a light on at the end of the hall. Room was a stretch. The space was half the size of his closet back home. There was barely enough room for both him and Ivan to be in there at the same time. The oak-paneled walls, planked floors, and ivory ceiling provided either a dull backdrop or a clean palette, depending on a person's opinion. Rory couldn't decide which direction he leaned. The patchwork quilt on the double bed reminded him of the ones his grandma, Eustice Stuart, had sewn by hand until arthritis made it impossible. In fact, the small room reminded him of the one he shared with Nick during the summers spent on their grandparents' farm in Oklahoma. Rory immediately thought of nightly cricket serenades through open windows as he drifted to sleep. He didn't want to think about those happy childhood memories because they made him pine for things he would never have again. Instead, Rory wanted to create a new collection with the gorgeous hunk staring a hole in his head.

He turned and met Ivan's gaze, catching the smug smirk on his face before he wiped it off. Did he expect Rory to be a diva and pitch a fit to demand better lodgings? What the fuck had Nick said to him during their brief meeting? It had to have been bad to make this guy yell like he had. In his heart, Rory knew Nick was trying to do the right thing by him, even if his actions seemed a tad extreme. Then he remembered the man who'd come after him, his face contorted with rage and spittle foaming at his mouth as he hurled nasty slurs at Rory. The dude expected Rory to back down and run, but that wasn't his nature. Rory had returned the volley of insults, and the fight was on. Ducking blows was one thing, but a car chase was something entirely different. A cold sweat broke out on Rory's forehead, ratcheting up his brattiness to higher levels.

Ivan continued to watch him with rapt attention. Bitching about his lodgings and proving Ivan's assessments right would not get him what he wanted. And what he wanted was for his Viking to make him forget all about the madness that existed outside the ranch. He needed to poke the bear and make him uncomfortable enough to shed his reservations and join Rory on the dark side, or… He glanced at the bed again and noted an old metal frame supported the mattress. Would it be sturdy enough to support both of them, or would they need to retreat to Ivan's room?

Rory leaned over, set both hands on the mattress, and gave it a few pushes to test the bounce and stability of the bed. He felt amber eyes boring into his backside and played it up. "Soft yet firm," Rory said. He pushed the mattress harder and smiled to himself when he didn't hear a single squeak. "Quiet and sturdy. Unlike the ones from summer camp. Thank goodness. Do you know how hard it is for a teenager to seduce his summer crush on one of those squeaky-ass things?" Rory shivered hard. "Bunk beds to boot, but one makes do to get the things he wants." He straightened up and faced his Viking. "And I always get what I want."

Ivan swallowed hard. *Score one for the brat.* "You went to summer camp?" he asked.

"Is that really the question you want to ask me, my liege?"

Ivan emitted a sexy little growl from his throat, followed by a cleansing breath. "What will it take for you to call me by my given name?"

Rory smiled seductively and took a few steps forward. Ivan's eyes widened because there was nowhere for him to go, and Rory could hear his gears grinding as he debated just how far Rory would take things. Ivan was several inches taller and at least fifty pounds heavier. He'd have no issues shaking Rory loose, but that wasn't what Rory wanted. When Ivan put his hands on him—and Rory was determined Ivan would— he wanted them to hold Rory close, not push him away.

What Rory truly wanted wasn't something he could buy, coerce, or seduce from Ivan. Though he struggled to put a name to his deepest desire, Rory needed it granted freely and wholeheartedly. So he stopped his forward advance before their bodies touched. "There is something you can do for me."

Ivan chewed on his bottom lip as his amber eyes darkened to the color of a hot toddy, and damn, Rory wanted to drink him down. "Name it." The words sounded like someone had torn them from his soul. Ivan's eyes widened as if they came as a surprise to him too. His lips parted, and Rory knew he was seconds away from retracting his response or replacing it with a reaction that wasn't as genuine.

"Treat me like you would anyone else who comes to work on the ranch," Rory urged softly. "I don't know what Nicky told you about my situation, but it's obvious you've drawn some conclusions about me." Rory offered a wry smile before continuing. "Truth is, I'm probably worse than you've imagined, but I am not a freeloader. I pay my own way."

Ivan's eyes widened, and it was hard to say which one of them was more surprised by Rory's confession. That wasn't at all what he'd planned to say, but there was a softening around the big man's features that encouraged Rory to dial back the attitude and reveal a little more. He opened his mouth and more words tumbled out before he could stop them. "You don't like me, and I get it. Take a number and get in line. Hell, I'm pretty sure I can't stand myself at the moment. But maybe give me a fair shake. I might surprise you." *And maybe even myself.*

Ivan remained silent as he held Rory's gaze, making it impossible to miss the spark of emotion in Ivan's amber eyes. Rory had this eerie sensation that Ivan read him better than anyone he'd ever met, including the brother he adored. The notion was ludicrous, but it still rang true and unsettled Rory in ways he couldn't explain. He probably would've reverted to bratty behavior to reestablish boundaries if a vibrating noise hadn't caught him off guard.

"Excuse me." The big man reached into his front pocket and removed his phone.

"The food is ready. You hungry?"

Ivan's question wasn't the truce he'd asked for, or was it? Rory didn't think he was hungry until he recalled the smells coming from the grill. "Famished."

"Do you want me to find a storage space for the guitar to give you more room in here?"

Rory stepped back and assessed the room once more. "I'll just tuck it under the bed."

Ivan nodded and eased out of the room. "Unfortunately, there's no bathroom on the first floor. There was a half bath down here, but we converted it into a laundry room a few years back. There's a full bathroom upstairs with a shower and a tub. You'll share it with Finley, Dylan, and me, though Fin is rarely here. It's not a huge space, but it's tidy, and we want to keep it that way. We stow our personal hygiene stuff in individual shower kits under the sink to maximize space."

"Understood, and it won't be a problem since I'm a clean freak. Which ones are Finley and Dylan?"

"Finley is the blond guy we passed on the way out of the house. Dylan is the guy who's manning the grill."

"The one who was running his fingers through your hair?" Rory asked.

Ivan stopped suddenly and turned around. It was Rory's turn to take a few steps back in surprise that a big man could move that fast. Ivan scowled at Rory's reaction and eased backward. "Didn't mean to startle you. I sometimes forget my size."

I assure you no one else does, big guy. Rory kept his comment to himself, though he wondered if his expression gave his thoughts away when Ivan scowled.

"Dylan was messing up my new hairstyle. There was nothing romantic in his gesture. His heart belongs to another."

"What a romantic thing to say." Rory changed his impression of Ivan from scholar to poet.

Ivan snorted. "Before you ask, Finley is involved with Kieran."

"The guy from the kitchen? They make a smoking-hot couple."

Ivan's scowl darkened, and Rory rolled his eyes. "What? I can't notice their attractiveness? I'm not here to wreck relationships." When Ivan didn't respond, Rory couldn't resist pushing his luck the tiniest bit. "And what of your heart? Does someone have a claim on it?"

Ivan's cheeks turned a pretty shade of pink. "Many would say I don't have one."

"What do you say?" Rory asked.

"I say it's time to eat before Owen and Tyler devour all the ribs."

Rory ignored the nonanswer and gestured for Ivan to continue out of the house. Ivan acknowledged it with a nod, then turned around.

"Take the weekend to settle in and meet the rest of the crew," Ivan said over his shoulder. "Monday is soon enough for the real work to begin. We'll assess your skills and determine the best fit."

"Sounds like a plan to me," Rory said. He trailed behind Ivan at his normal pace and was pleased that the big man's posture and stride weren't as angry nor did it look like he was trying to escape Rory's presence. He counted that as a victory too.

Rory didn't expect to find the fed-mobile still in the driveway or his brother leaning against the gray sedan with his arms folded over his chest. Like Ivan, Nicky didn't look nearly as tense, and Rory knew it was because his brother had gotten to spend some time with Cash. A breeze kicked up, stirring the overlong hair hanging over Nicky's forehead. Rory couldn't remember a time when his brother had looked so unpolished, and his earlier fears returned.

"I'm going to say goodbye to Nick," Rory called out. Ivan acknowledged him with a wave and continued toward the tent where a banner congratulating Kieran now hung. Rory wondered what it was all about and figured he'd find out soon enough. He veered off to meet his brother, who offered him an amiable smile reminiscent of the old Nicky. Echoes of boyish giggles wrapped around Rory's heart and squeezed. "Figured you'd be long gone by now after dropping me off."

"Cash asked my opinion on some concerns he has about a nearby religious sect that's making trouble. They started targeting the surrounding town but have turned their attention toward the ranch. Apparently, there's been a small outbreak of thefts and vandalism, and the religious leaders have been pointing fingers at the farm felons. Cash fielded a call from a reporter this morning. He categorically denied the allegations and declined further comment."

"Cash is making the same mistakes as Charles's campaign manager. I think he should get out in front of it. You and I both know Cash is a media darling and could easily sway the tone of the conversation."

"Once a brand manager, always a brand manager," Nick said.

Rory's stint in the Snyder Global Industries marketing department had been short but not nearly as contentious as currently portrayed in the media. Charles hadn't heartlessly fired Rory over creative differences, though they had disagreed on every campaign he introduced. Rory had resigned to pursue his own ambitions when it was obvious the corporate life wasn't for him. He'd used every marketing tool he'd gleaned from school and pursued his passion. Rory was very aware of what people thought about his decision to become a conservation influencer. They scoffed at his ambitions, but the joke was on them. With paid sponsor-ships, more than a million subscribers, and weekly videos that garnered hundreds of thousands of views, he regularly banked six figures a month. A career that could be in jeopardy if the media didn't stop dragging his name through the mud. The pressure had also clobbered his creativity, and he struggled to find projects that appealed to him. Rory exhaled his frustration and turned his attention to something productive.

"I could help Cash with the PR."

"You will help him by working on the ranch like everyone else. I'm going to set up an appointment for Cash to speak with people who investigate cults. Not sure Salvation Anew falls under their purview, but Cash feels strongly the organization is heading into cult territory."

He looked at his watch and met Rory's gaze again. "I really do need to get going, but I didn't want to leave without saying goodbye."

Rory put his hands on his hips and narrowed his eyes. "A favor, Nicky? Really?"

"You heard that, huh?"

"Yeah. I wouldn't mind being Ivan's party favor, so maybe I'll let you off the hook."

Nick reached out, hooked an arm around Rory's neck, and pulled him into a hug. "Behave, brat."

"Don't hold your breath," Rory said as he wrapped his arms around Nick's waist. "Christ, you're so skinny." He dropped his arms and stood back so he could look at his brother's face. "Doesn't the Bureau give you lunch breaks?"

Nick rolled his eyes, then rubbed his knuckles over Rory's head. "You sound like Cash." Some things never changed, like Rory pretend-ing he didn't love one ounce of attention his brother gave him. He took a moment to soak it in before he pulled free and feigned a punch to Nick's abdomen. His brother grimaced as he tensed to block the blow that would've never landed. Rory's concern must've registered on his face. "I'm fine, Rory. I've just been working a complicated case that re-sulted in a scuffle a few days ago."

Rory crossed his arms over his chest. "I thought you were in charge now."

"Doesn't mean less work."

Rory swallowed hard. Nick's answers could account for the changes in his brother, but he suspected there was more to it.

"You've got your own problems to deal with," Nick said, cutting off anything else he might've said about the matter. "That's why I stuck around while you harassed Ivan in the small house."

Rory snorted and held up his fingers in the Boy Scout salute. "I promise I was on my best behavior."

"Still think Ivan should sleep with his door locked and one eye open," Nick replied.

Rory shook his head and laughed. "I'm a shameless flirt, but I'm not a creep." A slow smile spread across his face. "If that man ever invites me into his room, I can promise he will never be the same, though."

Nick tipped his head back and laughed. "There's the cocky little bastard I know and love."

Rory shrugged and gave him his expression that said *what can I say?*

Nick sobered after a second, and his expression grew serious. "And I love you, Rory. You'll always be my favorite person on the planet. That's why I brought you here to my second-favorite person." Rory suspected the correct order was actually reversed, but a lump of emotion lodged in his throat, making it impossible for him to speak. "It's doubtful anyone knows you here, and if they do, I think they'll be cool. These are good people, and they'd love to know the real you. Work hard and stay out of trouble."

"I'll do my best to make you proud."

Nick wrapped him in another tight hug. "You always make me proud, baby brother.

Nick pulled back, then reached inside his jacket pocket. He retrieved an iPhone and passed it to Rory. "It's clean. No one can track you. I think it's better if you take this and give me your phone for the time being. I'll tuck it away someplace safe." Nick puffed up his cheeks and exhaled. "Listen, I'm going to be on the East Coast for a few months at least. I have meetings in DC and I'm filling in for a Quantico instructor taking paternity leave. I might be hard to reach at times, but I want to hear from you."

Rory swallowed hard and nodded. "I understand."

"This might feel like the dark period after Mom died when I was away and you were estranged from Charles, but this situation is different. And temporary. Remember that when the demons start to whisper in your ear."

"I will." Rory retrieved his mobile device and willingly swapped them out. Funny how such a simple gesture could be so freeing. Laughter echoed from the tent, pulling Rory's attention in that direction. Everyone seemed to be enjoying one another's company, except for the Viking standing next to the grill with his arms crossed over his chest. Ivan was staring in their direction, but Rory couldn't read his expression over the distance.

"Looks like the gentle giant is making sure everyone doesn't eat all the food before you get there."

Rory figured there was a better explanation, but he didn't want to keep Ivan waiting, just in case. He gave Nick one last hug. "Thanks, Nicky. I love you too." He took a few steps back. "Want me to make you a to-go plate? You look like the tiniest breeze could knock you over."

Nick chuckled and shook his head. "Bye, squirt."

God, he hadn't called Rory that since he was ten or eleven. Strange how something so simple and silly could mean so much. He swallowed hard to clear the lump in his throat. "Bye, Nicky."

Rory turned around and headed toward the tent. He wanted to say he scanned the crowd to gauge his reception, but he only had eyes for Ivan.

chapter
THREE

"**C**AN'T SEEM TO TAKE YOUR EYES OFF THE NEW GUY,**"** Rueben Sanchez said softly from beside Ivan.

He turned his head and met the farrier's curious, soft brown eyes. "Are you here to be closer to the meat when I give the signal, or are you here to charm information out of me?"

A wide smile met his question. "Can't a guy do both?"

Rue had to be the most affable person Ivan had ever met. He'd been quiet and cautious when he'd arrived two years ago but had quickly taken to the ranch and its inhabitants. Rue made it hard to stay grouchy and guarded when faced with his disarming smiles and effervescent personality. The situation with Rory had made him incredibly grumpy for a host of reasons—both the original gripes he'd had when learning why he was there and some new and unnerving ones he didn't want to explore. Ivan glowered until Rue held his hands up in surrender and walked away.

"I tried," he called out to Owen and Tyler, who'd done a poor job of feigning disinterest.

Alone once more, Ivan's thoughts returned to Rory, who slowly ambled toward the tent. His pale blue eyes seemed zeroed in on him, and Ivan couldn't tear his gaze away, no matter how much he willed it. Rory's words from earlier still bounced around in his head.

"You don't like me, and I get it. Take a number and get in line. Hell, I'm pretty sure I can't stand myself at the moment. But maybe give me a fair shake. I might surprise you."

Ivan had lived an existence of self-loathing for longer than he wanted to admit. It had taken a traumatic event, a stint in jail, and Cash's unwavering mentorship to learn to accept himself and build a bridge back to his family after his incarceration. Ivan had no way of knowing how tattered the fabric of Rory's family was, but it was obvious how much Nick loved him. The embrace he'd witnessed between the brothers had touched him deeply and made Ivan reach for his phone. He'd quickly tapped out, *You're an okay guy*, to his younger brother, Innes. He hadn't expected the new father to respond right away, but a text and a photograph came through before he could return the device to his pocket.

Innes was stretched out on the sofa with his newborn daughter peacefully sleeping on his chest. As tired as his brother looked, the megawatt smile on his face broadcast the joy he'd discovered in fatherhood. The text beneath the photo read, *We love you too. Can't wait for you to meet your niece this summer.* Sweet baby Claire had a head full of red hair like her daddy and the cutest chubby cheeks Ivan had ever seen.

Innes had taken the helm at their family's farm two years ago after their father died suddenly. Early spring was a busy time for both of them, so Ivan had planned a long vacation in August. Maybe he could get away for a long weekend before then. He didn't want to miss out on too much of Claire's life.

Or sooner if I can swing it, he replied. *Proud of you.*

Innes replied with a winking emoji and *Right back atcha.*

A commotion in the yard caught his attention. Patsy, Cash's border collie, barked excitedly and raced over to meet Rory before he reached the tent. Ivan judged people by how they treated animals. He expected Rory to be fastidious about his clothes and standoffish about getting dog hair and slobber on him. Instead, the man dropped to his knees and let the dog shower him with kisses between enthusiastic barks.

Patsy put her paws on his knee and wriggled closer until he wrapped his arms around her for a hug.

Cash put two fingers in his mouth and whistled sharply. Rory dropped his arms, and the dog darted back to her master. Patsy was a brilliant dog and an excellent judge of character. Ivan wouldn't admit it out loud, but Patsy had convinced him of Kieran's good nature before anyone else had. She'd taken to him during K9 training at Arrowhead and had showered him with devotion when he arrived at the ranch last year. Even the most cantankerous horse in the stable had warmed up to Kieran, so Ivan had known there was goodness there. He'd just been slow to admit it because of jealousy. He smirked at his own stupidity.

Rory rose to his feet and continued toward the tent, but this time, he seemed to assess his reception from the others instead of seeking Ivan. Something about this guy triggered Ivan's protective instincts. He itched to intercede but maintained his position by the grill. If Rory was going to fit in, he'd have to make the effort. Ivan was curious if he'd get flirty with the others or if he'd saved the act just for him. Recalling the heat shimmering in Rory's blue eyes made it hard to convince himself it was all a ruse. But doing so would be best for Ivan's peace of mind, so he'd just have to try harder.

Cash stepped forward when Rory reached the tent and placed a hand on the younger man's shoulder. A low growl formed in his throat, but Ivan subdued the sound before it escaped his mouth. What the hell was his problem? It seemed protectiveness wasn't the only unwelcome emotion the troublemaker sparked. Rory glanced in Ivan's direction, and a slight smile tugged at his lips as if he'd somehow heard the possessive reaction. He just as quickly diverted his full attention to Cash as he introduced Rory to the others.

One by one, the crew politely greeted Rory and Cash as they moved closer to where he stood. Ivan saw recognition on several of their faces and guardedness on others. He hoped Cash knew what the hell he was doing because he risked messing up the chemistry on the ranch with this stunt. The last cluster of people between Rory and him were Finley, Kieran, and Finley's family.

"Hello again," Kieran said to Rory as they shook hands.

"Not sure what you're celebrating, but congratulations," Rory told him.

Finley placed his hand on Kieran's shoulder and said, "A judge overturned Kieran's conviction today." He punctuated the statement by kissing his boyfriend's cheek.

He watched Rory closely for his reaction to Finley's remark. Had Nick or Cash told the man he'd landed on a ranch mostly comprised of convicted felons? If he was surprised, he didn't let it show.

"That's definitely something worth celebrating," he said before moving to shake Finley's hand. "Sorry I didn't introduce myself earlier when I nearly ran you over." Rory tipped his head in Ivan's direction. "I was trying to keep up with Ivan."

"No problem," Finley said. "It's good to meet you." Finley wasn't as skilled at hiding his reaction. "I really like your YouTube channel."

"Thank you," Rory said. "I'm a fan of your cheek bones."

"Good genetics as you'll soon see," Finley said. He introduced Rory to his sister, Harry, who kept the crew well fed and Cash's house in pristine order. They exchanged pleasantries before Finley introduced him to his mother and stepfather.

It turned out Finley's entire family subscribed to Rory's channel, though Ivan had no idea what that was. Rory seemed to be just as enamored with Hope. "Yes, I can see where your children get their exceptional looks," Rory told her.

She cupped Rory's cheeks and assessed him with her vivid green eyes. She'd pulled her wavy gray and white hair back into a ponytail and wore very little makeup. Hope had been Ivan's second mom since the moment they'd met, and she'd eased the ache in his heart until he'd made amends with his own mother. Ivan figured Rory could use a little of her TLC right about then and maybe even a little of her guidance. She always knew the right thing to say, even when it was the last thing you wanted to hear.

Ivan held his breath while waiting for Hope to speak. She might offer Rory sage life hacks, or she could remark on the state of his sex or love life. Either way, her takes were ridiculously accurate. Hope surprised Ivan by simply pulling Rory into a long hug.

"Cougar," Finley mock whispered. He turned to his stepdad with a raised brow, but Gary just shrugged as if to say *you know how she is.* When the hug lingered, Finley said, "Blink twice if you want to be rescued, Rory."

Hope snorted and pulled back to smile at her son. "Don't be jealous. I have plenty of love to go around." She gave Rory her full attention again and kissed his cheek. "Come see me at my studio. We'll have tea and chat."

Rory smiled and nodded before shaking Gary's hand. And then he was standing in front of Ivan, who was suddenly at a loss for words. Rory seemed like a different person than the one he'd first met. His blue eyes were clear of artifice and mischief, but it was hard to say which of the versions of Rory was real.

"I think maybe I'd like a do-over to make up for my bratty behavior earlier," Rory said.

Had it been an act? A defense mechanism after being dropped in unfamiliar surroundings, perhaps? Ivan knew that was the reality he should want, but the mere thought made his stomach tighten and twist with dread. No one had ever looked at him so hungrily. Rory made Ivan feel like he could be the version of himself that had only existed in his fantasies—proud, powerful, assertive, and sexy. Had any of it been real, though? Ivan knew one way to find out. It was entirely possible to fake emotions and attraction, but a person couldn't manufacture chemistry. There had definitely been some zing, pop, and sizzle when they'd touched the first time.

Ivan stuck out his hand. "Hi, I'm Ivan. I'm Redemption Ridge's foreman and—" His words died when Rory's fingers and palm connected with his. The dark-haired beauty's lips parted, and his blue eyes shimmered with awareness. Ivan felt like an insect beneath a microscope as everyone around them scrutinized their interaction. Rory took a step closer, tightening his grip as he'd done the first time. Ivan wasn't sure if Rory was even aware of the action.

Drop his hand and disengage, idiot. A step back would send him colliding with the hot grill. Dylan had killed the flames a while ago but shut the lid to keep the meat warm. Stepping forward would put

Ivan in closer proximity to Rory's heat. One would physically burn him while the other could scorch the healed pieces of his soul Ivan wanted to protect.

Rory quirked a brow. "You're also the grill dragon?" he asked when the silence stretched between them too long.

"Not normally," Dylan said, coming to stand beside Ivan. His best friend leaned closer and whispered, "Turn loose of the pretty man. Let's feed Rory and welcome him to the ranch properly."

Ivan flexed his fingers as if that was the last thing he wanted to do, but he forced them to relax and withdrew his arm. It was quiet enough under the tent to hear a pin drop, and heat crawled up his chest and neck. Ivan forced his gaze away from Rory to glance around the tent. The various smirks and grins spread the flush to his face. Ivan probably looked like a flaming tomato, but he pretended not to notice. "First pick of meat goes to Kieran to celebrate his exoneration and to Rory as a welcome to the ranch."

A collective groan echoed around the tent, giving Dylan cover to say, "A hundred bucks says you finish what you started before the night's out."

Ivan glared at his friend as he stepped away from the grill so the honorees could grab a plate and choose their food. If he were smart, he would've made an excuse to leave the gathering to find himself some peace and settle his frayed nerves. Then again, that would just amp up the speculation and betting. And if Rory sought him out and pushed the boundaries Ivan desperately needed to set? He feared Dylan was right. He was drawn to Rory in ways he'd never experienced before, not even with his first love. Hell, his only love.

Maybe that's why he ended up sharing a picnic table with Rory, Kieran, Finley, Harry, Hope, and Gary. He'd breathed a sigh of relief when Rory sat across from him instead of beside him, but that relief didn't last long. His attention kept straying to Rory's blue eyes and the myriad expressions he witnessed there. He'd enjoyed seeing his humor and quick wit at work when he bantered with Finley or teased Kieran between bites of food. His irises shimmered with interest when he discussed grill techniques with Dylan and guessed at the special ingredients

Harry had used to enhance the side dishes. Rory talked to Hope at length about her wellness center and the various classes she offered there.

"I find the concepts interesting and appealing, but I'm not patient enough for yoga or meditation," he said.

"You just haven't had the right instructor," Hope replied with a wink. "Until now."

Rory didn't commit to taking classes, but he asked additional questions about the products she created and distributed from the store.

Finley groaned when Hope shifted the conversation from standard hygiene and self-care products to the sexual health aids she made. "Mom, please don't. It's his first day here."

Rory placed both elbows on the table. "Please do."

Hope happily launched into a discussion about her lubes, Monkey Grease and Butt Stuff, and how they were so much better than the mass-produced products on the market. Finley seemed to shrink with every vivid description, and Ivan didn't think his cheeks could get any hotter. He kept his head down and ate like he didn't want to test out each of the products with Rory. Ivan also wanted to tell Finley what a little shit he was for not telling the rest of them about the lube his mom made. Then again, how would that conversation have gone down?

Ivan met Hope's gaze and said, "Seems to me you could've put samples in the Christmas stockings you make for us every year."

Hope tilted her head to acknowledge him. "Touché."

Ivan lowered his head and tucked back into his food while Rory and Gary talked about the state of the housing market and the economy. Rory's interests and scope of knowledge were vast, and Ivan was impressed, albeit against his will. Just when Ivan didn't think he could eat another bite, Harry and Hope brought out the dessert offerings.

Rory leaned across the table toward him. "Please tell me you don't eat like this every meal. I won't be able to fit into my clothes by Sunday."

Since it was Friday afternoon, Ivan thought that probability was low. Nick had told Ivan to work Rory like he would anyone else on the ranch, and Rory had pretty much said the same thing. Ivan had every intention of taking them up on their suggestion. "Don't worry," Ivan said,

"I'll help you burn off the calories." Then he realized just how loaded the comment sounded and wished he could take it back.

Rory's dark brows shot up, and his mouth trembled with obvious restraint. He cleared his throat after a moment and said, "Good to know."

Christ, he had no idea what he was going to do with Rory. Did Cash want to go all in and put Rory on the payroll and extend the same perks to him as he did to the others? And would that be fair? Most of the guys who arrived at Redemption Ridge didn't have a penny to their names and their worldly possessions amounted to the clothes they wore. That had been his reality at least. Cash, who'd found himself in similar circumstances decades ago, included clothes and housing as part of the crew's employment perks. Would it be fair to extend the same to Rory, whose father was the richest man in Colorado and was in the top ten in the entire country? Ivan checked himself because he was making a lot of assumptions about a man he didn't know. *Not your business, idiot. Just find him a suitable job on the ranch and forget about everything else.*

"Blueberry cobbler," Harry singsonged, cutting into Ivan's thoughts. He sat upright at her announcement. "Any takers?"

Ivan threw an elbow into Kieran's ribs to keep him from getting to the dessert table first.

"Damn it, Ivan," Kieran groused, holding a hand to his side. "So much for celebrating my exoneration."

"Hey," Ivan said calmly, "you got first pick of the meat. I saw you take the juiciest rack of ribs, so zip it."

Rory smiled as he watched their bantering but made no move to join the growing line at the dessert table. Something about the curve of his lips twisted Ivan's insides. Before he knew what he was doing, Ivan said, "Want something sweet?"

Rory's brow arched upward, and the smile spread. "I'll take some of that cobbler you nearly trampled Kieran over."

Ivan grabbed a second plate and heaped on a sizable portion for Rory.

"You took half the dish," Kieran shouted.

"Who cares as long as he doesn't eat the triple chocolate brownies," Dylan hollered from somewhere in the back of the line.

"This body requires a lot of fuel," Ivan told Kieran as he added a brownie to his plate and Rory's. "If I know Harry, she has at least two more dishes of cobbler in the kitchen."

"Three," she added with a smile. "I take care of my guys."

Ivan took his time checking over the treats on offer but passed on the other cookies, cakes, and pastries.

"About damn time," Finley grumbled when Ivan finally stepped aside.

Rory's smile was huge, and Ivan might've added a little swagger to his stride back to the picnic table.

"Must be some cobbler," Rory said as Ivan set his plate down in front of him.

"The best," Ivan said. He forked a big bite into his mouth, then stopped midchew. Ivan had thought Harry's past cobblers were perfection, but this was even better. He looked over at her while he swallowed and caught her smug grin. "You changed your recipe."

"And I see you heartily approve," she replied when Ivan immediately went back for more. "Want to guess what's different?"

"It's earthier?" Ivan guessed. He thought back to the comment Rory made about some of the side dishes. "You've added something savory."

"Basil," Rory said. "It's perfection."

"How do you know so much about cooking and baking?" Ivan asked. The surrounding conversation stalled, and he knew everyone else was just as curious about the answer.

Rory smiled and lifted another forkful, stopping just shy of his mouth. "I've been blessed to know people with incredible culinary skills." He saluted Harry and added, "You rank right up there with the best." Then he shoved the cobbler into his mouth and emitted a happy little grunt that made Ivan's dick twitch.

Harry covered her heart. "Thank you for such a lovely compliment. And what of your culinary skills?" she asked him.

He shrugged. "I can hold my own. I'm better with flavor profiles than execution, but I think I could sharpen my skills under the right instructor."

Harry smiled and looked around the tent until she found the

person she sought. "Cash!" she called out. The rancher turned from the dessert table with a partially eaten tartlet in his hand.

"Busted," he said. "I couldn't wait until I got back to the table. It's mostly your fault."

Harry laughed. "I'm not complaining about your etiquette or your offhanded compliment. I want you to make Ivan share Rory with me."

"Wow," Rory said. "A custody battle."

Cash arched a brow as he chewed the second half of the tartlet, leaving a smear of chocolate at the corner of his mouth. Ivan gestured to his own mouth, and Cash wiped the chocolate off with his thumb, then licked the cream from the digit before giving Harry his attention again. "And how does Rory feel about that?"

"Sounds great to me," he replied. "I'll go wherever I'm needed."

Ivan should've been relieved that Rory wouldn't be constantly underfoot. Living in the same house would be hard enough. But elation was the last thing he felt when Harry whisked Rory off to give him a tour of her operations. His annoyance grew when Finley and Kieran sat on either side of him like bookends and Dylan slid down the opposite bench to take Rory's vacated seat.

He looked over at Finley and Kieran. "Do you mind?"

They rolled their eyes and scooted over a few inches. "Better?"

"Don't you two have kissy faces to make at each other somewhere else?" Ivan asked.

"Not until you tell us the scoop on the new guy," Kieran said.

Ivan shook his head. "You're getting as bad as Tyler and Owen. Bunch of damn nosy church busybodies." His gaze strayed back to Harry and Rory, who had nearly reached the ranch house. Harry was laughing at something Rory said, and seeing him fit in did funny things to Ivan's insides. Then he recalled Rory's confession that he couldn't stand himself. "Just be nice to him, okay?"

"Like you were with me?" Kieran asked.

Ivan leveled him with a dark look. "How many times do I need to apologize for our rough start?"

Kieran shrugged. "At least once more it seems."

"You're still within striking range."

Kieran rubbed his ribcage and scooted down another foot just as Cash approached the table.

"Can we talk for a minute?" his boss asked.

"Of course." Ivan stood up and took care of his trash before following Cash a respectful distance away from the tent and the nosy Nellies watching them.

"I know I've ambushed you already today, but I took an important call right before Nick showed up that I need to discuss with you. It seems your honey is creating quite a buzz."

Ivan smiled at the word play. "*Our* honey," Ivan reminded him. Rocky Mountain Liquid Gold was Ivan's brainchild, but Cash had backed him financially and emotionally.

Cash dismissed him with a wave. "I know nothing about honey production, but you're a genius, which is why *Colorado Fine Cuisine* wants to do a piece about your liquid gold."

Ivan tried to stave off the panic that arose when he thought about dealing with media types. Too late. He heard the frenzied clicks and whirs of cameras, felt the heat from the lights, and heard the urgent pleas from journalists. *Mr. Gallagher, over here. A word please, Mr. Gallagher. Do you regret your actions, Mr. Gallagher? Was he worth it, Mr. Gallagher?* The frenzied media scrutiny after his arrest and during his trial had been insufferable, and the fallout had nearly destroyed his family.

"Ivan," Cash said. His voice was a gentle lifeline back to reality.

Blinking, he brought his friend into focus. Dark brows slashed down to form a deep vee, marring the handsome man's forehead. Ivan plastered on what he hoped was a radiant smile. "That's exciting news," he said, though his strained voiced revealed the lie. No, that wasn't fair. Ivan could acknowledge that the exposure would be excellent for their company while wanting nothing to do with it. A quick solution came to him. "You should totally do the interview."

Cash crossed his arms over his chest. The weight of his shrewd stare pressed against Ivan's chest. It reminded him of the time he'd overestimated his prowess during a bench press session in the weight room in high school. Ivan's arms had cramped under the strain, and the weight bar would've crushed his chest if his spotter hadn't bailed him out of trouble. Ivan rubbed his chest as if that alone could ease the pressure. It helped in the sense that he knew the suffocating sensation was in his head. Nothing was actually suffocating him, not a weight bar or Cash's disapproval. He only saw empathy in his friend's steely blue gaze. Cash knew what he'd gone through because he'd patiently listened as Ivan processed his trauma both during and after his incarceration.

"I'm afraid Roberto isn't interested in what I have to say about the honey."

"Who's Roberto?" Ivan asked.

"Roberto Vincente. The magazine's editor-in-chief. We met several years ago when mutual friends set us up on a blind date."

That little nugget of information intrigued Ivan and nearly quelled his rising panic. He knew next to nothing about Cash's romantic life. He was the most private person Ivan had ever met. "Didn't work out?" he asked, pressing for more information.

Cash's lips hooked into a wry smile because he knew Ivan was fishing. "No, but I made an excellent friend. We share many interests and a lot of them center on food and spirits."

"And you told him about Rocky Mountain Liquid Gold?" Ivan asked.

"No. Roberto experienced your brilliance firsthand at John Carlo's. Your honey was featured heavily in the baklava he ordered. Roberto loved the dish so much he asked for the brand of honey used. The server passed his compliments and question on to the pastry chef and learned about our company. Roberto made a note on his phone but forgot about it until he had a similar experience at Wyatt's Chophouse last night." Cash chuckled for a few moments. "He was talking so fast about some intricate dessert that I could hardly understand him. Anyway, after hearing the company's name twice, he did an internet search and saw my name listed as a partner."

"Which is why you should do the interview," Ivan said.

Cash shook his head. "I already told Roberto I'm a silent partner in the operation. I don't know jack about bees, their hives, or honey production. That's all you, big guy. I believed in your mission and wanted to see your dreams come true. That's the extent of my involvement."

Ivan snorted. Cash had provided so much more than the startup money he'd needed to establish his hives. "Don't downplay your role."

Cash held up his hands in surrender. "I speak the truth." He lowered his arms and offered Ivan an encouraging smile. "You're the genius behind the brand and the only one who can properly convey the magic of the honey. I told Roberto I would speak to you. I didn't tell him you were gun-shy around reporters, but I think he sensed the reasons for my hesitation. He's familiar with my mission for the ranch." Cash smiled, and Ivan wondered what was going on inside the man's brain. "Roberto just said, 'Pretty please. I don't bite.' And I promised to discuss it with you. The ball is in your court, Ivan. I would never force you to do anything that was detrimental to your health."

Ivan swallowed down the surging panic before it could take hold again. "But you'd like to push me outside my comfort zone."

Cash didn't need to respond; the answer was obvious in the man's kind and patient expression. But letting Ivan guess his thoughts or make assumptions about his frame of mind wasn't in Cash's nature. "Would I be a good friend, employer, or business partner if I didn't want to push you a little?"

Ivan shook his head because he knew Cash was right. A feature in *Colorado Fine Cuisine* could be a real game changer for their honey business. He'd worked hard to get their product into quality grocers and restaurants. His effort had paid off…if only he could get past his phobia and bitterness to separate the good media types from the bad. Rocky Mountain Liquid Gold deserved the attention. Ivan would need to work through his issues because he knew Cash wouldn't relent. And why should he? This opportunity was one Ivan had orchestrated with research, ingenuity, and perseverance. It was within his grasp. All he had to do was reach out and grab it. "When?"

"Roberto said he wouldn't get to the interview and photoshoot for a few weeks, possibly longer."

"Which would give me time to work through my issues." Ivan said it so Cash wouldn't have to. He took a deep breath and nodded.

Cash clapped him on the shoulder. "Read some of Roberto's pieces. It might help put some concerns to rest." He tilted his head as if considering his next words. "You know, Rory would be an excellent source to tap for insight on interviews."

Source to tap? Ivan had a hard time stifling a moan but managed. "I appreciate the suggestion." But he had no intention of taking it. He blew out a breath. "But I have one of my own."

"I'm listening," Cash said.

"Let's do this interview and photoshoot together," Ivan said. "It will help me break the ice and assign positive memories to dealing with press types."

Cash held his gaze for a few seconds before nodding briefly. "I think that's an excellent compromise. Would you like me to contact Roberto to confirm, or would you like to do it?"

"I'll do it," Ivan said. Cash retrieved his phone and started typing. "I just need his contact information—" Ivan's phone pinged with an incoming email from Cash. He smirked and shook his head. "I'll reach out and let him know we're interested."

"This is the right decision, and I'm proud of you for making it."

"Hold your praise until I survive the interview. There's still time for me to ruin it."

"You're going to be great, and it will get easier each time you field these requests. I'm telling you, Ivan, this is the beginning of something wonderful."

Did he dare hope? He wanted to, he truly did.

"And I'm sorry for springing Rory on you like I did."

Ivan waved it off. "I got the impression you only found out about five minutes before I did. I shouldn't have gotten so angry. I'm sorry I yelled at you. That was disrespectful."

Cash clapped him on the back. "Think nothing of it." But Ivan would. He admired Cash more than anyone he knew, and he was ashamed of his reaction. "Rory could stay at the big ranch house if things feel a little tight at your place."

Ivan thought of the flirty smile Rory had given Cash, and he hated that idea so much it soured his stomach. He needed to think on his feet and offer a believable excuse why that was such a bad idea. "Nick and Rory both instructed me to work him like I would anyone else,"

Ivan said. "New crew members don't stay in the swanky guest rooms at your place."

Cash assessed him through cool blue eyes. "Are you sure?"

Ivan felt like Cash was asking so much more with those three words. The only certainty he knew was that Rory Snyder was going to cause a fuckton of trouble, and lord help him, Ivan didn't want to miss a single moment of it. "Everything's going to be fine."

Cash held his gaze for an awkward pause, and Ivan tensed while waiting for a rebuttal, but his boss didn't have more to add. He changed the subject to Ivan's beloved beehives, and his tension faded on his next breath.

Everything's going to be fine. Everything's going to be fine. The words bounced around in his skull while Ivan continued working on the beehive after the celebration broke up. He busied himself in the barn doing anything and everything to avoid going to the old homestead until he figured Rory was asleep. Ivan was still chanting the sentiment when he finally drifted into a fitful sleep filled with dark, delicious dreams that left him achingly hard and damp with sweat. His skin felt prickly, almost like he had a fever or his flesh no longer fit his frame. Ivan knew damn well his condition had nothing to do with an illness and everything to do with the gorgeous man sleeping downstairs.

Ivan noted the time and decided he might as well get up. He tossed the covers back, careful not to disrupt his cats, and eased out of his bedroom wearing only his boxers. He had plenty of things on his agenda to attack, and he'd start with relieving the ache in his balls while the rest of the house slept. The hallway was black as pitch, but he could make the trip in his sleep. A few steps away from his destination, the door swung open. Light slashed through the darkness and a cloud of fragrant steam billowed out of the room. Ivan blinked to clear his brain, which felt as hazy as the hallway. What was Dylan doing up so early, and had he bought new shower stuff to impress Harry?

Before his brain could consider any other possibilities, Rory stepped out of the bathroom wearing nothing but a towel wrapped around his waist. *Holy shit.* He was tanned, toned, and dewy perfection. His tousled hair looked as if he'd run the towel over his head a few times before wrapping it around his waist. A droplet of water cascaded down Rory's torso, and Ivan watched with rapt attention until the light blue terry-cloth absorbed it. Everything inside him urged Ivan to drop to his knees and see if Rory's skin looked as soft as it appeared. He wanted to jerk that towel off and—

"Hey," Ivan said abruptly, snapping his head up to meet Rory's gaze. "That's my towel."

"Oops," Rory replied. "I saw a beige set and a blue set hanging up. They looked clean."

Because Ivan had washed them the previous day. "Dylan's are beige. Mine are blue. There are extras in the linen closet."

Rory's hands went to his waist, and before Ivan could even think to stop him, he whipped the towel off and tossed it at Ivan. The material smacked Ivan in the chest and landed on the floor. "My bad."

Ivan told himself not to look even as his eyes devoured the gorgeous flesh on display. Rory made no attempt to cover himself. He just stood there proudly as Ivan looked his fill. Every greedy pass discovered something new. Perfectly sculpted abs, a tiny scar on his right hip. Rory was smooth *everywhere*. Ivan forced his gaze up to meet Rory's. He arched a dark brow and tilted his head toward the bathroom in invitation. God, how easy it would be to close themselves inside and give in to their attraction. Somehow, Ivan found the will to shake his head, even if the words wouldn't form on his tongue.

"Seems to me not everyone agrees," Rory said, gesturing toward Ivan's crotch. "You make it so hard for me to behave, even though I promised myself I would."

Ivan looked down to see his thick erection jutting through the opening in his boxers. If he reached down to tuck it away, he feared he might start stroking it instead. Fuck, he needed to…fuck. "I'll see you at breakfast," Ivan said as he picked up his towel from the floor and stepped into the bathroom.

"Or you could let me watch you jerk off."

Ivan slammed the door. "No."

"Okay, what if I stay out here, and you just narrate your actions through the door?"

Ivan ignored him and turned on the shower. He would not give Rory the satisfaction of knowing he was jerking off, so he kept the water cold and his shower short. When he got dressed and went downstairs, Rory was nowhere in sight, but Dylan was in the kitchen doctoring a cup of coffee. Ivan took one look at his friend's smug smile and knew he'd overheard the entire exchange. "Shut the hell up. And you owe me a hundred bucks."

"Only because you hid in the barn until midnight," Dylan said. "You're both consenting adults. Live a little, buddy." His friend patted him on the shoulder and headed out the back door.

Dylan was right. Ivan needed to let off some steam. He just absolutely refused to do it with Rory. Luckily, Ivan had that upcoming business trip to Denver where there would be plenty of men looking for hookups. He might even extend his stay to two nights for extra insurance before he returned to the ranch. All he needed to do was keep his mind busy and his hands off Rory for a week. No problem.

chapter

FOUR

"M Y BRAZENNESS HAS REACHED NEW HEIGHTS," RORY told Harry several hours later as they toiled in her greenhouse.

Even though Ivan had been considerate enough to give him the weekend off, the last thing Rory wanted to do was sit with his thoughts. He'd hardly slept the night before because he'd spent too much time reading the media coverage on his dad's campaign. Charles was doing his best to divert attention to the issues the state was facing, but all the reporters wanted to discuss was Rory's troubled teenage years after his mom had died. They were having a field day with Rory's stint in rehab from when his underage drinking to dull his ache became a full-blown addiction. According to their sources, Rory had turned to the bottle when he couldn't find the solace he'd needed from his father. The truth hurt worse than lies, and that particular blow hit him hard. Rory had felt adrift with no anchor. His father had felt the same, but instead of turning toward each other, they'd grown apart. They were good now...or at least they had been. Rory feared they would revert to the bad habits that had ripped them apart the last time as the media sharks circled looking for anything they could use to poke holes in his dad's platform.

So he'd been primed to find trouble when he stepped out of the shower and saw Ivan clad only in his underwear. The man's muscles had muscles for heaven's sake. But seeing his long, thick erection jutting from the opening in his boxers had stirred Rory's imagination, among other things, and produced some additional nicknames that could just as easily apply. Ivan the Blessed, Ivan the Gifted, and Ivan the Hung were among his top three new favorites.

Harry looked up from planting carrots. "Is that a good or bad thing?"

Rory straightened up and set his trowel on the soil. He wiped his brow with his arm and grimaced when he realized he'd probably just smeared dirt all over his face. "You saw the thundercloud at breakfast this morning. What do you think?"

Harry snorted and went back to work. "Ivan is all bark and no bite. He's just not used to people challenging him the way you do." She stilled and looked over her shoulder. "I am dying to know what you did to him."

Rory worked his bottom lip between his teeth. He was only at the ranch because he'd trusted the wrong people. Then again, he already knew Harry was a much better person than his so-called friends from home. "I'm afraid you won't like me anymore."

Harry snorted. "You've met my mother. Nothing you can say will shock me."

So Rory told her most of what had occurred in the hallway outside the bathroom. He left out the part where he asked to watch or listen to Ivan jerking off. Harry opened and closed her mouth a few times, but no sound escaped.

"I lied," she said finally. "You've shocked me." Then she burst into a fit of giggles. She paused every few minutes to look at Rory before laughing harder. Harry waved her hands in front of her face as if she couldn't breathe, so Rory stood up and fetched her water bottle. Harry had to turn away from him so she could drink without choking. Rory would've felt self-conscious, but he knew she wasn't laughing at *him* just at his antics. "So sorry about that," she said when she finally settled down. "Dude, you've got some serious cojones." Harry tipped her bottle back and took another long drink.

"Nah, they're just average." He waggled his brows. "Ivan, though… Those things must be the size of boulders to balance out that monster—"

Harry sprayed water like a hose, blasting the front of his shirt. Her eyes widened in horror, but it was his turn to laugh raucously. "What happened after that?" Harry asked. "I know you didn't just strut down the hallway without some parting remark."

Heat crept up Rory's face, and he fought the urge to cover his cheeks like a blushing maiden. "I won't be sharing that part. It's too personal." Harry's eyes bulged, and he realized the conclusion she'd jumped to erroneously. "No, nothing like you're thinking," Rory said. "I just said a few things that are too…slutty for me to admit after knowing you for only a day."

Harry clapped her gloved hands and squealed. "Oh, Rory, I'm so glad you're here. You're just what we needed, especially Ivan."

Rory wasn't so sure about that. Tyler and Owen seemed pretty guarded around him, and Rory was pretty sure Ivan was ready to send him packing. Nicky hadn't told him much about the ranch during their drive, so Harry had filled in the blanks while he helped her in the kitchen and greenhouse. He could understand why some of the guys weren't eager to embrace his presence. Hopefully, the media firestorm would blow over soon, and he'd be out of their hair. Rory wasn't sure he wanted to go back to living in his father's pool house, but he could start fresh on his own somewhere else.

In the meantime, he needed to lay off the big guy and stop harassing him. He'd take a page out of Ivan's book and avoid the foreman as much as possible. Later that night, when several of the crew went to the old homestead for poker, Rory joined Harry for facials and movies at the main ranch house. Aside from mealtimes, he steered clear of Ivan most of Sunday too. He didn't face his first real challenge until answering a summons to the barn after breakfast on Monday morning. Ivan wanted to assess his skill set to see where he'd fit in best around the ranch.

"I'm not as blue-blooded as you're thinking," Rory told him. "I spent summers at my grandparents' farm in Oklahoma as a kid." He'd also dedicated his life to conservation studies, which included traveling to countries with rudimentary farming. He helped sow fields with horses and mules instead of the fancy equipment Redemption Ridge used. There was a doubtful look in Ivan's eyes that challenged Rory. Ivan the Hung didn't think Rory could keep up with the rest of the crew, and there was only one way to prove just how wrong he was. "Take off your kid gloves and put me to work," Rory urged. The air seemed to crackle around them, their ever-present sexual chemistry leaching into other parts of their dynamic. "What are you afraid of, Ivan? Worried I'll prove you wrong?"

A responding challenge sparked in Ivan's amber gaze, holding Rory spellbound for a few moments. "All right. Just remember you asked for it. Tap out if the going gets too tough."

Rory wouldn't tap out if it killed him. The only satisfaction he wanted to give Ivan would come from his hands, mouth, or ass. *Tap out if the going gets too tough.* That wasn't the Snyder way. Rory had heard that sentiment from his dad a hundred times. When he was little, it bolstered his confidence. But those words had the opposite effect once Rory had become a sullen teenager, especially when applied to Rory's grief after losing his mother. Though Charles had never been that callous with Rory, others in their circle had been, but that old fighting spirit returned tenfold when standing in front of a smirking Ivan Gallagher, who didn't think Rory could hang with the big boys. Rory wasn't so mad he wouldn't take Ivan to bed or the nearest surface that could support their weight. He'd ride that glorious cock, but he'd just be damn stingy with his compliments before, during, and after.

Ivan's first task was to unload the seed they'd soon plant in the fields. Someone had backed a flatbed truck into the barn. Rows of stacked bags were waiting to be lifted and stored along the back wall. Tyler, Owen, and a few others were there to pitch in, but Rory decided he would pack and stack the most bags if it killed him. And it damn near did. He grinned victoriously through the discomfort once they finished and waited patiently for Ivan to heap praise upon him. But the foreman barely glanced in his direction.

"Damn, Rory," Owen said, leaning against the side of the truck. He wasn't full-on panting, but he was definitely winded. "Was there some kind of prize on the line I didn't know about?"

Rory glanced over at Ivan, whose glare warned him to keep his mouth shut. *Or what?* Rory really didn't want to fuck around and find out, so he plastered a good-natured smile on his face when he replied to Owen. "Nah. Just carrying my weight. I appreciate all of you putting up with me."

Owen slapped him on the back, and it was his first friendly overture toward Rory. It made all the extra effort worthwhile and made his aches feel less achy. "Tyler and I watched a few of your videos last night. They really impressed us." Owen smiled sheepishly and rubbed his chin as if embarrassed about something.

"Dude, it's not an Only Fans account. Why the angst?" Rory figured he knew, but he'd let Owen tell him instead of putting words into the guy's mouth.

Owen grimaced. "Honestly?" Rory nodded because there was no other way. "When I'd heard you were a social media influencer, I assumed the worst."

"What did you expect?" Rory prodded. He felt Ivan's interest and knew he was listening, even if he was staring at the clipboard in his hands like it contained the secrets of the universe. Maybe answering Owen's questions would put some of Ivan's concerns to rest too.

"I figured your videos would be a sequence of Jackass-style stunts. Those accounts seem to rake in all the money."

Rory nodded because it was true. "I didn't start my conservation channel to get rich, although I appreciate the income. It allows me to travel and expose myself to more possibilities, which I then get to share with my large audience. It amazed me when I got my first ten thousand subscribers. I never expected that even a thousand people would tune in to my channel and watch my videos on conservation and preservation, let alone a million."

"That's really amazing," Owen said.

"I'm sure it doesn't hurt that you're a cute guy and often travel around without a shirt on," Tyler tossed in.

The barn grew eerily quiet. Rory didn't get the impression that Tyler was remotely interested in him. He assumed Tyler was just vocalizing an observation he'd made. Owen's and Ivan's reactions were very interesting. Owen suddenly couldn't seem to look away from the ground, and Ivan snapped his pencil in half.

Rory looked over at him with a quirked brow. Was Ivan the Blessed threatened by that comment? Rory sure as hell wouldn't press the issue and find out with an audience around. He risked undoing all the progress he'd made with Owen if he so much as batted an eyelash in Tyler's direction. Ivan probably thought Rory was a shameless flirt and a provocateur, but only Ivan brought out those characteristics in him.

"Could it be that easy?" Rory asked. He rubbed his thumb and forefinger over his trimmed beard. "I'll have to give it some thought. And to think I stress myself out choosing destinations and content."

Owen shifted his booted foot in the gravel and snorted. "There's always the Only Fans option you mentioned."

It was Rory's turn to laugh as he slapped Owen on the back. "Never." He turned to Ivan and caught a murderous expression on his face before he wiped the slate clean. "What's next, boss?" Rory reckoned the title was okay since the others called him that.

"Repairing fences in the lower pastures," Ivan said. "You could head inside the ranch house and help Harry for the rest of the afternoon if you'd prefer. I promised to share custody of you."

Rory would've found the comment funny if Ivan's previous remarks and obvious doubt hadn't pissed him off. It was clear Rory still needed to prove himself, so he turned his back on Ivan to address Owen and Tyler. "Do we head out on four legs or four tires?"

Tyler and Owen both smiled. "Horseback for this job. You ride?"

"Sure do, though it's been a while."

Ivan stayed back at the barn, but Finley joined them since his precious horses benefited from the repairs. Rory wasn't sure if Finley always joined his crew on those types of tasks or if he was curious about Rory. It didn't take him long to discover Finley was there to work his ass off. Rory fed off his positive energy when his muscles whined for a break and his stomach pleaded for food. The sack lunches Harry made for them had seemed excessive, but Rory had burned through the calories in record time. The trio was curious about his career and asked a lot of questions, mostly about the rainforest and farming practices in other countries. It made the afternoon go by fast and helped him ignore his body's incessant complaints.

"I'm sure my sister is fit to be tied that we hogged you all day," Finley said when they arrived back at the equine barn. "Give me your horse, and I'll get her settled. You better clean up and check in with the real boss on the ranch."

"Thought that was me," Ivan said.

Rory hadn't even heard him walk up behind them. "Damn, you move stealthily for a big man."

"We all know who really runs the show around here, and it's Harry," Finley said. "Queen of the kitchen always gets her way."

"Well, the queen is looking for her…"

Rory crossed his arms over his chest and dared Ivan to say joker or jester.

Ivan cleared his throat and said, "Protégé." He looked and sounded irritated. "I told you before you set out that you should report to Harry. Remember the custody comment?"

Rory wasn't the least bit mollified. "You said *could* and only gave me the option because you didn't think I could handle nailing up fence line after packing and stacking bags of seed."

Ivan scowled, placed his hands on his hips, and took two steps closer to Rory. "You think I was going easy on you?"

Rory matched his two steps, then added another. Any closer, and he'd be within climbing range. "Yes, and I told you I didn't want that. All I asked you to do was treat me like you would anyone else."

"We need popcorn," Tyler whispered.

"And a cold beer," Owen added.

Rory and Ivan were too busy staring each other down like gunslingers at high noon to pay them much attention.

"Since you two knuckleheads technically report to me, I'm telling you to take your horses to the barn and cool them down," Finley said. Tyler and Owen mumbled their displeasure but did as they were told. "Will you guys be okay out here, or do I need to get the hose?"

That got Rory's attention, and he looked at Finley with a raised brow. "Hose?"

"My grandmother used to take the water hose to her two dogs if they got to bickering too much. She'd open up the door at the first sign of trouble and holler, 'Do I need to get the hose?' They'd usually straighten right up."

The story had eased the tension between Ivan and Rory, which was clearly exactly what Finley had wanted. Rory walked back to the horse he'd ridden to the lower pasture and back. He stroked a hand over her soft muzzle and patted her chest. "Miss Loretta, it was a real pleasure meeting you. Thanks for being such a patient girl with me." She nickered softly and bumped him with her muzzle. "Thanks for a fun afternoon, Finley," Rory called over his shoulder as he walked away.

"Anytime," he replied.

Rory debated heading straight to the kitchen until he looked down the length of his body. He was covered in dirt and dust from a long, physical day and had no business stepping into a room where someone prepared food. Rory hadn't made it far when the sound of heavy footfalls reached his ears.

So the big man wasn't always stealthy.

"I wasn't done talking to you," Ivan said.

"In front of the others you are."

"Fine," Ivan growled. "We'll take this inside."

Rory whirled on him the minute they crossed the threshold into the kitchen at the old homestead. "Look, the way I acted the other morning was reprehensible, but at least I did it in private." Ivan's cheeks turned pink as he closed the door behind them, telling Rory he knew exactly what he was talking about. "I was out of line with my towel stunt and… the rest," he said, unable to repeat the exact words. They'd felt right in the moment, but he'd been ruminating on them ever since. He should just get this off his chest and move on. Ivan scowled and crossed his arms over his chest, not making it any easier. Rory took a few seconds to admire the way his biceps bulged before forcing his gaze to meet Ivan's. "My behavior was borderline predatory, and I'm sorry."

"Apology accepted, but I'm not sure what that has to do with what happened this morning. I get the sense I said the wrong thing, and I don't understand."

"If Cash had picked me up from one of the correctional facilities and brought me to the farm, would you have given me an option to tap out? Reassigned me to easier tasks because you thought I was too soft?" Ivan's eyes darkened, making it clear he didn't like Rory questioning him. Unfortunately, that only brought out Rory's brattier side. "Does my lack of body hair and the effort I put into my appearance make you think I can't handle manly tasks around the farm? Do you think I'm too soft?"

Ivan stiffened, and his eyes burned with molten intensity. His nostrils flared as he stepped closer to Rory. "You're making a whole lot of assumptions."

That wasn't a no, so Rory kept pushing. He moved closer to Ivan too. "Or maybe you're just afraid other parts of you will like me as much as your dick does?"

"You think I want you? Is that it?" Ivan growled.

Rory's heart pounded so hard he could feel it in his throat. "I—" Dizziness washed over him like a tidal wave, and he leaned against the counter for support.

"Rory," Ivan said, his voice softer but urgent. "Are you okay?"

"I think my blood sugar tanked." Rory swayed a little and gripped the edge of the counter. "Feeling pretty stupid about my big speech now."

"Here," Ivan said, gently gripping Rory's upper arms. "Let's sit down at the table. I'll get you a snack, and we'll calmly talk this out when you feel better." Once Rory was sitting down, Ivan released him to rummage through the cabinet. "I think we're both operating under some false assumptions here. It's not healthy for either of us to continue like this."

"My fault," Rory said wearily. "I came in here like a master seducer and set the wrong tone. I just couldn't seem to stop myself. You're so damn yummy. And your dick is just…" Rory sighed. "I'm doing it again."

Ivan dropped something on the counter, and it sounded like a shotgun blast in the small room. Rory jerked in his seat as if he'd been shot. His head felt really heavy, but Rory still turned to see what Ivan was doing. He held a jar of peanut butter in his hands. "Rory, do you have any food allergies?"

"Nope. Just give me a spoon. I'll eat the entire jar."

Ivan's lips quirked into a brief grin before he turned away to pull a loaf of bread out of a bin on the counter and a banana from the fruit basket. Moments later, Ivan slid a peanut butter and banana sandwich in front of him. "Start there." He went to the refrigerator and poured a tall glass of orange juice. "Sip on this." Ivan sat across from him and waited quietly for Rory to eat his snack and drink some of the juice.

"I'm already feeling better," Rory said when he was halfway through his snack.

"Keep eating please. I think you overdid it today." Ivan's voice was gentler and more patient than Rory deserved. Something about his tone made Rory want to nestle against his broad chest instead of provoking another argument. That reaction was far scarier. "I think we need to determine why you felt the need to push yourself."

Rory set his sandwich down and met Ivan's concerned gaze. The big guy tapped the table near his food, indicating he should eat some more. Rory obliged by taking two more bites and followed it with a long drink of juice. "I already told you why I was upset. I didn't want you treating me differently than any recruit."

"That's a fair place to start," Ivan said. "We'll address the other parts afterward." Ivan's gaze never wavered, and it made Rory want to wilt like a flower. Oh, wait. He'd already done that. "It's not fair to compare yourself to the crew we hire from the correctional facilities because they all have agricultural experiences through numerous programs. That's where I learned to care for beehives for instance. Both Ty and Owen worked with horses through programs, and Dylan and Kieran started working with dogs at their facilities. Rue learned how to weld and fix machinery and has shifted those skills to blacksmithing, so each of the recruits who show up here already have a head start."

Rory knew that and felt foolish for his line of questioning.

"And, yes, I would offer them extra breaks or a lighter load to carry if I saw them struggling. This isn't a hardcore boot camp where I'm trying to turn guys into superbutch cowboys. Now about your other comments," Ivan said. "If you haven't figured it out by now, most of us are queer on this ranch. There's no one way to be queer." He swallowed hard and ghosted his gaze over Rory for a few moments before making eye contact again. "I don't think you're too soft because…you're smooth all over. Masculinity isn't defined by body hair." Ivan tilted his head to the left and right as if stretching his neck. He followed that up with small shoulder rolls. Rory wasn't sure what this display meant. Was he uncomfortable? Stalling? Finally, Ivan settled in his chair and cleared his throat. "I'd never judge you harshly over your hygiene habits and preferences nor would they sway my opinion about your capabilities. Let's just leave it at that."

Rory sagged against his chair as he exhaled a long sigh, doing a fine impression of a deflating balloon. "I made the mistake of checking headlines before work this morning to see if the scandal was dying down. I didn't read the articles, but a quick skim of headlines revealed that interest is increasing instead of waning." Rory had briefly thought about reaching out to his dad to plead with him to take a more assertive stance on these attacks. Refusing to comment on personal matters and diverting attention back to pertinent topics wasn't working. It only made him look guiltier. But Rory had decided his opinions wouldn't be welcomed and didn't reach out in the end.

"Don't do that," Ivan said.

Rory's muddled brain struggled to focus. "Do what?"

"Don't read the articles. Most of it is probably conjecture and rubbish to entice clicks and sell papers."

Rory sighed. "You're right. It really got in my head this morning. I've sensed that some of the guys are uncomfortable around me, and I guess I wanted to prove I'm not that spoiled punk often represented in the articles. Call me silly, but I want people to like me. I want to like me." Rory buried his head in his hands. "Damn, I've made a real mess of things."

Ivan scooted his plate closer until it bumped into Rory's arm. Taking the hint, Rory lowered his hands and finished the sandwich. Ivan's gaze softened further. "Look, the first thing you need to understand is that every single one of us on this ranch has trust issues. Life taught us to be guarded and cynical before we went to jail, and time in lockup didn't change that. We've built trust and respect among each other, but it takes time to adjust when someone new arrives. I promise no one intended to make you feel unwanted or excluded. Just be yourself and give them a chance to get to know you." Ivan tilted his head to the side. "I'd say you made quite the impression today. Relax and patiently build on that. And maybe eat more protein and complex carbs, especially at breakfast. I'll make sure you get a healthy snack from now on until your body adjusts to the new demands you're putting on it."

"You're being way nicer than I deserve," Rory said. "And I'm sorry I misjudged you."

Ivan shook his head. "Kindness shouldn't be a rare occurrence. I'm sorry I gave you a reason to make those leaps in judgment."

The urge to lean forward and test the suppleness of Ivan's lips was almost too strong to resist. Those thick thighs looked as if they were made to cradle Rory's weight. Ivan's broad chest would make the best pillow, and his brawny arms would hold Rory safely. How nice would it be to curl up on his lap like one of his cats?

"You look like you're ready to crash," Ivan said.

Rory tried to nod, but his head was too heavy to lift. He held his hand up to show his thumb and forefinger an inch apart. "Maybe a little."

"You need a power nap," Ivan suggested.

"Have work to do. Harry is expecting me."

"I'll take care of it," Ivan promised. "The others might fear her, but I don't." Ivan stood up, cupped Rory's bicep, and helped him up.

"Your bed or mine?" Rory asked.

Ivan snorted. "I'm going to settle you on the couch. If I put you in bed—"

"You'll do wicked things to me?"

"You just can't help yourself, can you?" Ivan teased.

"You bring it out in me. I swear I'm not like this with anyone else."

"Uh-huh," Ivan said as they reached the couch. "This is the perfect spot for napping. Just ask the cats."

The sofa might've looked outdated, but it was a pillow of perfection for Rory's weary body. Ivan unfolded the throw blanket from the top of the couch and draped it over him. Though Rory's eyes were heavy, he couldn't seem to stop tracking Ivan's movements through the room. It surprised Rory when Ivan sat down in the recliner and retrieved a book from the armrest. The cats came running, thinking they were getting another treat but settling for cuddles when none were forthcoming. The last thing Rory remembered was thinking how lucky those cats were.

chapter FIVE

IVAN KNOCKED ON CASH'S DOORJAMB TO GET HIS ATTENTION. His boss looked up from the paperwork on his desk and smiled. "What's up?"

"I just got off the phone with Roberto," Ivan said casually as if his heart wasn't trying to beat out of his chest. "He let me know that he'll be in the area much sooner than he expected and wants to move the interview up."

"Great news." Cash picked up his phone and tapped the screen before meeting Ivan's gaze. "When will he be here?"

Ivan's stomach pitched, threatening to reject his breakfast. He was already nervous about his meeting with Valentino Russo in Denver and the phone call from Roberto might just push Ivan over the edge. "Um, Sunday."

Cash narrowed his eyes. "Next Sunday?"

"No," Ivan replied. "In two days." He ran a hand through his hair. "I'm not ready."

Cash's eyes widened. "Oh, wow. I'm glad he's eager to meet with us, but the timing presents a problem. Nick arranged for me to meet with some FBI agents who specialize in cult investigations this weekend. I leave tomorrow morning and might not make it back in time." Cash rose from his chair and crossed the office. "Don't you dare reschedule this meeting," he said firmly. "You've worked too damn hard to blow this opportunity. Talk to Rory. Get some tips and pointers. The kid is a damn natural in front of a camera."

Ivan nodded because words failed him. On one hand, he knew Cash was right, but he was too fixated on his past experiences to focus on what his future needed. He forced a nod and said, "I'll talk to him before I leave for Denver."

Cash squeezed his arm. "You're going to do great. I promise."

Ivan wasn't convinced but he nodded and headed to the kitchen to find Rory. If he put off asking for help, he might not do it. Best to get this conversation behind him since he needed to get cleaned up and on the road to Denver soon. Ivan found Harry stirring something on the stove that smelled delicious.

"Where's Trouble?"

She pointed to her chest and said, "You've found it."

"Trouble Junior, then," Ivan said.

Harry snorted. "Rory is collecting eggs with Tyler and Owen."

He suspected shenanigans were afoot if those two were involved and headed that direction. He could ask Rory for his help and make sure he didn't get caught up in whatever schemes the troublesome twosome had cooked up.

After Monday's conversation, Ivan attempted to find the right balance of give and take with Rory. Something about the guy incited a surge of protectiveness he normally reserved for the people he loved dearly. Rory didn't fall into that category. Hell, Ivan wasn't sure he even liked the guy, but he admired the effort Rory put into every task. It didn't matter how big or small; the guy gave it his all. Ivan wasn't the only one who'd noticed. The guys who'd been the most reserved around Rory had all warmed up to him. Owen looked a little worried that Rory's shine drew Tyler too close to his orbit, but Owen had nothing to worry about there. Ivan figured eventually those two would figure out their bond extended beyond friendship, but that was their business.

Ivan saw Rory approach the chicken coop with the egg basket in hand while Tyler and Owen stood off to the side with their heads together. Definitely shenanigans afoot. They were probably wagering on Rory's success. Those two fools were each other's constant shadows and caused trouble nine times out of ten. Ivan was determined that Rory wouldn't become a victim of their chaos. Most of the hens were docile animals who didn't mind them reaching into the nesting boxes, but two of them would sooner peck your eye out than let you take their eggs.

Rory was sporting safety goggles, so Owen and Tyler had at least warned him about the vicious hens. Once Rory approached the coop, it became obvious the guys hadn't told him which hens had the propensity for violence since their names were painted above their nesting boxes. Rory gingerly reached into Helga's little house like she might attack him at any minute. His lips were moving, but Ivan couldn't hear what he was saying from his hiding spot. Sweet, docile Helga sat there like she did every morning. Ivan had seen her savagely devour a worm in the hen yard, but she was a total sweetheart the rest of the time. Helga clucked and shifted her wings just as Rory would've reached the egg. He jumped like he'd stuck his hand in a mousetrap and jerked his arm out of the nesting box.

Owen and Tyler looked at each other and fought back laughter for a few moments before calling out encouragement to Rory. Damn those assholes for their troublemaking. Rory reached over and gingerly stroked Helga's breast feathers, and Ivan imagined him sweetly talking to her like he did the cats. Ivan had noticed the treat bag was considerably lighter, and his felines were as enamored with Rory as Helga seemed to be at the moment. Rory reached back under the hen, cautiously removed the egg, and gently placed it in the basket. He didn't immediately move to the next hen, though. Rory took a few moments to stroke Helga's feathers, and Ivan found himself jealous of a chicken for the first time in his life.

He could almost feel Rory's long fingers brushing over his skin. And yeah, he'd noticed the length of the man's fingers, eyelashes, and other things he never paid much attention to on other men. Ivan didn't allow the image of Rory's cock to fully form in his brain. He wouldn't let himself imagine how smooth Rory's bare skin would feel against his lips. He hadn't needed an Only Fans subscription to see Rory in all his glory. Ivan reached the coop before Rory reached Bloody Mary's nesting box.

"Hey, Rory," Ivan called out. "Got a minute."

Rory turned around and smiled at him. "Sure."

Owen and Tyler exchanged a glance, and Ty slipped his best friend a folded bill. Did they assume Ivan was going to haul Rory off for midday sex? Ivan thought he'd hidden his attraction to Rory from the rest of the ranch crew. There was no way in hell they could know he'd googled everything he could find on Rory or that he'd started watching his YouTube channel at night. They weren't privy to Ivan's raunchy, nightly dreams, where he explored every inch of Rory's body. They sure as hell weren't in the bathroom when Ivan eased the ache in his balls in the shower while the rest of the house slept. Something in Ivan's demeanor must've tipped Owen and Tyler off, though. Ivan never considered them to be exceptionally intuitive or observant, so if they recognized Ivan's interest, the others had as well. Had Harry read more into Ivan's insistence that Rory get extra protein and complex carbs in his lunch?

Knowing everyone was watching and discussing Ivan made him queasy. His love life had once been violated and exploited just as fervently as Rory's relationship with his father. Ivan couldn't bear the thought of being the subject of such intense scrutiny ever again, even if on a smaller scale vis-à-vis the gossiping crew, and to think he hadn't thought his nerves could get worse.

"Ivan," Rory said softly.

Snapping out of his thoughts, Ivan looked into the bluest eyes he'd ever seen. They studied Ivan with the kind of curiosity that made him want to strip down and stretch out. The tip of Rory's tongue darted out and licked his bottom lip before the plump flesh ended up between his teeth. Ivan had caught Rory doing that a few times and realized he was nervous or worried about something. He balled his hands into fists instead of reaching up to rescue Rory's lip.

"Where'd you go just now?" Rory asked. "You were standing right here with me, but you weren't really here."

Telling Rory the truth wouldn't do them any good. Rory might see that as an invitation to amp up his flirtations, and Ivan wasn't sure how much longer he could resist him. The tone of Rory's teasing had transformed over the past four days. He hadn't bared his skin or blatantly invited him into his body, but there was an undeniable something extra when Rory looked at Ivan or spoke to him. Rory had claimed he didn't flirt shamelessly with anyone else, and Ivan had witnessed that firsthand. Rory engaged, chatted, and laughed with everyone on the ranch, but he reserved the special sparkle in his eyes and coy tilt to his lips just for Ivan. And hell if he didn't like it too fucking much. It was a damn good thing he was heading to Denver soon. He'd screw this frustration out of his system and return a new man.

"I guess my mind wandered to the meeting I have this afternoon," Ivan said. "I've contracted with a few upscale restaurants to sell my honey, but this meeting is the most important one yet. This chef is Michelin-starred, and being able to claim the partnership on my website would be an enormous deal."

Rory released his lip to smile at Ivan, and damn, what a beauty it was. Either his maker had blessed Rory with incredible genetics or his folks had paid a small fortune to accomplish a smile so perfect. "I have every confidence you'll land the deal."

"Thank you." Ivan checked his watch and noted the time. He needed to shower and hit the road soon, but he didn't want to postpone this conversation.

"You wanted to talk to me?" Rory prodded.

"Um, yeah. I need your help." Ivan swallowed hard and told him about the interview. "I'm really anxious about it, and Cash suggested you could give me some tips and tricks to help settle my nerves."

"Roberto is a really nice guy. I've met him a few times at various events and fundraisers. You have nothing to worry about, but I'll happily give you some tips." He tilted his head to the side. "I wonder if we could agree to a trade-off. A little quid pro quo." Ivan quirked a brow and Rory smiled. "That wasn't a come-on. You've seen enough of those to recognize them by now." Ivan tried really hard not to think about Rory's gleaming, naked body.

"What do you suggest?"

"I've researched many sustainable farming sources, but I've never explored honey making. Would you consider teaching me some things? You don't have to do anything on camera," Rory rushed to say. "It doesn't have to be for my channel. I just see your passion for it, and I'm curious." Rory placed a hand over his heart. "I promise to mostly be good."

"Sure, I can show you a few things," Ivan said, surprising both of them.

"When do you want to get started?" Rory asked. "I'm watching a *Dateline* marathon with Cash and Harry tonight, but I could work with you instead."

"I might be staying over in Denver tonight. I haven't decided for sure. Depends on how things pan out, I guess." He really needed to get laid because being so close to this man was driving him slowly mad. Rory's eyes darkened, and Ivan suspected he'd read between the lines and didn't like what he'd discovered. Ivan refused to feel sorry about putting his needs first for once. "My queen bee is due to arrive tomorrow afternoon, so I'll definitely be back in time for that."

Rory tilted his head to the side. "Beyoncé?"

Ivan chuckled. "My newest queen honeybee. She doesn't have a name yet, but I have big ambitions for her. I want to be here to ensure she gets settled in."

"Sounds like the perfect time for me to shadow you and learn what honey making entails."

"It would. We can work on tips afterward." Ivan took two steps backward. "Enjoy your *Dateline* marathon."

Rory raked a knowing gaze over Ivan's body. "Enjoy…whatever you get up to tonight."

Since Ivan nearly tripped over his own feet, he forced himself to turn around and head to the homestead to clean up and head out. Ivan stopped for gas halfway to Denver and heard several stupid news headlines regarding Rory and his dad when he restarted his truck. It was the same regurgitated bullshit with the latest polls thrown in to emphasize how much the scandal was hurting Charles Snyder's candidacy. Ivan switched over to his favorite agriculture podcast to catch up on the new episodes. Bob Harlow had the type of personality that took sometimes dry subjects and made them fun. Ivan figured it had to be exhausting to be so positive all the time. There were several memes circulating that called him Bob the Farmer and compared him to the kid's show character Bob the Builder. Instead of "Can we fix it? Yes, we can!" Harlow's lines were, "Can we grow it? Yes, we can!"

To his shock, Ivan couldn't even escape Rory halfway to Denver because he appeared as Bob's guest on the very next episode. Rory came across as laid-back and humorous when he told a story about an encounter with wild boars during one of his excursions. But then the conversation morphed into why he was so passionate about conservation and preservation.

"It's not just about saving the environment," Rory said, "though that is really important to me. What really tugs at my heartstrings are the traditions families pass down. You see that represented a lot in agriculture, where the goal is to preserve the land to sustain future generations by putting food on the table and money in the bank. You also see the same preservation passion in cooking and crafting. Recipes are shared and skills are taught to keep the older generations present with us long after they've passed. It's a beautiful thing, and family is at the very core of those principles."

"Wow," Ivan and Bob said at the same time.

"So we know why you're passionate about conservation and preservation, but who inspired you?" Bob asked.

"My grandparents," Rory replied. "They owned a farm in Oklahoma, and I spent summers there with my older brother, Nick."

Bob led Rory through some of his fondest memories, and Ivan became so enraptured that he nearly missed his exit. The episode was still playing when Ivan pulled up to the restaurant, and he looked forward to hearing the rest. Ivan shut the podcast off and organized his thoughts before stepping out of the truck and slipping into his suit jacket. He didn't dress up often because it reminded him of his childhood church and his time in a courtroom. Ivan checked his reflection in the side window and had to admit he cut an impressive figure in his navy suit and crisp white dress shirt. He'd skipped the tie and finished the look with a brown leather belt and matching dress shoes. With the custom crate he'd built for presentations such as these, Ivan headed into Russo's on Main. They wouldn't serve patrons until five, but the staff was bustling around, prepping for the night.

Valentino Russo sat in the back corner of the restaurant with a stunning blonde woman. Both of them wore chef's coats—white for Valentino and gray for his guest. A server had told Ivan to go on over to the table because Val was expecting him. He debated waiting for the chefs' conversation to end first, but Russo saw him and waved him over.

Both chefs rose when he approached, and Valentino made introductions. The blonde woman, Stephanie Borsch, was Val's wife and the head chef at another popular restaurant—one on Ivan's contact list.

"Please call us Val and Steph," Russo said. "Have a seat. Would you like something to drink or eat after the long drive?"

Ivan was way too nervous to eat, but he asked for a cup of coffee. A server brought over a gorgeous silver set, and Val poured them all a cup.

"We both have full houses tonight, so we could use the caffeine too." Val took a sip and set the cup down. He exchanged a glance with his wife before smiling at Ivan. "We've already sampled your honey when we were scouting out a competitor's restaurant. I've experienced it drizzled over a scone, used as a sweetener in my tea, and featured as a principal ingredient in a dessert." Val folded his hands on the table and said, "Both of us would like to use it in our kitchens, and we've come up with signature dishes that will make your honey the star."

Ivan sat flummoxed for a few seconds before a broad grin spread across his face. "You're kidding?"

Steph smiled and shook her head. "The question is…would you like to try them before anyone else?"

"Having renowned chefs prepare special dishes just for me that just happen to feature my honey?" Ivan asked. He cocked his head to the side and stroked his beard as if mulling it over. "Okay, you've twisted my arm."

Stephanie clapped and pulled the honey crate toward her while Val saluted him with the coffee cup. Seconds later, both chefs rose from the table.

"Should I leave and come back?" Ivan asked.

"No, no," Stephanie said. "Relax and be our guest. The first course will be out soon."

"First course," Ivan said to himself, wishing he'd brought Cash with him for the meeting. This was too fun to do by himself. Rory would get a kick out of it too. Ivan shoved the thought aside and decided it would be a good time to search Grindr for a hookup before he left the city. He'd just opened the app when a sexy bartender with smoldering good looks stopped by his table.

"Hello, I'm Jack. Are you ready to kick off your experience on the right foot, Mr. Gallagher? Perhaps something made with your honey?"

The sparkle in his dark eyes said more than a beverage was up for grabs. Damn. Ivan might refer to this as his lucky suit from now on. As handsome as this guy was, he didn't quite fit the bill for what Ivan had in mind.

"I could use something slightly stronger than coffee." Ivan had a few hours, and it sounded like plenty of food to counter the effects of a single cocktail. "What do you recommend? I'd like something with a little kick but nothing too sweet."

The bartender winked and said, "I know just the thing. I'll be right back."

Before Jack returned with his drink, a Latina server named Emilia placed a tray of halved figs topped with goat cheese crumbles and drizzled with honey on the table.

"This looks incredible," Ivan told her.

"Enjoy."

Ivan remembered to take a picture of the plate before he popped a fig into his mouth. Sweet Jesus, it was divine. He'd just bitten into a third fig when Jack returned with his drink. It was dark orange, so Ivan expected something citrusy. He took a tentative sip and tasted gin and lemon. His honey and something spicy came on later. Chili pepper, perhaps. "What is this?"

"Spicy bee's knees," Jack said. "It's more potent than you realize, so proceed with caution if you're driving."

Ivan saluted him and took a small sip. He popped another fig into his mouth and picked up his phone. That's when he remembered to take a picture of his cocktail. He made a note on his phone for future consideration: flavored honeys. After that, he attempted to open the Grindr app. He'd passed on two or three candidates when Emilia returned with a salad.

"You'll find your honey in the toasted walnuts and in the vinaigrette drizzled on top."

Ivan snapped a picture of the salad then dug in. The feta cheese on top of spring greens provided a salty balance to the sweetened nuts and dressing. The experience was a dream come true, and Ivan nearly pinched himself to make sure he was actually awake. There was a brief lull between the salad and the main course, so he again looked at Grindr. He kept passing on sexy men with thoughts like too tall, too blond, eyes aren't blue enough, eyelashes aren't long enough, too—

Ivan's brain screeched to a halt, and he nearly dropped his phone. He'd discounted probably a dozen hot, horny guys simply because they didn't look enough like Rory. That little shit had somehow infiltrated every aspect of his life with very little effort. Sure, he'd made a big sexy production on his first day, and okay, his third, but he'd kept his distance from Ivan since. This…infatuation was all Ivan's doing, and he just couldn't fathom what it was about Rory Snyder that had gripped him by the balls.

When Emilia brought out his entrée, Ivan nearly leapt to his feet and hugged her. He was desperate for a distraction from his thoughts. She set the plate in front of him and smiled. "Honey truffle fried chicken, garlic mashed potatoes, and asparagus."

Ivan leaned closer and inhaled the sweet and earthy combination of truffles and honey. "Heaven on earth."

"Enjoy," she said.

Ivan was convinced he didn't have room to clean his plate, but he enjoyed every bite. He'd have to rent a room to sleep off a food coma instead of finding a place to fuck. When Emilia strolled to him with dessert, he waved his white napkin in surrender. Val and Stephanie were a few steps behind and laughed at his antics.

"I can't," Ivan said when she set down the plate.

"Oh, come on," Emilia teased. "Live a little." She didn't know how often he heard that phrase from the crew at the ranch.

He smiled at her when everyone else would've earned a glare. "I'll give it my best shot."

"Mind if we join you?" Val asked.

"Please do."

"The dessert you have now is a crêpe. We used your honey to sweeten the Greek yogurt and fruit filling. We both plan to introduce cakes and other desserts with the honey as well, but this was something we could do quickly."

Ivan took a picture of the final course and tucked his phone away. "I'm not sharing these images publicly. I just want to tease everyone back at the ranch." The husband and wife laughed and gestured for him to dig in. Ivan took a bite and groaned a little. "So light and flavorful. It's the perfect thing to end a heavy meal. Just the right mix of sweet and tangy." He could only eat one of the crêpes on the plate and waved the other away. "Seriously, I won't be able to walk to my truck. I can't thank you enough for this experience."

"It is our pleasure," Steph said. "Let's do it again, and next time you can bring a special guest."

Rory's face appeared unbidden in Ivan's mind. "That would be wonderful."

Val called for more coffee, and the trio got down to business before they were both needed in their respective kitchens. When Ivan exited the restaurant, the doors had just opened, and the hostess was seating people with five o'clock reservations. He practically floated out to his truck. He couldn't wait to call Cash.

"Ivan?" Nine years had passed since he'd heard that voice, but Ivan recognized it immediately. It belonged to the first and only man he'd ever loved.

Ivan turned around and faced Curt Washington. It had been nine years since Ivan had found Curt unconscious on his dorm room floor after an intentional overdose. Nine fucking years since Curt had cut Ivan out of his life without even a goodbye or fuck off. Curt had changed very little. His black hair was shorter and showed a hint of gray at the temples. His dark brown eyes looked at Ivan with wariness instead of the adoration they'd once held. The men had both traveled a lot of miles since then, so it was understandable. But they'd never said their good-byes or had any sort of closure. One minute they were riding high on their love, and the next, their lives were turned upside down.

Ivan recognized the man standing with Curt as his husband and business partner, though they'd never met. He purposely never searched out a single thing about Curt because he'd never wanted to resurrect the pain Ivan associated with him. But one day, when he'd been minding his own business, he'd come across an ad for their real estate business in Colorado Springs. The smiling husbands and their adoptive son were featured front and center in the promo that vowed to find forever homes for their potential clients.

"Curt," Ivan said, aiming for an ambivalent tone.

Curt's husband, Gavin Truman, looked at Curt and said, "Is this *the* Ivan?" At Curt's nod, Gavin closed the small distance separating them and threw his arms around Ivan. "Thank you for saving his life. Thank you, thank you, thank you."

Ivan held Curt's gaze the entire time and didn't miss the tears filling his ex-boyfriend's eyes. Curt's lips trembled like he wanted to speak but couldn't. And what more was there to say? Maybe Curt had never said goodbye when their relationship ended or expressed his gratitude, but Ivan saw both things in his dark gaze. Ivan patted Gavin's back. "You're welcome," he said, addressing them both.

Gavin sniffled, pulled back, and returned to his husband's side. "Have you already eaten? We'd love to treat you to dinner if not."

Ivan smiled and politely refused the offer. "I'm just leaving. I had an earlier meeting with the chef." He could tell they were curious, but he wasn't interested in sharing the details of his personal or professional life with them. "You guys enjoy your dinner."

There was no offer to keep in touch or to clear the air. They wouldn't be friends or even acquaintances. Curt was just somebody Ivan used to love, and that was good enough for him. He gave them a small wave, told them again to enjoy their evening, and continued toward his truck.

Ivan drove on autopilot while his brain tried to process everything that had happened in the last few hours, hell the past week. All the euphoria he'd felt after signing the deal with both restaurants fizzled out as exhaustion moved in. Ivan was halfway home before he remembered to call Cash, but then decided against it when he remembered the marathon he'd planned with Harry and Rory. The morning would come soon enough. All Ivan wanted was a hot shower, his bed, and his cats. He rolled down the windows so the breeze could ruffle his hair and cranked up the radio.

Ivan rolled up to the ranch a little after eight o'clock. He parked his truck and headed into the old homestead, where the cats were the only ones around to greet him. Mindful of his suit, he only bent down to pet them instead of picking them up. They weren't happy about it, but he promised cuddles after his shower.

Once upstairs, he was too damn tired and decided to just return his suit to the closet and get into bed. He'd planned to watch television for a bit but fell asleep before he'd even found the remote to switch the TV on. He crashed hard for a long time, but his slumber turned fitful around three in the morning when sexy dreams of Rory invaded. Ivan would wake up hard, sweaty, and yearning, his heart racing and dick throbbing. He'd ignore the urge to fuck his fist to find relief and eventually drift back to sleep for more of the same torture. Sometime around five, he gave up and threw back the covers. He'd take a shower and head to his office to double-check the preparations for his new queen.

He didn't switch on any lights because he knew the way frontward and backward. Just outside the bathroom, Ivan collided with a warm, half-naked body. He wasn't sure if he recognized the gasp or the scent, but he knew damn well who he'd collided with in the hallway. Loneliness and lust formed an electric synergy, and it must've fried his circuits because Ivan pulled Rory tighter against his body instead of pushing him away.

chapter
SIX

W ARM, CALLUSED FINGERS GHOSTED OVER RORY'S BARE
back before settling on his hips. He didn't need to turn a
light on to know whose body was pressed so deliciously
against his. If Ivan had taken liberty with wandering hands, Rory could
do the same. He leaned forward and rubbed his face against Ivan's chest,
inhaling his masculine scent as crisp chest hair teased his nose and
cheek. Rory expected the big man to come to his senses, but a guttural
groan eased past his lips, and Ivan pressed his fingers deeper into Rory's
flesh.

This was real, right? Broad shoulders, brawny arms, a firm chest,
thicker than thick thighs, and a mouthwatering hard-on pressed against
his stomach. He had to be dreaming, and if so, he was going to live it
up until reality invaded his nocturnal sandbox. Rory planted a kiss in
the center of Ivan's chest, his mouth slightly open to brush the tip of
his tongue against flesh and fur. Ivan released his left hip to tangle that
hand in Rory's hair. Fingernails lightly grazed Rory's scalp, making his
dick jump in his briefs. He rocked his hips forward, but the difference
in their heights meant their dicks didn't align perfectly. He emitted a

hungry growl and stood on his tiptoes to get his sensitive cockhead closer to the promised land.

Rory shifted open-mouth kisses to the right, loving the way Ivan's heart pounded beneath flesh and bone. He let sensation and instinct guide him. When he reached Ivan's nipple, Rory swiped his tongue upward to lave the hard bud with wet heat.

"Fuck," Ivan whispered hoarsely as the fingers on both hands dug in deeper.

Rory circled Ivan's nipple with his tongue, sucked it between his lips, and gently raked his teeth over the extended flesh before pulling back.

"Again," Ivan demanded.

"So bossy," Rory replied between kisses to the other side. He repeated the pattern of kiss, lave, suck, and scrape. Ivan thrust his hips upward, rubbing his erection against Rory's abdomen and leaving a wet streak. The big man's excitement was a buffet for the senses. Ivan's earthy musk teased Rory's nose, his heavy breathing was a perfect soundtrack of seduction, and his body heat seeped into his skin, warming him better than any electric blanket could.

When Rory lifted his head from Ivan's chest, strong fingers tugged his hair until Rory raised his chin. Firm lips smashed against his, hot and insistent. Rory gasped his pleasure, and Ivan pressed his advantage to slip his tongue inside. Rory fisted one hand in Ivan's hair and gripped one of Ivan's ass cheeks with the other. Thick muscles bunched beneath his underwear as Ivan rutted against Rory harder and faster. Rory wanted to make him come in more interesting ways, but he'd settle for a horny frotting session in a dark hallway.

Without warning, Ivan took two steps to the right, pulling Rory with him. A doorjamb scraped against his back, and Rory noticed the transition from wood to tile beneath his feet. Ivan had moved them into the bathroom. The edge of the vanity pressed into Rory's ass a moment later and a gentle whoosh of air brushed against his skin when Ivan shut the door with a soft click. There was no window in the upstairs bathroom, so the room was pitch black. Rory fumbled around for the light switch, but Ivan captured his hand and used it to turn him around to face the sink. Ivan's dick pressed against his ass. Need and lust throbbed in the long shaft rutting hungrily against him. Rory knew the massive erection didn't have a mind of its own, but it felt like a heaving beast hell-bent on possession. And Rory was desperate to be claimed. He grunted and leaned forward, thrusting himself tighter against the friction, signaling that anything Ivan wanted was his for the taking.

A hungry snarl answered Rory's invitation. Ivan leaned forward and pressed a wall of muscle to Rory's back, then wrapped a powerful arm around Rory's chest, holding him in place for…whatever the fuck he wanted. Rory's brain was already several minutes ahead of them as he imagined Ivan yanking down his underwear and thrusting hard and deep inside him. He didn't want to miss a second of it, so Rory fumbled around for the light switch again.

"Leave it." Ivan's voice sounded terse, and his words felt like scabs he'd ripped off to reveal a wound Rory didn't understand.

Why did they have to stay in the dark? Did he have ugly scars he wanted to hide? If Rory pushed, the dream would end, and he didn't want that. So he braced his hands in front of him instead. The mirror was cold beneath Rory's hands, and he wished again that he could see the look on Ivan's face when he buried his dick inside him to the hilt. Ivan slowly slid his hand down the front of Rory's chest, eliciting fire in his wake, and didn't stop until he reached the elastic waistband of his briefs. Rory's blood rushed through his veins, deafening him to everything but his desire for a man he hardly knew. He'd had hookups with strangers before, but this was so much different. Ivan's touch felt like it had branded his flesh, creating a map of the places he'd caressed, unlike past lovers who'd never so much as made a mark—on his skin or his soul.

Rory gasped when Ivan shoved his hand down the front of his underwear, thick fingers encircling his shaft. Precum spilled onto Ivan's fist, aiding the glide as he dragged his palm up and down Rory's erection. Everything inside Rory urged him to scream for more, but he didn't want his voice to break the spell or disturb his dream. Instead, he reached back with a hand to tug one side of his underwear down before shifting to the other side and repeating his action. His briefs snagged beneath the swell of his ass cheeks, but it was enough for what he wanted—needed. He spread his legs as far as the fabric prison permitted and stepped back from the vanity. Rory lowered his torso over the sink, which put his puckered hole right where he needed it to be.

"Fuck, I want you." The snarled confession made Rory's dick leak more as Ivan's fat cockhead rubbed against his sensitive nerve endings. Rory didn't need the words to know Ivan was just as turned on as he was. The growing wet spot on the front of Ivan's underwear told him everything he needed to know as did the aggressive thrusts against his eager flesh.

Ivan moved the hand from Rory's hip up to cup his chin and rained fervent kisses along his neck and jaw. Soft beard bristles tickled Rory's skin, eliciting tingly goose bumps and sending shivers down his spine. And all the while, Ivan's hand dragged lazily up and down Rory's cock while he slid his drooling monster between Rory's ass cheeks. The sensation overload made him crazy, and it wasn't nearly enough.

"More," he said, hoping his greedy demand wasn't a bucket of ice water on their fun.

A chuckle rumbled deep in Ivan's chest, but instead of yanking his underwear down for full skin-on-skin action, Ivan used his grip on Rory's chin to turn his head. Firm lips landed on his, softer than he would've expected from someone so big and brawny. Ivan used the tip of his tongue to tease Rory's lips apart, then licked into his mouth once he surrendered. Rory moaned like a needy slut because the angle didn't allow for a deep kiss, and he was desperate for Ivan's penetration somewhere. He greedily twirled his tongue around Ivan's before forming an O and sucking on it.

Ivan grunted and released Rory's chin so he could tug his underwear down to midthigh. The heat from before magnified tenfold when Ivan's bare dick rubbed against Rory's trembling hole, glazing the ring with precum. Rory's pleas were carnal and shameless.

Ivan loosely covered Rory's mouth, and he realized just how loud he'd gotten. Instead of being turned off, the needy begging seemed to amp Ivan up. He rocked his hips faster, tunneling his dick between Rory's ass cheeks. Had he been able to see, Rory was sure dots would've danced before his eyes as intense pleasure built until his entire body went tense. His climax slammed into him hard, the intensity catching him by surprise. He bit down on the meaty heel of Ivan's palm to keep from screaming his pleasure. Ivan groaned and pumped him to completion. The slickness of his release coated the thick fingers now pressed against Rory's stomach, holding him in place while Ivan rutted against him like a wild beast. Ivan didn't yell when his orgasm hit. He sucked in a sharp breath and held it while his release splattered over Rory's lower back and ass crack, then dribbled over his puckered hole.

Ivan rested his head between Rory's shoulder blades and braced his hands on the vanity to support his weight. Rory was seconds away from melting into a puddle of goo. The brain-rattling orgasm must've knocked his filter loose because he said, "Why didn't you want the lights on? I would've given everything I have to watch you come."

Ivan sighed heavily. "That would've made this too real. In the dark, I can pretend this was a delicious dream and that I didn't just step over a line I never allow myself to cross."

The words stung, though Rory knew Ivan hadn't meant to be cruel. The ranch crew had been extremely curious about the connection Rory and Ivan couldn't seem to hide. The scent of their combined releases was heavy on the air but not as thick as the tension between them.

"It'll be our secret," Rory said as he shifted out from between Ivan and the vanity.

Ivan said nothing as he stepped back to put more distance between them. Rory had seen the size of the bathroom. Ivan couldn't have been more than a foot away, but it might as well have been a country mile. Rory pulled up his underwear, feeling cheap and stupid for the first time in his life. Nearby rustling signaled Ivan was doing the same. Rory was grateful the lights weren't on to reveal the stupid tears filling his eyes. He should go downstairs and let Ivan clean up first. Then he could do his own thing before heading over to the big house for breakfast. Yeah, that's what he would do.

"I'll just, um…" Rory fumbled for the door, his hands suddenly clumsy. "Head out." His fingers finally found the knob, and he twisted it harder than necessary. He pulled the handle, but the door wouldn't budge. Rory gave it another yank but still nothing. The knob had turned, so it wasn't stuck, but something pressed against it toward the top.

"Not so fast," Ivan said.

Rory released the knob and stepped back into a wall of muscle. Ivan slid his hand down the length of the door, revealing the source of the blockage, then he placed it against Rory's stomach. The second hand, the sticky one, landed on Rory's hip and held him flush against Ivan's chest. If he didn't get the hell out of there, he'd break down and sob in front of Ivan, and that was the last thing he wanted. Rory wasn't usually a crier, but the emotional highs and lows of the past week had taken their toll.

"I'm not sorry," Ivan said huskily. "And I didn't mean to make you feel ashamed of what happened." Rory hated that Ivan could read him so well even in the dark. "I just like to keep my personal business away from the ranch. We've already drawn too much attention. If Owen and Tyler are placing bets on how quickly I come running when I think you might be in trouble, I guarantee others have noticed I can't keep my fucking eyes off you."

"I knew you were out there somewhere," Rory said. "I felt you."

"That's a problem."

Rory remembered the conversation they'd had about when Ivan would return from Denver. He'd gotten the distinct impression Ivan was going there for something more than business. "Did you plan to fuck out your frustrations with someone else last night?"

"Yes," Ivan replied without hesitation. He kissed a spot behind Rory's ear that made him shiver. "And I just kept swiping because they weren't who I wanted." A soft growl rumbled through Ivan's chest. "You've been on my mind too much, and that was before I knew the breathy sounds you make when you orgasm and what your cum smells like."

"I'm not looking for commitment and romance," Rory said, feeling a little hopeful that this wasn't a one-off when Ivan didn't seem to be in a hurry to release him. As if to prove his point, Ivan ran his nose along the side of his neck.

"You going to let me go?"

Ivan nipped his shoulder, then licked it. "I should want to…"

"But you don't." An idea, albeit a stupid one, popped into Rory's mind and exited his mouth before he could stop it. "Neither of us are looking for a relationship. We both want me to ride your gorgeous cock. I think we could come to a mutually pleasing arrangement."

Ivan bit the sensitive bend in Rory's neck and chuckled when he trembled. "I'm listening."

"I propose a no-strings fuck fest until the media moves on to a fresh scandal and I can go home." Rory figured it would be another two weeks tops. He could make and store tons of sexy memories with Ivan in fourteen days. His hyperactive brain was already plotting day six's sexy adventures before Ivan reacted on day one.

"It's a terrible idea." Ivan's words expressed doubt, but his hands explored the plains and valleys of Rory's abdomen, and he nuzzled his nose in Rory's hair. "We've drawn too much attention already."

"So we'll just have to be smarter and stealthier. Interview practice will give us an excuse today." Rory pushed his ass against Ivan's bulge. "I'm heading to Last Chance Creek with Harry to do some grocery shopping and meet Hope for lunch. I can buy us the good lube."

Ivan groaned and lowered his hand to cup Rory's crotch. "You're making it hard to say no."

Rory's dick twitched like it might have life left in it. "You're just making me hard."

Ivan sighed heavily, and Rory braced himself for rejection. He expected the big man to release him and step back, and Rory fought the urge to turn in his embrace and hold him one last time. That right there should've been the red flag needed to rescind his offer, but he couldn't form the words to take it back.

"I have concerns," Ivan said.

Rory nearly sagged with relief. "Name them."

"I have a position of authority and respect to maintain. I don't want to act in a way that jeopardizes that or to have my personal life become gossip fodder." Rory sensed there was more to Ivan's attention phobia, but he didn't press. Ivan dipped his fingers under Rory's waistband and caressed the bare skin at the base of his cock. Was Ivan aware of the sexy little growl he made?

"You think you're so irresistible that I won't be able to keep my hands off you in front of the crew?" Rory asked. He'd meant the words to come out as a tease, but they hung in the space like a husky challenge.

Ivan nipped his neck again, then licked a long stripe up to Rory's ear. He sank his teeth into Rory's tender earlobe and slowly pulled back until the flesh popped free. "Not normally, but then you showed up on the ranch and eye-fucked me in front of everyone." Ivan dropped his hand to cup Rory's smooth balls. He parted his legs to give him full access to the goods, and Ivan took advantage. His middle finger circled his taint and inched backward, stopping just shy of his sticky hole. "And my thoughts were just as carnal. I don't have a lot of confidence we can pull this off."

Rory dropped his head back to rest on Ivan's shoulder, exposing more of his neck to seeking lips. "I can be good." *The best you'll ever have.*

Ivan shifted his hands to turn Rory around and pinned him to the door. Firm lips captured his in a hot, devastating kiss that felt more like sealing the deal than nixing it. Ivan's tongue was persistent and oh so talented. Rory couldn't wait to experience it in other places. Ivan worked him up to a semihard state before breaking the kiss and leaning his forehead against Rory's.

"Continue this tonight?" Rory asked. "We can practice your interview."

"Yes," Ivan replied. Then he groaned. "Oh, damn. It's poker night again."

"How long do they usually last?" The fun had already broken up by the time Rory had returned from the big ranch house the previous week.

"A few hours at most." Ivan snorted.

Rory settled his hands on Ivan's narrow hips, fingers aching to explore the expanse of flesh and muscle. "All we need to do is avoid giving them something to talk about. We practice our poker faces right away, and they'll stop watching us like hawks and go home at a decent time."

"You underestimate their nose for gossip. I'm pretty sure some of them are part bloodhound, but we'll give it a shot." Ivan stepped back, taking his heat with him. "Get out of here while you still can."

"That line might work in a horror film, but it's not motivating me to budge."

"Go downstairs now, and I'll go down on you later," Ivan said gruffly.

Rory knew in his heart that it wouldn't take much persuasion to change Ivan's mind, but he might resent it—and Rory, once the post-orgasmic fog lifted. Rory rose on his tiptoes to kiss Ivan's mouth, but the kiss landed on his cheek instead.

"I'm going, but we're doing it with the lights on next time," Rory said. "See you at breakfast."

"Where you won't eye-fuck me in front of the others."

"Not even a figurative fondle. They won't have a clue about what we got up to this morning nor will they know about our future plans."

Ivan captured his mouth in one last sweet kiss before stepping back. "See you at breakfast."

Rory forced his feet to move and exited the bathroom. He crept quietly down the hallway, hoping like hell they hadn't woken Dylan. When he returned to his room and turned on the light, Rory found Scruffy stretched out on his bed. Rory lay down beside the plus-sized purr machine while waiting for Ivan to finish showering. He usually hated being sticky after sex, but he didn't relish washing away the memories of what he'd shared with Ivan. Scruffy crawled onto his chest and headbutted his chin, seeking attention.

"Just like your master," Rory said as he complied.

The cat purred louder, easing tension Rory hadn't realized he was carrying. The shower continued overhead, triggering images of a wet, naked Ivan soaping up. He'd talked a huge game upstairs, but keeping his eyes and hands to himself around Ivan would be hard. The reward would be more than worth it.

"I've got this under control." *I've totally got this under control.*

Meow.

Rory's eyes popped open. He wasn't even aware he'd closed them until Scruffy meowed. Weak sunlight filtered in through the crack in the curtains, and Rory jackknifed into a sitting position, dislodging the cat.

"Fuck!" He'd overslept.

A quick glance at the clock told him he wasn't that late to breakfast.

He leapt off the bed and dressed in a hurry. He made a quick pass in the bathroom to scrub his teeth before heading up to the big house. His face felt dry, and he wished he'd taken a few minutes to wash his face or even check his reflection in the mirror. But memories of what they'd done in the bathroom threatened to sabotage the promise he'd made to Ivan. Rory hauled ass to the main house, lecturing himself the entire way. Laughter and conversation drifted from the dining room, reminding him of how much these people cared for one another. It made him suddenly shy about going in. Rory stood just outside the dining room entrance, trying to breathe through his nervousness.

Toenails clicked on the hardwood, and Patsy appeared in the hallway. She made a cute little growly noise and wiggled until he leaned over to pet her. She raised her paw and placed it over his hand as if to assure him everything would be okay. Rory straightened and followed her into the dining room with an apology for his tardiness on the tip of his tongue. He forgot what he was going to say when everyone turned their attention to him. Rory was confused about the various smirks and smiles on their faces. Surely, someone had accidentally overslept on the ranch before him. When his eyes connected with Ivan's, his amber gaze dropped to Rory's neck, making him suddenly aware of the tenderness there. He recalled the brush of Ivan's beard against his neck during their fevered make-out session. *Oh shit.*

Ivan averted his gaze, but Rory could tell the tops of his ears were red. He turned to grab a plate and caught his reflection in the mirror over the buffet, confirming his suspicions. He could practically hear "Taps" playing for their now dead arrangement.

chapter
SEVEN

THAT FREAKING BEARD BURN IVAN HAD LEFT ON RORY'S NECK
screamed, "Look at me! Look at me! Look at me!" And everyone
did, and then they looked at Ivan. It got so quiet in the dining room
that a mouse fart would've sounded like a cannon blast. A wave of heat
engulfed Ivan's body but only some of it came from embarrassment. He
ducked his head and turned his gaze to his food, but he knew it was
too late. Anyone with eyes on him, which was everyone in the room,
would've seen the blush staining his cheeks. He might as well have stood
up and shouted, "I did it! I rubbed his neck raw with my beard while
rubbing one out between his perky ass cheeks!" And to be sure no one
thought him a scoundrel who took pleasure without giving it in equal or
better measure, he would add, "And he came so hard he nearly collapsed."

But Ivan did no such thing. He speared a sausage link with so much
force someone might think it had insulted his mama. He lifted the pork
to his mouth and bit off half its length, reverting to the little kid who'd
wolfed down his food at mealtimes. Instead of eagerness to go back outside and play, Ivan wanted to retreat to the barn to hide from prying
eyes. It reminded him too much of a previous time in his life when his

name had been dragged through the mud and his face splashed across newspapers and media reports. First the run-in with Curt and now everyone staring at him in the dining room. It felt like history repeating itself, just on a smaller scale. The fork in his hand shook, and he tightened his grip on both the utensil and his composure. *Think of something else, damn it.* Memories of Rory coming apart in his arms danced across his brain, but he tossed up a wall to block them. *Anything but that.* Ivan forced his thoughts to the tasks he needed to accomplish before his new queen arrived, and calm washed over him.

Not a single person uttered a word or maybe even breathed while Rory made his plate. The only open chair was the one across from Ivan, and he shifted his eyes without lifting his head to assess Rory's expression when he sat down. Their gazes met and held for a brief second. Ivan was pretty sure he caught a spark of pure mischief in Rory's arctic eyes, an expression he'd label *hold my beer*, and oddly, that made Ivan feel calmer.

"What are y'all gawking at?" Rory asked. "You act like you've never seen razor burn until now. And take a damn breath for crying out loud. Some of you are turning purple."

A combination of laughter, exhaled breaths, and utensils scraping against plates followed Rory's comment. Ivan admired his quick wit and unflappable demeanor, but he didn't trust himself to communicate it through body language or eye contact.

"Razor burn?" Owen asked a few minutes later. "You sure about that?"

Ivan wanted to tell him to mind his own business, but that would just draw more unwanted attention.

"Positive," Rory said. "I forgot to bring my shaving cream upstairs with me. Ivan had already left. Made do with what I had since I was already late." Rory forked up a bite of fluffy scrambled eggs and chewed thoughtfully. "I also skipped my three-step face routine and didn't exfoliate my skin. Want to bust my balls over that too?"

Ivan shifted his eyes to the right and saw Owen raise his hands in surrender while Tyler chuckled at Rory's admonishment.

Rueben changed the topic to future projects Rory had planned for his channel. Grateful for the shift, Ivan continued to eat while everyone else hung on Rory's every word. He finished long before anyone else and pushed back from the table. "I have a lot to do before my queen bee arrives," Ivan said. "See you all at lunch."

"Which will be cold-cut sandwiches and chips or various leftovers from previous meals," Harry added. "Rory and I are headed into town this afternoon."

"Congratulations on landing another deal," Rueben called out. Ivan had just finished filling everyone in on his successful meeting the previous night when Rory had entered the dining room. "Rocky Mountain Liquid Gold could become a household name someday."

"Thanks, Rue," Ivan said, even though he didn't aspire to reach that particular milestone.

Once in the kitchen, he rinsed his dishes and put them in the dishwasher before topping off his travel mug and heading to the barn. He breathed in the familiar scents of lumber, equipment, and the fluids they used to keep the machinery maintained. The hardest part about farming was timing the planting and harvesting seasons just right. If the seed went into the ground too soon, melting snow from the mountains and spring rain would flush them from the soil. If he waited too long, he risked low field production. And harvesting had its own set of weather-related obstacles.

Agriculture was in Ivan's blood. He couldn't recall a time when his life hadn't revolved around weather forecasts—past, present, and future. Like any industry, agriculture had advanced its technology, but the success of a healthy crop and prosperous harvest came down to the weather. It was one part planning and planting and three parts luck. Ivan sought solace in the data on the forecast sheets. He'd studied them over the last few weeks, comparing historical numbers to the futures available. His mama was fond of an old saying: *If you want to make God laugh, tell him what you're going to do later*, but Ivan had changed it to *if you want to make Mother Nature laugh, tell her when you're going to plant your fields.*

The newest reports aligned with the plan he'd made last week, and Ivan realized the data was probably as good as it was going to get. He needed to shift his brain out of planning mode and into planting mode, which meant he needed to ready the winterized equipment. It wasn't just possible they'd see a spring snowfall; it was probable. The temperatures should remain high enough to prevent mechanical damage after he changed the fluids in the various machines. Ivan wrote out a schedule for each piece of machinery and assigned the tasks. He wished he could say thoughts of Rory didn't intrude, but he'd be a liar. A montage of images of the things they shared flashed through his brain. The lights might've been out, but his brain had no problem imagining the way Rory looked—wild and wanton—in the bathroom. And the sounds he made? If Ivan allowed his mind to go there, he'd be hard as stone in no time.

Once he'd completed his spring planting agenda, Ivan shifted his attention to his bees. Rocky Mountain Liquid Gold was more than a moneymaker; it was his passion project. The Gallaghers had never raised bees in Kansas, and Ivan's first experience came when he'd been sent to Arrowhead Correctional Facility. He never could've anticipated how much he'd enjoy watching the bees build their hives or the absolute satisfaction he would get from making honey. Ivan had always taken pride in whatever task he tackled, but he had some serious hubris when it came to his precious bees and their liquid gold. A smile curved his lips as he thought about the shit Rory would give him over the brand name. *No, no, no. We are not thinking about him right now.* We? Had his brain become its own entity? Seemed like maybe it had happened since Rory had arrived on the ranch.

Ivan forced his attention to the schematics for hive improvements. New flower species and water source upgrades topped the priority list. His plans were ambitious but solid, yet Ivan was unsettled. He scanned his information again and realized his malaise didn't have anything to do with the bees. Ivan didn't like the way he'd left the dining room. Hindsight could either be his best friend or provide a swift kick to the balls. Ivan's present reflection fell into the latter category. The knot in his stomach had nothing to do with illness or hunger. Ivan knew without a doubt that Rory would've interpreted his hasty retreat as rejection when self-preservation was his only aim. Ivan had wanted to reach across the table and kiss Rory or pull him into his lap and soothe the skin he'd abraded, but he hadn't wanted to get a raging hard-on while surrounded by the rest of the crew, so he'd hightailed it out of there.

Ivan alternated between staring off into space and rereading the same lines without comprehending the words. "I gotta make this right."

He took a few moments to straighten his desk before leaving his office. Cleanliness had been another recurring theme throughout his life. The message had started in Bible school and been reinforced in all the influential arenas of his youth and young adulthood. Maybe that was why he was so insistent that no one know his personal business. It was too messy. *That's not it.* Indoctrination was a factor in the equation but not the sum.

By the time Ivan stepped out of the barn, Harry and Rory were already striding toward the zippy red convertible Harry drove. Ivan stopped and observed Rory's posture and body language, noting his quick pace, downturned head, and hunched shoulders. Gone was the confident, slow swagger the gorgeous man usually favored. Guilt slammed into Ivan like a fist to the gut. What kind of asshole allowed their hang-ups to inflict so much damage on others? His hastily devoured breakfast threatened to make a return. Acid burned his throat, and the regret tasted awful on his tongue.

Ivan choked it down and forced his feet into action, quickening his pace to a jog so he could reach Rory. He could've called out to stop him, but that would've grabbed too much attention. As if his giant frame hauling ass across the barnyard didn't stick out like a sore thumb. Ivan could practically feel the curious gazes burning holes into him, but he kept pushing forward. This hang-up was his to deal with, and Rory's kicked puppy demeanor made Ivan realize just how deep the attention phobia's roots had dug into his psyche. He should really work on that before the weeds choked out all the light in his life.

"Hey," Ivan said softly as he approached the car.

Rory stiffened and dropped his hand from the door handle. He turned slowly to face Ivan as he closed the remaining few feet. Rory wore an oversized pair of sunglasses, making it impossible to see his expressive eyes, but his lush mouth was set in a firm line.

"Can we talk a minute?" Ivan asked gently.

Rory swallowed hard, and his body visibly tensed in front of Ivan as if he was bracing himself for a verbal blow. The fierce urge to kiss his lips until they softened and curved into a wry smile caught Ivan completely off guard. He braced his hand on the top of the car to keep from reaching for Rory, but then it looked like Ivan was trying to prevent Rory's escape.

"I want to apologize," Ivan said, his voice low and meant for Rory's ears only.

"You know," Harry piped in a little too loudly, "I forgot something back at the house. Y'all talk among yourselves, and I'll run back and get it."

Ivan knew she was making an excuse to give them privacy, and he reminded himself to pick up a big bag of her favorite chocolate candies the next time he went to town.

Rory didn't tear his gaze away from Ivan but nodded to acknowledge Harry's thoughtfulness.

Alone, Ivan gave himself permission to really look Rory over, and that's when he noticed the beard burn was gone. His lack of control had humiliated him and stirred his possessiveness. Seeing it gone created equally conflicting feelings.

Noticing Ivan's interest, Rory said, "I borrowed some concealer from Harry for our trip into town." The corner of his mouth ticked up slightly, and he added, "I'll take it off when we get back because otherwise, it confirms their suspicions."

"I'm really sorry I was so careless with you this morning." Ivan balled his right hand into a fist to keep from caressing the abraded flesh he knew was there. The car shielded most of their bodies from prying eyes, so Ivan relaxed his hand and settled it on Rory's hip. He circled a spot above the waistband of his jeans with his thumb, wishing there was no fabric between them. "You sure thought fast on your feet this morning."

A soft tremble rumbled through Rory, and he inched slightly closer. "Still ran you off."

Ivan swallowed hard. It was so much easier to whisper desires and confess truths in the dark. "Push your sunglasses up. I want to see your pretty eyes." Rory did as he was told, and Ivan drank in the sheer beauty of the man. "You misunderstood my abrupt departure." His fingers flexed against Rory's hip, digging deeper. "Seeing my marks on your skin aroused me, and I couldn't stop thinking about what we did together and what we we're going to do later."

Rory swayed a little toward Ivan, and his relief was evident in his features. "You haven't changed your mind?"

"Fuck no. Not about any of it. I still want you naked in my bed, and I need your help with the interview tomorrow." Ivan shifted his hand to the upper swell of Rory's ass cheek. "My hang-ups are my albatross, not yours. I'm sorry I projected those onto you."

Rory shook his head slightly. "I fully understand why you established the parameters you did, and I don't have a problem with it. I'm here to hide away from the press's scrutiny for crying out loud."

Old memories tried to intrude, but Ivan wouldn't let them spoil this sweet moment with Rory.

"And I'm sorry too," Rory said. I should've paid closer attention before coming to breakfast. I have concealer in my kit."

Ivan narrowed his eyes as a foreign feeling emerged from his emotional toolkit with a big *ta-dah*! He tried to wrestle the jealousy into submission, but the oily fucker evaded his grasp. "Need to cover up beard burns often?"

Heat flared in Rory's eyes. "Jealous?"

"Very."

"Well, we're even. I didn't enjoy hearing how you planned to hook up with random guys in Denver last night either. Red flags should be going off. I have no right to feel jealous because I have no claim on you. I don't understand what's happening."

"Maybe we can fuck it out of our systems." Ivan knew the notion was ludicrous as soon as he suggested it. The level of intimacy he craved with Rory would only bring them closer.

Rory snorted and shook his head. "Doubt it."

Ivan winked and said, "Get the biggest bottle of lube available from Hope's store and we'll give it our best."

After a shaky breath and another sway, Rory said, "Condoms?"

"Got us covered." Calmly discussing all the fucking they would do made Ivan restless.

"*Psst,*" Rory whispered. "You're eye-fucking me right now."

Ivan cleared his throat and turned his head. Harry was almost back to the car, and he wanted to get one last parting shot in before she returned. "Just a preview of what awaits you tonight." He dropped his hand from Rory's body and tucked it into his front jeans pocket. The tips of his fingers brushed over his semierection, and he marveled that such a brief exchange could amp him up.

"Oh, good," Harry said breezily when she reached the driver's side. She tossed a Redemption Ridge ball cap to Rory. Between the hat and sunglasses, it was unlikely anyone in Last Chance Creek would recognize him. "The buildings are still standing, and you haven't melted my car."

Ivan chuckled but silently downgraded the amount of candy he'd buy her. He turned and headed back toward his office. "Drive safe," he called over his shoulder.

Harry zoomed past him with a little honk and wave before he reached the solitude of his barn. Ivan forced his attention back to the schematics and prepping for his new queen's arrival. "I'm trading one high-maintenance obsession for another."

chapter
EIGHT

"Whew," Harry said as they passed Ivan. She fanned herself for emphasis.

Whew, indeed, though Rory didn't comment. He couldn't. The memory of Ivan's intense expression incapacitated his ability to deflect and bullshit. Rory had to interlace his fingers to keep his hands from shaking. *Keep your cool, buddy.*

Harry glanced over at his face, then giggled the entire length of the ranch's long driveway. Rory just smirked and shook his head, unsure of what he should do or say. Once she cleared the gate, Harry gave the convertible some gas and shot down the road. She drove fast enough to turn the landscape into a colorful blur outside his window. Rory pictured her in the summer with the top down and her long red hair blowing in the wind. The sunlight would bring freckles out on her pixie nose.

"Damn, girl. Are you a stunt driver in your spare time?"

Rory knew there was no way in hell she had room for a side hustle. She'd loosely referred to herself as a housekeeper, but he thought Cash's CEO of domestic operations was more apt. Overseeing the small staff that kept the mountainside manor in pristine condition was only a small part of her daily tasks.

Harry threw her head back and laughed at his silly question. "Just a girl who has one mode: full steam ahead."

Rory had already figured that out when she rolled out her spring agenda, which encompassed every aspect of the homestead from cleaning to inventory. There wouldn't be a pantry, refrigerator, or walk-in freezer shelf left unanalyzed. "I'm kind of surprised you haven't gone into business for yourself," Rory said. "A restaurant or maybe even a B and B. You have the knowledge, skills, and drive to see it through."

"Not the capital," she replied. "And I'm not much of a risk taker, even if I had the money. I have the best of both worlds. Cash gives me free rein so I can live the life of a chef without the financial risk or stress."

Rory had to admit, she seemed very content. "How'd you come to work for Cash?"

"You don't believe he met me in jail?" she asked.

"Nope," Rory replied without hesitation. "You wouldn't have gotten caught."

Harry laughed and executed a sharp turn on two wheels. "I answered an ad he'd placed in the local paper soon after we moved to Colorado from Tennessee. How do you know so much about food?"

Rory snorted. "I just love to eat. I grew up around people who excelled at cooking and baking. They were patient and indulged my curiosity when I was young and encouraged it when I was older. My interest in food transformed from preparing and consuming it to figuring out why it binds people. During my travels, I learned that food is a love language every culture speaks. You may not speak the actual language, but you know love and joy when you taste it."

"That's beautiful," Harry replied. "And so very true. We should recreate some of your favorite meals from your expeditions and share them with the ranch," Harry said. "We could all stand a little culture."

"Count me in."

Rory didn't know where the closest international store was but quickly realized he didn't need to worry about it. The market in Last Chance Creek was a miniature version of the ones he found in big cities.

The vast selections of fruits, vegetables, meats, and pantry staples blew Rory away. Did he attempt true replicas of his favorite meals, or should he try fusions, using unique ingredients to enhance the meals the crew expected? His mind went into overdrive with all the possibilities in front of him. He expected smoke to escape through his ears at any minute.

Harry laughed and hooked her arm around his. "We can stick to my list for now and plan a thorough menu later."

"I like that idea," Rory agreed. Let him work Ivan out of his system a little and free up some room in his brain for something besides the sexual positions and maneuvers he wanted to try on Ivan the Hung.

Harry spent a long time in the aisles dedicated to baking, checking out the various chips on hand. "Can't decide on toffee or chocolate chips for the cookies."

"I say both," Rory replied.

She beamed up at him. "I say you're a genius."

Rory grabbed a bag each of white, sweet, and dark chocolate and held them toward her to choose from. Harry chose milk and dark, and he put the white chocolate back on the shelf and eased the cart forward. "What are the cookies for?"

"Poker," she replied.

Rory stopped and arched a brow. "You're coming too?"

"Honey," she drawled like a Southern belle, "everyone will be at poker tonight. I know that's the last thing Ivan wants, so I came up with a strategy."

He wasn't too pleased with this news either. "And that is?"

"Put them in a sugar coma so they won't stick around long," Harry replied.

"And if that doesn't work?"

Harry winked and said, "I have a backup plan. Have no fear."

"You've piqued my interest," Rory said. "Do tell."

The grin Harry aimed his way was downright cheeky. "Oh, you'll know when I deploy it."

Laughing, Rory said, "When? Don't you mean *if*?"

"I mean what I say and say what I mean, love," Harry replied. "Though my baking skills are legendary on the ranch, I believe the chemistry sparking between you and the big guy outshines even my talents."

"I love your well-earned swagger," Rory said. He thought she was teasing about the latter part of her statement, but Harry's stone-cold sober expression said otherwise.

"Are you prepared for that level of scrutiny?" she asked.

"I'm tougher than I look."

"I have no doubt about that," Harry said. "Would you care to guess whose sweet tooth is as big as the rest of him?"

"You've seen the rest of Ivan?" The words were out before Rory could clamp his smart mouth shut. "Sorry," he said, tightly gripping the shopping cart so he didn't fall into the trapdoor that opened straight to hell. Would he at least have time to pass go and collect two hundred dollars first? He had staples to buy before his extended stay like moisturizer to keep his skin from drying out in the heat and booze for cocktails. According to the zealots, any person with a spark of creativity or personality would burn in hell for all eternity. And every good gay knows you don't arrive at a party empty-handed. Harry snorted, and it snapped Rory back from his ambling thoughts. If he had a dime for every time a teacher commented on his lack of attention, he'd have blown his fortune on booze and boys a long time ago.

"Do I even want to know where your mind went just now?" she asked.

"I'd like to say I was racking my brain for a good cookie recipe to make for Ivan. Just because and for no other reason," he added when Harry smirked.

"But you don't want to lie?"

"That's right," Rory said. "But now I'm thinking about cookies for Ivan." He narrowed his eyes and cycled through some of his favorite recipes from over the years. "He seemed to really like the touch of savory in his blueberry cobbler yesterday. I bet he'd equally enjoy a salty and sweet combo." The perfect recipe came to him. "Kitchen sink cookies."

Harry arched a brow. "Not sure I've heard of those."

"You throw in everything but the kitchen sink. It's about texture combinations as much as flavors." It was one of his mama's favorite recipes.

"Sounds fun."

"Does Ivan like coconut?" he asked.

"Yes, but he's probably the only one besides me."

Rory added the smallest package of coconut flakes to the cart, but Harry swapped it out for the largest bag.

"A big man eats a lot of cookies."

They doubled back and added more chocolate to the cart. White chocolate was hit or miss with most people, but the naysayers usually didn't like it because it was so much sweeter than its cousins. The macadamia nuts, dried cranberries, and pretzel bits would counter the sweetness of the triple chocolate chips he used.

"I have never been so excited to try a cookie before in my life," Harry said when they loaded the groceries in the trunk of her car. "I think you might be hazardous to my waistline."

"Nah," Rory scoffed. "I've seen your to-do list, remember?"

The next stop was a diner in the center of Main Street. Last Chance Creek was a charming town, a throwback to a different era but thankfully one with electricity and running water. Hope was already seated inside. She waved to them from a vinyl booth overlooking the bustling street. Whatever was happening there captured Hope's full attention and caused her to glower out the window. The feisty woman practically vibrated with tension.

When they arrived at the booth, Rory followed her line of sight and noticed a large gathering of people dressed in simple, old-timey clothes. The women wore simple dresses in drab colors and the men wore white shirts and equally boring pants. In the center of the group, a white-haired man stood on something that elevated him above everyone else. He lifted a leather book in one arm, and Rory assumed it was a Bible. "Are those people actors?" Rory asked, then forced his gaze back to Harry and Hope, who sat across from him.

Harry snorted. "Kieran thought something similar when he arrived last year. He thought it was a reenactment for tourists."

"It's not?" Rory asked.

"I wish," Hope said bitterly before forcing her gaze away from the window.

"Blasted any of them with a Super Soaker lately?" Harry asked her mother.

Hope's frown turned upside down, and she grinned like the Cheshire cat, which was apropos since Rory was feeling a little like Alice. "No, but the day is still young." She darted a glance at the gathering once again, and Rory noticed the mischievous gleam in her eyes.

"So who are they if they're not actors?"

"Salvation Anew," Hope and Harry said at once.

The women looked at each other and giggled. Rory couldn't help but grin in response, though he didn't know what was so funny.

"We better be careful," Harry whispered. "That sounded too much like a summoning." She smiled and leaned toward Rory. "At best, they're a cluster of religious fanatics who moved to Last Chance Creek to make everyone's life hell on earth."

That must've been the organization Cash had mentioned to Nick. Intrigued, Rory placed his elbow on the table and rested his chin in the curve of his cupped palm. "And at worst?"

Harry had just taken a sip of water, so Hope fielded his question. "A cult of religious fanatics who've moved to Last Chance Creek to indoctrinate us all into their way of thinking."

"And is it working?"

"Fuck no," Hope replied with fervor.

Harry's expression wasn't as adamant. "Some have fallen prey to them." The women shared a brief glance, but Rory could tell they'd silently communicated a lot in so little time. Harry met his gaze once more and told her about Finley's ex-boyfriend, Keegan, a confused guy who'd turned to Salvation Anew for answers.

"Poor guy," Rory said. He'd known lots of people who'd struggled with their sexuality. Some remained firmly in the closet, only coming out when the loneliness became too strong. Others lived a complete lie, pretending to be someone they weren't. Most found their footing in the sunlight, even if the journey wasn't an easy one. Rory was fortunate his parents were open-minded in that regard. Nicky had come out as bi in college, paving the way for Rory to come out in middle school. It had been one of the last big conversations he'd had with his mom before cancer claimed her. "What's the deal with the Super Soaker?"

Thank goodness he didn't take a sip while Hope answered. He might've choked to death when she recounted the afternoon when she'd chased them from her shop with the water gun. "I found one of them spewing hate at my son on the sidewalk and blasted him too."

"Don't leave out the best part, Mama."

Hope groaned and covered her face with her hands. Rory hadn't known her long, but the gesture seemed out of character for her. She dropped her hands to her lap and smiled meekly. "Finley had brought Kieran to meet me. I got so excited that my finger slipped, and I blasted him with water too."

Rory laughed as he pictured the incident. "I bet he wasn't mad."

Hope smiled and shook her head. "We just laughed and laughed at the ridiculousness."

"Then Mama proceeded to get Kieran out of his shirt." Harry waggled her brows and coaxed another smile from Rory.

Hope swatted her daughter playfully. "And into a dry shirt from my yoga studio."

"A real cougar, this one," Harry said, hooking her thumb in Hope's direction.

"Keep it up and I'll put a curse on you."

Harry rolled her eyes. "The cult leader thinks Mom is a witch. That's why they harassed her in the store. They think she's selling spells to unsuspecting people."

"I guaran-damn-tee those assholes could benefit from using some of my lubes or lotions. No one is more miserable than sexually oppressed people." The words came out a little louder than Hope probably intended.

"Mom," Harry whispered, looking around to see who might've overheard.

Rory was utterly charmed by Hope and reached for her hand across the table. "Your children are lucky to have a mother with so much warmth and humor."

Hope batted her eyelashes. "You charmer."

Harry groaned. "Don't encourage her, Rory." She playfully whacked her mom's arm with the menu. "And turn loose of Ivan's man."

Ivan's man. Rory knew damn well he needed to correct her or at least recalibrate his own thoughts before they triggered feelings that would cause him a lot of heartache. They weren't destined to be together. They weren't in love. Rory and Ivan were horny as hell for one another, and they planned to fuck each other out of their systems. Plain and simple in concept but a folly if ever he'd heard one. Rory couldn't even think of himself as Ivan's man when they were alone, tangled up in each other. Those would be the moments when Rory needed to keep a tight grip on reality and not let himself get swept out to sea on a tide of pleasure.

"I'm my own man, thank you very much," he said saucily. He too grabbed a menu from behind the condiment rack but didn't whack anyone with it. "What's good to eat here?"

"Everything," Harry said with a sigh. "Makes it hard to choose."

Rory glanced up and caught Hope watching him with a twinkle in her eye that said she saw right through him. Maybe that uptight, sexually repressed cult leader was onto something. Maybe Hope had special powers, though Rory suspected she'd use them for good. He was even more convinced of it when she packed a bag full of lube, massage oil, and samples from her new line of men's products and refused his cash.

Rory couldn't wait to test them all out, especially the Butt Stuff, with Ivan. Their time together might be limited, but that didn't mean they couldn't enjoy it down to the last drop of lube. Rory's first stop once they got back to the ranch would be the large kitchen to bake cookies for poker night. If he stayed busy enough, maybe he'd stop hearing the echo of Harry's words in his head. *Ivan's man.*

When they left the shop, Rory noticed the group of protesters had grown considerably, and his thoughts took a drastic turn. As disturbing as the scene was on its own merit, the oddly dressed cluster wasn't responsible for the icy fingers of dread marching up his spine. A solitary reporter stood off to the side with her cameraman. They spoke animatedly as if preparing to go live. Rory knew the score. Attention-seeking groups like Salvation Anew often drew one journalist's attention in the beginning, usually a newbie looking for their break. The subject would like the attention they garnered and would amp up their activity to draw more attention and feed their insatiable ego. One journalist would quickly multiply into three, and the stakes and antics would only rise. Before long, a media frenzy would unfold. That pretty brunette checking her makeup in a compact mirror just might hold the fate of the little town in her palm. Rory didn't think anyone would recognize him under the cap and sunglasses, but he kept his gaze averted as he and Harry put some distance between themselves and the chaos.

Staying busy on the ranch wasn't an issue, and he and Harry made a dangerous duo. They cooked and baked for hours, only stopping to hydrate and maybe sample each new baked good that came out of the oven. He was grateful Nick had brought him to Redemption Ridge. No matter the duration of his stay, Rory knew the ranch would change him for the better. That sexy conqueror with the sweet tooth wasn't the only reason, but he sure as hell was the biggest one. Of course, that thought steered the rest of his thoughts off the rails until Harry playfully swatted him with an oven mitt when he didn't hear the timer go off for Ivan's cookies.

"Sorry," he said sheepishly. "I was thinking about my next steps."

Harry snorted. "I just bet you were."

He could deny it and claim he was only thinking about baking, but it wasn't worth expending the energy. He needed to save that for the marathon sex he wanted to have with Ivan. Rory grabbed a cookie from the cooling rack and shrugged. "Guilty as charged."

Harry giggled and handed him two more cookies. "Pretty sure you're going to need all the fuel you can get."

chapter

NINE

ANTICIPATION THRUMMED THROUGH IVAN AS HE thoroughly soaped his body from head to toe, then repeated the process. He didn't linger on his crotch too long because he didn't need more stimulation in that department. Ivan had felt like a walking live wire since he'd seen Rory carrying a purple canvas bag with Hope's logo on it. Had he headed straight to the original homestead with it, Ivan would've followed without regard for who saw him. That's how amped up and ready to fuck he was. He debated rubbing one out in the shower and had nearly convinced himself Rory would be better off for it. Ivan would last longer and draw out Rory's pleasure, but those just sounded like easy excuses to jerk off instead of tempering his lust.

He'd been too curious about the contents of the bag to give his queen the full attention she deserved. Ivan had kept one eye out the window for signs of Rory and the other on her temporary hive. She was a magnificent queen and deserved better, and he vowed to show up with renewed vigor in the morning. Ivan just needed one night with Rory. He wasn't foolish enough to think a few rounds of sex would get Rory out of his system, but he thought it might lessen the ache so he could concentrate. He didn't even have a name for his new lady yet. And that was something he usually came up with soon after observing her interaction with the drones in her shipping box.

Thinking about his bees got his mind off his balls, so Ivan snapped off the water and toweled off with vigor. Wiping the steam off the mirror, he unpacked the hair shit from his previous week's barber trip and tried his best to style his hair like Danielle had. Dylan kept a round brush and hairdryer in the vanity drawer, so Ivan figured he'd give it a whirl. He'd always considered himself to be a well-coordinated man until he was trying to hold the hairdryer with one hand and the brush with the other. At one point, he got the bristles tangled in his hair and had to set the dryer down to pull his hair loose from the brush. He got the hang of the brush and the wrist action required first, then added the heat. After two more false starts, Ivan had a better grasp on the process.

He set the tools on the vanity when he finished and admired his handiwork with a satisfied nod. He hadn't mastered Danielle's skill, but his first attempt was downright respectable. Ivan continued to study his face, trying to figure out what Rory saw when he looked at him. He'd always thought of himself as ordinary if not borderline homely. His sexual conquests were with guys who were sober enough and consenting, but their beer goggles elevated his hotness to a ten. Ivan prided himself on pleasing his partners and would rock their worlds and move on before they realized he was actually a two. But Rory made Ivan feel sexy and virile, and just thinking about Rory made him straighten his posture and jut out his square jaw. There was a sparkle in his amber eyes he'd never noticed before, and it had nothing to do with the new bulbs he'd installed in the bathroom light fixture. It was the Rory Effect. That's what Rory had named his YouTube channel. His intentions to conserve and preserve were obvious, but Rory's influence on his life after just a week felt substantial. Ivan waited for alarm bells to sound, but they remained silent. He blew out a breath and reached for the hair goop that was supposed to finish the look.

"Painter's putty," Ivan grumbled. The tin looked tiny in his hands, but most things did. He brought it to his nose and cautiously sniffed the contents. It smelled woodsy and smoky, and he vowed to give it his best shot. Danielle had told him to start with a small amount, work it with his fingers for a few moments to warm the product up, and then apply it to his hair. He raised his hands toward his hair a few times but stopped, reworked the product a little more, then finally dove in. Danielle assured him it was foolproof. If he put too much in his hair or got too close to the roots, he just had to go over the sections again with the hair dryer to loosen the product up again.

It took Ivan three attempts and twenty minutes before he didn't look like he'd smeared jizz in the front of his hair. At one point, he placed the dryer too close to his head, and it smelled like his hair was on fire.

"Fuck me. Looking pretty is hard work," Ivan said to his reflection.

But he looked damn good. He imagined the pleasure on Rory's face when he realized the lengths Ivan had gone to for their sexy times. Speaking of length, Ivan dropped his gaze toward his crotch and decided he could use a trim down below. He loved how smooth and bare Rory was, but that wasn't his style. Ivan retrieved his beard trimmer and attachments from under the sink and made sure his bush was tight and trim. He wrapped the towel around his waist and picked up his discarded clothes from the floor. Ivan opened the door and stepped into the hallway, hoping to find Rory waiting for him. He'd drag him down the hallway and work through the insane energy buzzing through him before everyone arrived.

But Rory wasn't there, and in fact, he still hadn't returned from the main house when Ivan went downstairs. He retrieved his phone to order pizza when he saw a text from Harry that told him she and Rory had dinner covered for poker night and not to worry about ordering food. That was fine with him. Anything Harry made would be better than Giovanni's. He was curious about Rory's cooking skills, but then again, he was curious about everything when it came to Rory.

"Guess I'll get to taste a few of his skills tonight," Ivan said as he pulled the pitcher of water from the refrigerator.

He poured himself a tall glass and had knocked back half of it when he caught movement in his periphery. Ivan turned and saw Rory sauntering across the barnyard with the purple canvas bag in one hand and a plastic storage container in the other. He was so glad to see Rory's swagger had returned that Ivan's first instinct was to meet him at the door. He wanted to play it cool, though, so he smothered the urge with both hands. Ivan leaned back against the counter and sipped his water with the urgency of a sloth. And that's where Rory found him when he entered the house.

Arctic eyes devoured Ivan from head to toe before meeting his gaze. "Hi," Rory said, his voice a husky promise of things to come. "Nice hair."

"Thanks."

Ivan set the empty glass down on the counter and crossed the room. He cupped Rory's neck and brushed his thumb over the angry red marks on his skin. Then he planted a hard kiss on Rory's lips. So much for playing it cool. Rory gasped softly and parted his mouth, inviting Ivan inside. He'd meant it to be a quick exchange to assure Rory—but mostly himself—that they were really okay. His reaction at breakfast had left a bitter taste in his mouth. Figuratively, of course, or Rory wouldn't have moaned and leaned deeper into the kiss, sucking Ivan's tongue into his mouth just as he'd done that morning.

Ivan pulled back, breathing harder than the exchange warranted. But arousal had held him in its grip for hours and now hummed beneath his skin louder than a colony of his beloved bees. "What's in the bag?"

Before Rory could respond, he shifted his gaze to the window, and his beautiful eyes widened. Ivan had sneakily watched enough horror films in his youth to recognize that Rory's expression spelled imminent doom.

Ivan groaned, and the hair on his arms stood up. "Just tell me. I'm brave and strong."

Rory darted a quick glance at him and licked his lips nervously. "Were you supposed to say that last part out loud? It sounded more like a private pep talk you'd give yourself before facing a horde of zombies or a swarm of ranch hands that want to stick their nose in your business."

Ivan relaxed and chuckled. "Only you get to stick your nose in my business."

Rory gave Ivan his full attention, and his icy gaze grew impossibly hotter. "Wasn't referring to your junk, but okay."

It took little imagination to picture Rory on his knees, getting up close and personal with his cock and balls. But that did nothing to dispel the need gathering strength inside him. If he wasn't careful, lust would seep into his marrow and rattle his bones. He tore his gaze off Rory and turned to see just how many people were descending toward them. *Zombie horde indeed.* But instead of brains, these assholes were ravenous for gossip.

"Christ," Ivan groused. "Did you and Harry count on the extra people when planning the food?" There was no way in hell he was missing out on the grub. The people who rarely or never came to poker night had to get in the back of the line. And hell yes, Ivan would use his clout to insist. There was a tiny part of him that said he'd give them a show if that's what they wanted, but it was just a teeny voice that his growling stomach drowned out.

"Yes, we did, and here." Rory stepped forward and extended a cookie that was nearly the size of his hand—Rory's, not Ivan's. "This will stave off the hanger for a bit."

"What other goodies do you have?" he asked.

"We don't have time to discuss it." Rory stepped back into the hallway. "I'm going to put my stuff away and take a quick shower so I can help Harry set up the food."

"I'll help her," Ivan said, though he wanted to toss Rory over his shoulder and carry him up to his bedroom.

"Fine. Eat your cookie." Rory said the last part slowly as if talking to a child on the verge of a tantrum.

He wasn't far off the mark. "Don't think you can distract me with a cookie," Ivan called out. But then he bit into it and barely resisted falling to his knees in worship. Ivan chewed slowly, picking out all the flavors and textures in one bite.

Rory ducked his head back into the kitchen. "Maybe not just any ole cookie. But I made those especially for you."

The sweet gesture touched Ivan. Then he narrowed his eyes. "Where are the rest of them?" Rory patted the purple canvas bag. "Tucked away until we're alone again."

"Hurry." But did he mean Rory or the passage of time? Ivan decided it was both and took another big bite of cookie after Rory disappeared out of sight again. He'd wolfed down the entire thing by the time the first wave of rubberneckers arrived.

Ivan knew they were in for a treat when Harry had to commandeer Dylan's truck to get all the food she'd made from one house to the other.

"Though I could use the exercise the back-and-forth trips would've afforded me," Harry said when they'd arranged huge foil platters on every available surface in the kitchen.

She and Rory had made a variety of sliders and chicken wings, which would've been enough on their own. But they also made hash brown casserole, macaroni and cheese, baked beans, pasta salad, and a bunch of brownies and cookies.

"Wow," Ivan said once they had everything set out. "You guys made enough food for an army of nosy-ass ranchers."

"Figured I'd put them in a food coma so they didn't linger down here too long. If that doesn't work, I have a surefire backup plan that will draw them out of the house."

"Yeah?" Ivan asked.

Harry smiled. "You'll know it when you see it." She faced him with her hands on her hips and a smile on her face. "Cash left for a few days, so Dylan is going to stay with me at the main house."

Ivan knew Cash had headed to Denver because he'd stopped by the barn on his way out. Apparently, Cash had expressed his concerns about Salvation Anew to Nick after Ivan had stomped out of the house like an immature brat. Nick was introducing Cash to a special agent who investigated cults. Or that was the excuse the guys were using to spend time together, but that was their business.

Harry winked and said, "We got you covered."

Ivan's cheeks heated, and he wanted to dispute Harry's assumptions, but he *let it go*. They were grown-ass adults who didn't need anyone's blessing or permission. Besides, their interest would wane soon enough, and they'd find something or someone else to gossip over instead. "Appreciate it," Ivan said instead of a rebuttal.

"Trust me," Harry said, placing a hand over her heart. "I'm not doing this for you. If left up to me, I'd never kick that man out of my bed."

"I'm happy for you both," Ivan said, though he was dying to know when and how Harry had come around.

Dylan's crush on her had been obvious as hell, but she'd acted impervious. Ivan suspected the age difference bugged her since Dylan was younger. Harry was surprisingly cautious for being Hope Newton's firstborn. Then again, Harry and Finley had talked about the mistakes Hope had made when they were younger. They must've left an indelible mark on her impressionable kids, and it manifested in opposite ways. Harry, who was pure fire and sass, went to the extreme opposite of her mom. Finley had followed in her footsteps until the ill-fated romance with Keegan, who'd broken up with him to enter the cult. The betrayal had spawned a hiatus that came to an abrupt end when Kieran arrived at the ranch a year ago.

"Thank you," Harry said. "Maybe it's time for you to let your hair down a little too, yeah?" She narrowed her eyes and studied his attempt to style his hair as Danielle had. "Did you go back to the barber today?"

"Nope. Did this myself," he replied breezily as if the entire process hadn't eaten over thirty minutes of his time. Seeing the ravenous look in Rory's eyes made the effort worth it.

"You better not be hoovering up all the food," Kieran yelled from the living room. The asshole had gotten awfully brazen over the past twelve months, and Ivan couldn't help but smile.

"Give him a break," Owen said. "He needs to fuel up for tonight's activities."

A cacophony of laughter followed the remark but broke into catcalls and whistles. Curious, Ivan poked his head out of the doorway and saw Rory had descended the stairs. He wore a pale gray, long-sleeved shirt made from a material that looked ridiculously soft. Rory's jeans were faded and distressed, but Ivan suspected that was by design rather than from wear and tear. He still hadn't forgotten the sticker shock when he'd tried to buy a pair from a department store in the mall during college. His folks couldn't afford to buy their kids designer clothes and wouldn't have bought them even if money wasn't an issue. Rory's jeans looked soft and some of the holes on his upper thighs were strategically close to where Ivan wanted to put his tongue.

Rory shook his head and waved off the crew's silliness, making a beeline for the kitchen.

"Why does he get to go in there while the rest of us have to stay in the living room?" Tyler called out.

"You know why," Owen said. He followed it with a kissy face that drew more laughter.

"Because Rory and Harry prepared all this delicious food for you, so they get to fill their plates first," Ivan said. Tyler and Owen had the good grace to look slightly chastised.

"It's a rough crowd tonight," Rory said when he reached the safety of the kitchen. "Maybe we should throw a few sliders out there to appease them."

"Fill your plate," Ivan said, reaching for him without thinking.

Rory rose and pressed a quick kiss to his lips.

"Awwwwww," a chorus of grown men said from the fucking doorway.

Rory stiffened as if he'd done something wrong, and Ivan didn't want a repeat of that morning's miscommunication. Ivan kept his hand on Rory to hold him in place. Damn, he smelled so good. Like fresh air, sunshine, and something slightly earthy like freshly mown grass. Ivan wanted to roll over and under him and was grateful he'd get his chance to do just that in a few hours.

"The next person to make a smartass comment about us or stick their nose in our business will live to regret it come Monday when I hand out the weekly assignments."

Harry spun around and said, "And you can count on a week of cold cereal for breakfast and bologna sandwiches and chips for lunch."

Groans met Harry's threat. Ivan laughed because that was by far a much worse fate than he would've dealt them. True to his word, Ivan held the ravenous group at bay while Harry and Rory filled their plates, then he jumped to the front of the line once they finished. A few protested his audacity, but most of them weren't willing to incur Harry's wrath. There were too many people to cram inside the small dining room, so the gawkers spilled over into the living room and kitchen too.

Ivan wondered how they'd manage the poker games if everyone stuck around after dinner. Multiple tables and tournament style?

Harry and Rory's cooking skills rendered the crowd nearly mute with the occasional groan and hum of approval. A soft belch broke the silence, and Ivan hoped like hell it wasn't him, though he wouldn't mind a discreet one if it allowed more room to shovel food into his gullet.

"Sorry," Owen said, sounding mortified.

"Don't be," Rory replied. "I took it as a compliment."

Tyler glanced up from his plate, halting with his fork midway to his mouth. "How much of this food did you make?"

Rory rattled off a long list, comprising half the sandwiches and wings and a sizable chunk of the desserts. His cheeks flushed with pride, and Ivan wanted to send them all home—with no leftovers—so he could get to the Rory appreciation party he'd planned.

"What are the cookies you made with a bunch of ingredients?" Dylan asked. "They had bits of crushed pretzel, nuts, and different chocolate chips in them."

"I didn't see those," Rueben said, sounding disappointed.

Ivan knew and recalled the surprising combo of salty and sweet ingredients and the mix of textures. He couldn't wait to eat more of them, preferably with Rory's nude body acting as a serving platter.

"Oh," Rory said, casting a furtive glance in his direction. "They weren't for poker night."

"Really?" Tyler asked, turning a suspicious gaze on Ivan. He mouthed, "Lucky bastard," before turning his head back toward his plate.

"You wouldn't like them," Ivan said. "They have coconut."

"I'd sure give it a try," Rue grumbled and stabbed a bite of hash brown casserole.

Ivan caught Rory's gaze and winked before tucking back into his dinner. He'd always loved food, especially the dishes the women in his family made. He learned early on to recognize the singular secret ingredient they put into their dishes—love. It was the universal spice that made the ordinary extraordinary, and Harry poured love into her cooking. He glanced at Rory, who smiled as he observed those around him wolfing down the food he'd helped create. It seemed he was blessed with the innate ability too.

"So what went into the cookies you made just for Ivan?" Owen asked, clearly not ready to let the slight go.

Rory wore a cute smirk on his lips before rattling off the ingredients.

"What do you even call a cookie with that much stuff in it?" Tyler asked.

Ivan smirked and said, "I call them delicious."

Rory's beaming smile was so bright that Ivan needed sunglasses. "Kitchen sink cookies," he said without breaking eye contact with Ivan.

"I get it," Rue said. "You throw in everything but the kitchen sink."

"Yep." Rory looked at him. "The dough starts with a standard versatile base that allows any combo of salty, sweet, and textured ingredients."

The group started tossing out their favorite ingredients, then debated how they'd pair.

"Maybe we'll have a bake-your-own party someday," Harry suggested. "Rory and I can make a huge batch of the dough and divvy it out, and you guys can add your own ingredients."

"We're not children," Owen grumbled, but his protest sounded halfhearted at best.

"Speak for yourself," Rueben replied. "It doesn't sound any different from make-your-own pizza night. Count me in."

Tyler nodded and said, "Me too."

Owen averted his gaze and exhaled. "Okay, fine. It sounds like a lot of fun."

The conversation shifted to other topics while they ate, though Ivan noticed the forks were moving slower. He shoved back from the table when he couldn't eat another bite. Rory pushed back too and offered to help tidy up.

"We leave the food out because we'll nosh on it while we play. Unless you think something will spoil," he added quickly, giving Rory an excuse to follow him if he chose.

Smartly, Rory reclaimed his seat next to Harry and finished eating the few bites on his plate. Ivan needed a few minutes to get his thoughts under control because all he wanted to do was run everyone off so he could have Rory to himself.

"Hey," Finley said softly behind him.

Ivan turned around and smiled at his friend. "Hey yourself."

"You doing okay with all the extra attention on you?"

That Finley knew him so well didn't come as a surprise. They'd lived together for most of the five years Finley had worked on the ranch. But their hallway run-ins had had vastly different outcomes than the ones Ivan had shared with Rory. "Yeah," Ivan said with a smirk. "It will blow over as soon as they find a new target."

Finley grinned. "True." He inched closer. "Surely, you'd share one of those special cookies with a good friend?"

Ivan wouldn't share them with his own mother. "Not you too." He assumed Rory had put them away in his bedroom when he got cleaned up for poker, but Ivan was wondering if he should stash them in the small safe he kept in his bedroom closet. There was no way he could keep his eyes on everyone at once. Ivan handed him a golden blondie square and said, "Eat this and quit busting my chops…even though I deserve it for how I acted last year."

Finley bit into the brownie, and his eyes nearly rolled back in his head. "What were we saying?"

Yeah, his guy could bake. *His guy?* Oh, hell no. He'd only known Rory for a week. It was way too soon for those types of thoughts. A year from now would be too soon. Ivan had been in love one time, and it had nearly destroyed him. He'd gotten by on hookups since he'd gotten out of jail six years ago and had zero plans to change his habits now. Rory was on the same page. They were going to engage in a horny spring fling, then go their separate ways.

Ivan would remind himself of that over the next few hours when he pretended not to be frustrated by the lingering crowd. The fellas had been too eager to retrieve card tables and folding chairs from the main ranch house. A few of the guys pushed back the furniture in the living room to set the tables up for tournament-style play. Ivan had a fun night, though he couldn't remember a single conversation or the outcome of the games. Ivan was fully attuned to Rory—his laughter, smiles, and the glances he'd sneak in Ivan's direction when he thought no one was looking. Everyone was looking, which was why none of the assholes would go home.

That is until Harry deployed her backup distraction technique. She said he'd recognize it when it happened, and boy did he ever. Harry sat on Dylan's lap, carded her fingers through his hair, and asked if he was ready to go home. Insert pin drop, mouse fart, or any other idiom about quiet noises sounding loud. The group held a collective breath while waiting for Dylan's response. He looked up at her with affection radiating from his eyes. She'd made her claim, and he couldn't be happier.

"I've been ready," he said.

Harry kissed his upturned lips to a chorus of catcalls, clapping, and well wishes. Everyone was eager to find out the details about how and when they'd taken the leap. They trailed out the door after the happy couple as if they were pied pipers playing a merry tune. Ivan turned the dead bolt in the front door, then hurried to do the same on the entrances off the kitchen and the utility room before one of the crew doubled back for leftovers.

Rory trailed behind him silently, and Ivan worried he'd misread the situation. A quick glance over his shoulder revealed Rory biting his lips but not seductively. Ivan stopped in front of him, gently tugged the abused flesh free, and placed a soft kiss on his mouth.

"Interview practice first?" Rory suggested.

"There's no way in hell I could concentrate. Grab the cookies and lube and anything else you want for the night. I'm not turning you loose until at least dawn."

Rory smiled but shook his head. Ivan's heart sank. Had he changed his mind? "Everything's already up in your room. I dropped it inside when I took a shower."

That was the only encouragement Ivan needed. Urgency surged and swelled inside him, making his heart race, his chest expand, and his fingers twitch. Ivan felt acutely aware of every hair follicle, cell, and nerve ending that made up his body, and they were of one accord, united in a singular purpose—to conquer. Not with swords and shields and in his bedroom instead of on a battlefield. Ivan would volley promises of carnal delights, not grenades. He would use his touch to incite pleasure, not pain. Ivan hadn't lied to Rory when he said he wasn't a conqueror because he'd never been brave enough to give in to his instincts. That morning was the first time he'd really come close to living out the version of himself in his fantasies. Ivan had wanted, and he'd taken.

That same instinct gripped him by the balls, but Ivan didn't give in to his body's demands. Instead of tossing Rory over his shoulder and sprinting up the stairs, Ivan laced his fingers through Rory's and tugged him into his embrace. He didn't maul and plunder Rory's upturned mouth. Ivan offered gentle kisses until the supple flesh trembled against his. Rory's next breath came out on a simpering sigh, a surrender Ivan's baser instincts wanted to explore. Ivan's suppressed urgency escaped in a throaty growl before he nipped Rory's plush bottom lip, teasing a sexy shiver from his lithe body.

Everything Ivan wanted was his for the taking, but it wasn't enough. The situation called for restraint and finesse, though he didn't understand why or how he even knew it. Having his instincts at war was a new and confusing sensation, and the timing couldn't be worse. Ivan had expected this moment ever since they parted ways in the cramped bathroom, and he'd be damned if he let anyone, including himself, ruin it. *All in due time, big fella.* Ivan wanted to seduce Rory's mind before conquering his body.

As if feeling the shift inside him, Rory broke their kiss and looked at him. Arctic eyes shimmered with desire, but Ivan could read the confusion in Rory's furrowed brow. He'd read Ivan's changed approach as doubt. Instead of verbally communicating just how wrong Rory was, Ivan recaptured his mouth and backed him toward the staircase. The maneuver exercised trust, navigating the steps while relying on someone else to guide you, and Rory executed it perfectly. He gave himself fully to the kiss, licking into Ivan's mouth, twining and twirling their tongues together, never breaking their embrace to check his surroundings even once. Rory stepped back when Ivan advanced forward, their bodies pressed tightly together in a symbiotic dance of senses. Ivan found Rory's trust illogically hotter than anything he'd experienced with other men, an aphrodisiac for a body already primed to fuck.

When they reached the top of the stairs, Ivan stopped and pressed Rory against the wall. Rory arched his neck, presenting a column of flesh Ivan couldn't resist, though his kisses were much gentler than the ones that had left angry red marks. Ivan swiped his tongue over the abrasions, then softly bit Rory's earlobe.

"I love having your marks on me," Rory said, his eyes begging Ivan to do it again.

"I loved seeing them on you," he confessed. "The next ones will be for my eyes only." Ivan trailed his hand over Rory's ribcage and down to his hip, dipping even lower to graze over his erection. Ivan settled his hand between his legs and pressed fingertips against Rory's inner thigh. "Right here."

Rory moaned and fisted Ivan's shirt. "Yes, please."

Urgency became desperation, digging its razor-like talons into Ivan's soul, but he resisted. Ivan slid his fingertips beneath the supersoft material of Rory's shirt and brushed the smooth skin above his low-rise jeans. Rotating his wrist, Ivan slid his callused fingers beneath the denim waistband and found unencumbered access to the smooth skin below. Ivan growled when he realized Rory had been bare beneath his jeans the entire night. Inching his curious fingers lower, he stroked them over Rory's erection. Ivan recalled the feel of Rory's dick jerking in his hand, the splash of hot cum on his fingers, and the scent of his release tickling his nose. And now he would get to see all those things.

Ivan pulled his hand back and hooked his finger in Rory's belt loop. This time, Ivan walked backward while Rory attacked his mouth with renewed fervor and worked Ivan's shirt loose from his jeans.

"Lights on this time," Rory insisted. "I want to see every glorious inch of you. I want to see your face when you fill my ass."

Ivan growled and forgot all about his determination not to mark Rory's neck. He fastened his lips to his flesh and nipped and sucked until they stumbled into his bedroom. Ivan didn't bother to close the door. Dylan was gone for the night, and he was nearly too far gone to care otherwise. A glance at the bed revealed his cats lounging on the bedspread.

"Daddy's got company, boys," he said.

They didn't budge from their cozy spots until Rory leaned forward and bit Ivan's nipple through his shirt. Ivan let out a hiss, and the felines bolted out the door. Rory shoved his hands under Ivan's shirt and pushed the material up and over his head. Hot lips pressed open-mouthed kisses across Ivan's chest just as they had this morning. Rory's tongue tasted and swirled against his skin each time it landed. He sucked one nipple into his mouth, then the other. Ivan cupped the back of Rory's head, holding him in place, but Rory wriggled free and continued his worship lower. He rubbed his face against Ivan's happy trail as he dropped to his knees between Ivan's feet. Rory tilted his head enough to peer up at him from beneath a fan of dark eyelashes, and the conqueror became the conquered.

Maybe that's what Ivan had been missing this entire time—someone he could relinquish his control to. That he would give it to someone he'd known so little time blew his mind. Ivan saw the curve of a smile forming on Rory's gorgeous lips seconds before they pressed against his belly. Rory nipped, sucked, and teased the flesh there, leaving his own marks behind. Ivan's core muscles quivered and quaked when Rory unfastened his jeans and tugged them down to his thighs. Only his briefs separated his cock from Rory's hungry mouth. He tongued Ivan's cockhead through the fabric, making the wet spot already there larger. Warm palms landed against his upper thighs and slipped upward until the tips of Rory's fingers brushed against the swell of his balls.

"Christ, I can't wait to have you in my mouth."

Ivan cupped Rory's chin and brushed his thumb over his lips. "Prove it."

Rory's eyes burned with intensity, and Ivan briefly wondered if he'd accept the challenge or defy it. Rory didn't keep him guessing for long. He hiked the leg band up on one side to reveal the wet and very eager head of Ivan's dick. Rory leaned forward to tongue the frenulum, lick the precum pearling at his slit, and suck the swollen head into his mouth.

Ivan's hips snapped forward, seeking more delicious friction against the supersensitive spot. Rory pressed his forearm against Ivan's thigh to still him.

"One of these days, I'm going to make you come just from this,"

Rory said. He continued teasing and tasting Ivan, working that sweet spot until his legs trembled, and some day was nearly now.

Rory sat back on his haunches and continued petting Ivan's thighs. Rory's wicked fingers brushed against the underside of his balls and the head of his dick still poking out the side of his briefs. "God, I love these thick, hairy thighs. I've been thinking about them all day and how I'm going to brace myself against them when I ride you."

Rory's fervent need for him went straight to Ivan's head—both of them. Rory pulled Ivan's briefs down to his thighs and reduced his five senses to one when he took the length of Ivan's dick into his hot mouth. Lust surged inside him, making him believe he was every bit the conqueror Rory saw. Ivan's chest swelled with the ferocious roar cresting inside. But the pressure escaped from his lips in a needy whimper when Rory fondled his balls with the perfect amount of tension. It was like a mighty lion opening his mouth to roar but a tiny kitten's meow came out instead. Ivan was too far gone to care. Wet, hot suction worked up and down the length of his cock, but the changing pace, angle, and intensity kept him off-balance.

Rory pulled back suddenly as he stopped and rocked back on his heels to catch his breath. His lips were swollen, cherry red, and slick with saliva. Ivan had never wanted to kiss anyone as much as he wanted to kiss Rory in that moment. He extended his hand to Rory and pulled him to his feet, claiming the mouth that had worked him to a fevered pitch. Ivan went to work on Rory's clothes and didn't stop until he'd revealed every inch of smooth, golden skin. He wanted to know how bronze Rory's skin would get beneath the scorching summer sun, preferably from lazing naked in Ivan's arms after vigorous sex. He knew tons of spots on the ranch that would make excellent rendezvous points. Ivan rested his hands on Rory's hips and pressed a tender kiss to his lips. "Damn, you're beautiful."

Rory flung his arms around Ivan's neck and pressed his nude body against his partially clothed one. "I was just about to say the same thing about you." Ivan had never thought of himself as handsome, let alone beautiful. Maybe Rory read Ivan's disbelief in his expression because he cupped his bristly cheek and said, "Absolutely breathtaking."

The night had taken a drastically different turn from the one Ivan had envisioned all day, but he wasn't disappointed. What they'd shared in the predawn hours was raw and gritty and beautiful in its simplicity. The energy sparking between them now was layered and maybe a little confusing but made gorgeous by the complexity. Rory was filling a void Ivan didn't know existed. Ivan recognized the same wondrous emotion shining back at him in Rory's luminous gaze.

Rory shoved Ivan's pants and underwear all the way off until they both stood naked. His fist immediately found Ivan's dick and worked it up and down a few times before he let go and led Ivan to the bed. Ivan climbed onto the mattress first, and Rory was on him before he could lie down. Wrapping his arms around Rory's waist, Ivan rolled him onto his back. It was his turn to do some exploration with his hands and mouth. Ivan was very thorough, and Rory was both responsive and vocal about what pleased him most.

Rory let out a soft gasp when Ivan kissed the back of one knee. "I didn't even know I liked that."

Ivan nibbled the inside of his calf. "Let's find out what else you like."

The urge to possess and claim was strong, but Ivan overrode it. He kept his touch gentle and steady, committing every shiver, moan, and plea to memory. When Ivan dug his thumbs into the arch of Rory's foot, he arched his back and cried out. Ivan turned his head and dropped a kiss there before lowering Rory's foot and inching higher up his body. The higher he climbed, the wider Rory spread his legs, revealing his tantalizing inner thighs. Ivan spent a lot of time there, kissing, nibbling, and rubbing his beard against the sensitive flesh until it was a pretty shade of red. Only then did he turn his full attention to Rory's leaking dick.

Ivan took his time kissing and rolling Rory's silky-smooth balls in his hand. They were as different as night and day; Rory was all soft and polished to his rough and hairy, but he loved their differences.

Rory fisted his hands in Ivan's hair and dragged his mouth over to where he wanted it most. "Suck me."

Ivan fought the urge to salute him and took Rory's dick into his mouth instead. He gave Rory a taste of his own medicine, keeping his sucks shallow and slow and not taking him down to the root like the squirming man beneath him wanted. The sexy little growls drove Ivan wild, so he used his broad shoulders to keep Rory's legs spread wide so he could tease his pretty pink pucker. Wetting his middle finger with saliva, Ivan traced the crinkled rim while Rory yanked his hair and cried, "Deeper."

Was he talking about his mouth or the finger at his entrance? Ivan gave him both, taking his cock down to the root and pushing his finger in to the second knuckle.

"About fucking time," Rory yelled. "I'm going to die if you don't fuck me."

Ivan let Rory's dick slip free from his lips and met his gaze. Rory's eyes were wide and desperate, but Ivan wasn't done with him yet. "You're not going to die." He eased his finger free and left the bed long enough to retrieve the bag with the lube. He lifted the container of cookies and grinned wickedly.

"Do not dare stop to eat a cookie," Rory growled, snagging the bag.

Ivan flopped down beside him and tucked his hands under his head. Rory eyed his submission and fumbled the containers.

"Um, do we want Monkey Grease or Butt Stuff?"

Ivan darted a glance at his dick—long, thick, and erect—then met Rory's gaze. "You're the one riding it, so you choose."

"Good call," Rory said, settling on a tube. He tore into the packaging like a madman before working the cap open. Not willing to lie idle anymore, Ivan snagged the tube from his hand and crooked a finger for Rory to come closer.

"I'm not done exploring you," Ivan said. He couldn't tell if Rory's groan was from excitement or dread over the potential delayed gratification. "Straddle me."

"Gladly." Rory settled his ass on Ivan's thighs, just where he wanted to be, and watched him slick up two fingers.

Ivan closed the flip cap and set the lube aside. Rory rose on his knees and scooted closer without being told. Ivan rubbed the liquid around the rim before pushing two fingers inside Rory's heat.

"Mmmmm," Rory moaned. He closed his eyes and let his head fall back. Pretty pink lips parted on a sigh when Ivan started moving the fingers in and out, spreading the lube and loosening the ring of muscle. "So good." Rory braced his weight with a hand on Ivan's lower abdomen, then started fucking himself on Ivan's fingers. "I could come just from this."

Someday, Ivan would love to watch it happen, but right now, he wanted Rory on his dick. He eased his hand free and grabbed a condom from the nightstand. Rory snatched it, tore the wrapper open, and rolled it onto Ivan's cock.

"Didn't know you could move that fast," Ivan teased.

"Want you," Rory replied, running on pure desperation.

"Have me."

Rory gripped the base of Ivan's dick and lined it up against his pucker. He didn't ease himself down; Rory took him to the hilt on his next exhale. Tight heat enveloped his shaft, and Ivan clenched his teeth and arched his neck. Rory remained still as he adjusted to the intrusion, keeping his eyes locked on Ivan's the entire time. Something passed between them—silent, beautiful, and completely unguarded. Ivan accepted then what he already knew. He was in over his head with Rory, and he wanted to make him come harder than he ever had in his life.

Ivan placed his hands above Rory's knees, then slid them up until they rested on his hips. "You promised me a ride."

Rory's hips bucked forward, lodging Ivan's dick impossibly deeper. He moaned long and sweet, then rode Ivan in earnest, his cock slapping against his stomach. Rory's hands became active participants instead of idle witnesses. He caressed his own stomach, torso, and chest. Rory pinched and rolled his nipples while riding Ivan so smoothly it had to be a crime. The entire time, Rory held Ivan's gaze, burrowing deeper into his psyche while taking pleasure from Ivan's body. Yeah, he was in so much trouble.

Ivan's body tensed as pleasure built into a painful crescendo. Just when he didn't think he could hold back anymore, Rory's breath hitched and he pitched forward, bracing his hands on Ivan's chest to keep from collapsing. Eyes wide, Rory came without even touching his dick. His channel tightened around Ivan's cock, triggering his climax too, but he needed more friction to finish. He bucked his hips upward, driving into Rory until he had nothing left to give.

Rory let him take his full weight. Ivan ran his hand up and down Rory's spine while their breathing returned to normal. Rory nuzzled his nose against Ivan's neck, and he expected him to purr at any minute. After a few moments of respite, Rory pushed up on one elbow and looked down at him. "So have you worked me out of your system yet?"

chapter

TEN

RORY HELD HIS BREATH WHILE WAITING FOR AN ANSWER TO his question.

Ivan smiled and rubbed the back of his fingers over the curve of Rory's cheek. "Not even close."

Leaning into his caress like a kitten, Rory said, "You know this spells trouble, right?"

Ivan slid his hand back to palm Rory's head and bring him closer. "Big trouble," he whispered against Rory's lips. "But I knew that the moment I laid eyes on you." Ivan swooped in for a fierce kiss.

Everything they'd shared was new to Rory. Well, not everything. He'd had plenty of sex before, but those encounters had been about finding physical release with an eager partner. Ivan had the enthusiasm in spades during their…coupling? Was that the right word? Christ, Rory couldn't even get his private thoughts in the right order, and he blamed the gorgeous man making love to his mouth.

Ivan pulled back and studied him with sleepy amber eyes. "You seem distracted. Are you okay with what happened between us tonight?"

"Okay?" Every muscle felt like a limp noodle, and he needed his voice to express the emotions he couldn't form on his face. "The reason I seem distracted is because my brain matter hasn't reformed after the orgasm you gave me." Rory pushed up higher, and his skin didn't immediately separate from Ivan's hairy belly. "We better get cleaned up. My liquid gold is turning into glue. You wait much longer and you're going to regret having it in your hair."

Ivan's chest rumbled with humor and his smile created a fluttering sensation in Rory's chest like a butterfly flitting about. Rory suspected the source was a sexy conqueror pitching a tent to make himself comfortable as he staked out his territory. "I knew it was only a matter of time before you started in with the liquid gold jokes," Ivan said, tugging Rory back down on top of him.

"Come on, man. What were you thinking?"

"Some of us aren't degenerates and perverts," Ivan said with a haughty sniff. "Some of us were good boys who spent all our free time in church."

Rory arched a brow. Was this a genuine factoid or Ivan teasing him? "Seriously?"

Ivan nodded with a wry grin. "We went to church a minimum of three days a week. Our parents restricted what we read, watched on television, or listened to on the radio. We worked our farm, worshipped God, fueled our bodies to do both those things, and that was it. I didn't lose my virginity until I was twenty." Rory envied the asshole who'd gotten to teach Ivan Gallagher all the beautiful things his body could do. Ivan reached a hand down to squeeze his ass cheek. "I've more than made up for the slow start, and I promise I have no intention of preaching the gospel to you."

"I'm stewing in jealousy."

Ivan arched a brow. "Of church revivals and lock-ins?"

"Of the lucky bastard who got to coax you out of the repression," Rory admitted. "The person who taught you how to kiss and who showed you how good it felt to have your dick in their mouth. I resent he got to see the look on your face the first time you went balls deep inside his ass." Rory cocked his head to the side. "I'm assuming it was a guy."

A dark shadow washed over Ivan's golden amber eyes, and Rory realized the subject was a painful one for him. He was on the verge of diverting the conversation to something safer when Ivan nodded. "Yeah, a guy. I've only been with men. What about you?"

"Same. Gave my V-card to my high school boyfriend. It was less than memorable." Not because the guy was a lousy lover but because Rory had started drowning his misery in booze. Their relationship hadn't survived Rory's stint in rehab, and he'd never attempted a serious relationship since.

Rory pushed up again, and this time, he barely pulled free without taking hair with him. "Let's hit the shower. I'll wash that off before it hardens to cement."

Ivan's gaze heated, and it didn't take a genius to know where his mind had gone. They didn't bother grabbing clothes but padded naked to the bathroom, where they kissed and touched while they waited for the water to get hot. Ivan stepped into the shower, and Rory became transfixed on the sight of Ivan naked and wet. When Rory didn't immediately follow, Ivan slid the glass door open again and crooked his finger. "It's lonely in here."

Rory held up his finger. "Give me just a second. Hope gave me some products to test out. Don't wash or touch anything until I get back."

Ivan gave him a wicked smile and placed his palms against the shower wall. "Alrighty."

Rory pivoted and rushed back to Ivan's room to retrieve the items from the men's line he'd chosen from Hope's store. She produced a variety of scents, but he'd gone with the one that made him think of Ivan. She called it the Billiard Room. It smelled like expensive bourbon, wood, leather, and a hint of something smoky and fruity that reminded him of his grandpa's pipe tobacco. The combination conjured a gentleman's escape, and for all his roughly hewn edges, Ivan had a poet's heart. No one would convince Rory otherwise. He'd only meant to grab the hair and body stuff, but he snatched the water-friendly lube she'd aptly named Splash Zone. Rory wasn't sure either of them had any giddy-up left in the tank, but he was game to find out if Ivan was. And it could be a while before they had the privacy to test the shower lube without Dylan overhearing them.

"Finally," Ivan said when he got back. His dick was amazingly at half-mast already.

"I thought I told you not to touch yourself," Rory said, pointing at the obvious infraction.

Ivan smiled wickedly. "I didn't. My current state happens when I think about how your wet body will feel against mine. I imagined running soapy hands over you from head to toe." Ivan lowered his voice to a whisper. "Spoiler alert: I plan to linger in a few places."

Miraculously, Ivan's dick went from semihard to fully erect as he verbally mapped out the plans he'd made.

"I wasn't gone long," Rory said.

"An eternity," Ivan whined. "Get in here." He looked down and also seemed surprised at how hard he'd gotten. "Wow. That hasn't happened for a long time." He met Rory's gaze once more. "The Rory Effect."

Rory smiled at the reference to his YouTube channel. Did that mean Ivan had watched some episodes? A question for another time. Seeing Ivan's desperation sparked his sleepy libido back to life. Rory didn't trip over his own two feet while getting into the shower with Ivan, but it was damn close.

Ivan settled his hands on Rory's hips and kick-started his heart. "What do you have there?"

"A two-in-one shampoo Hope swears won't dry out your scalp or weigh down your hair and make it oily. Those shampoo-conditioner combos usually do one or the other or both. There are vitamins and essential oils in it to keep your scalp healthy and your hair looking good." Rory set that bottle down on the noticeably barren ledge. He typically stocked his shower with a variety of body and hair care products. "This is a body wash with the same scent as the shampoo and conditioner." Rory rattled off the name and scents he detected.

"Hope is a pure genius at marketing."

"Absolutely," Rory agreed, and he should know. "Um, this is a face wash. I left the toner, moisturizer, and beard oil in your bedroom. Not sure how much of that you want to try, but I'm excited to—" Ivan cut him off with a passionate kiss. Firm lips lingered, teased his mouth open, and reduced Rory's limbs to the consistency of wet noodles. If not for the firm hands holding him upright, Rory would've been a puddle at Ivan's feet.

"What's that last one?" he asked. "Looks like water drops or jizz splatters."

"I think it's both," Rory said. "It's her newest lube called Splash Zone. It enhances—"

Ivan kissed him once more and snagged the product from his hand. He set the tube next to the body and hair care products, then hoisted Rory into the air and pinned him against the shower wall. The cold tile ripped the breath from his lungs in a ragged gasp, but the heat of Ivan's big, muscular body made him forget about the shock. Rory locked his legs around Ivan's hips and moaned where their dicks slid against each other. Ivan reached for the tube, tore the cellophane off with his teeth, and let it fall to the shower floor. His hips pinned Rory in place while he drizzled the liquid over their dicks as if he were pouring honey on biscuits. Ivan snapped the lid shut and set it aside, then he wrapped his fists around Rory's wrists and pinned both his arms over his head. He dipped his hips a little lower then slowly rolled them up, making the sweetest, wettest friction against Rory's dick.

"Ohhhhh." Rory's moan was long and needy.

Laughter rumbled from Ivan's chest, and he repeated his dip and roll again, eliciting even sluttier moans. Attaching his lips to Rory's neck, he kissed and licked the sensitive flesh while he frotted them to within an inch of their lives.

Rory's breathing turned choppy and fast. "If you don't let me c-c-come…"

Ivan nipped his neck and said, "You'll do what?"

He was at the bigger man's tender mercies, and he couldn't fathom there being anywhere else he wanted to be or anyone else to share this moment with. "Die." And it didn't feel like a dramatic response. Rory was acutely aware of his body in ways he'd never experienced, as if everything had boiled down to this one moment. He would know the secrets to the universe with this one orgasm. Stupid, he knew, but no less true.

Ivan slowed his thrusts instead of speeding up. Rory voiced his frustration in a jagged moan and struggled in his embrace until Ivan soothed him with gentle kisses. "Or you'll find out what it means to live," Ivan whispered before capturing Rory's mouth. The searing kiss amped the sexual tension right back up until they were rutting animals instead of men.

Rory came first, grunting and growling through his release. Ivan followed right after, not uttering a single sound as his facial features twisted and froze into a mask of pleasure and pain. God, it made Rory so fucking glad he was alive.

Ivan carefully set Rory down and firmly gripped his hips to make sure he was steady enough to stand on his own. "We won't have much hot water left," he said, steering Rory under the spray and reaching for the shampoo and conditioner. Ivan flipped the cap open and took a sniff. "This is how I imagine a billiard room would smell before I bent you over the table and fucked you."

Rory let out a little whimper and braced an arm on the tile wall to keep him upright.

Ivan poured a generous circle of amber liquid into his palm. The color was nearly a dead ringer for his eyes. Instead of lathering his own hair, Ivan went to work on Rory's, massaging his scalp and making him tingle in new and exciting ways. The wash ended much sooner than Rory wanted. Then he remembered the comment about limited hot water and tipped his head back to rinse the shampoo out while Ivan went to work on his own scalp.

"I like the amount of lather I get," Ivan said. "Makes me think the product is doing something. That's two checks in the pro column." He gave Rory the dirtiest smile he'd ever seen. "Pretty sure you know how I felt about Splash Zone."

Rory couldn't help but smile. Their sexy shower had turned into a consumer survey. "Might need another test before we can render a true opinion. The liquid was perfect for jerking off or frotting in the water, but how well would it hold up during a rigorous fucking?"

Ivan moved under the spray to rinse his hair. Rory tried to move to give him space, but Ivan snagged him by the hip and held him there. It seemed Ivan was in no hurry to part ways either. They turned to the body wash next and had just enough time to soap up and rinse off before the water temperature cooled significantly.

Rory turned the faucet off with a hard shiver. "I'll test out the face stuff tomorrow," he said as he accepted the towel Ivan handed him. He dried off but got distracted watching the light blue terrycloth move over Ivan's skin until a shiver racked his body.

Ivan snorted, threw his towel over the rack to dry, and gripped Rory's towel. He scrubbed the material over damp skin while grinning. He looped the towel around Rory's neck when he was done and gently tugged him forward for a quick kiss. Uncertainty settled in the pit of Rory's stomach. Should he tell Ivan good night and go to his own bed? Should he just follow Ivan back to his room and see what happened? The internal debate must've shown in his expression because Ivan smoothed his fingers over Rory's forehead. "Tell me what's wrong," he said.

"Do you want me to go downstairs now so you can sleep?"

"No, but I'll understand if you need your own space."

Rory shook his head. "I'd like to sprawl in your bed and feed you cookies."

Ivan placed a hand over his heart and feigned a hard swoon. "How could I refuse a suggestion like that?"

Rory hung up his towel, and they hurried to Ivan's room, where they could get warm under the covers. Once Rory was in bed, Ivan turned the overhead light off and flipped on a bedside lamp. True to his word, Rory fed Ivan two giant cookies and tucked the joyful sounds of the big man's moans of delight next to his heart. Once they finished, Ivan turned off the lamp and spooned up behind him.

"I can't remember the last time I've felt this relaxed," Ivan murmured.

"Good," Rory said. "Interview tip number one: Remember this feeling tomorrow. You're just engaging in an intimate conversation about your business."

"How intimate?" Ivan asked.

Rory rolled over in his embrace and kissed his lips. "What do you love most about raising bees?"

Ivan immediately tensed, so Rory rubbed his chest until he relaxed. "Roberto isn't out to get you. He wants to know what makes your honey such a standout. I can tell you right now it comes from passion. I can feel it humming under your skin."

"That's what happens when you're near."

Rory chuckled. "Be serious."

"I'm very serious about my bees," Ivan replied.

"See how loose you are? Let's keep it this way." Rory repeated his original question and raptly listened to his reply. This was a man who loved his job, and that was something they shared. Doubts about Rory's future tried to creep in, but he held them at bay to ask Ivan another question. They continued practicing until they spent more time yawning than talking.

"Rory?" Ivan whispered.

"Yeah."

"You make me really glad I stopped hating myself."

Rory's breath caught in his chest. No one had ever said anything half as beautiful to him. He wanted to give Ivan a truth equally as powerful, and the dark made confessions so much easier. "This is the first time I haven't felt lonely since my mom died."

Ivan tightened his arms around him and pressed a kiss to Rory's nape. "We're in so much fucking trouble."

"Yeah, but we're in it together." The significance of his words should've startled Rory and kept him awake, but the truth settled over him like a weighted blanket and lulled him to sleep.

The next thing Rory knew, early morning light filtered into the bedroom, and he noticed an erection pressed against his lower back. He stretched and pushed harder against Ivan's hot body, earning a grateful groan.

"Finally," Ivan said in a gravelly voice. "Can you take me again?"

Rory lifted his right leg and rested it on Ivan's outer thigh, opening himself to whatever Ivan wanted. A possessive growl and a rigorous fuck met Rory's offer.

And there was no better way to start the day.

ELEVEN

IVAN CROSSED HIS RIGHT ANKLE OVER HIS LEFT AND LEANED against the kitchen counter to observe Rory's purposeful stride toward the ranch house. He sighed, actually fucking sighed. It wasn't the annoyed kind he was used to either, though he might've been a little grumpy. Rory had seemed more eager to arrive on time for kitchen duties with Harry than to linger around kissing Ivan. The thought made him scowl, which Ivan only knew because he caught his expression in the shiny toaster next to the window. But the breathy sound escaping his lips sounded content, and when was the last time he'd felt that way?

Unfortunately for him, Ivan's brain accepted the question as a challenge and started replaying all the things that had led up to the big sigh. Kissing Rory. Making Rory come. Seeing Rory bond with the crew over poker. The hottest, tightest ass he'd ever experienced. Rory feeding him cookies. Confessions in the dark. Cuddling. Morning wood he fed to Rory's greedy body one throbbing inch at a time. Languid, indulgent strokes that lasted forever and not long enough. Kissing Rory awake again when he'd drifted to sleep in his arms. The joy on Rory's face when he accepted the cup of coffee Ivan had made for him.

Yeah, okay. I fucking get it. Rory, Rory, Rory.

Ivan's smiling reflection betrayed the joy he felt just thinking his name. He forced his gaze back out the window just as the object of his obsession—there was no better term—disappeared into the ranch house. Had he felt Ivan's eyes on him the entire walk? Had he turned around to confirm while Ivan stared at his reflection in the toaster?

Enough already! The admonition bounced around Ivan's skull loud enough to make him wince. He couldn't shake the feeling that he was on the cusp of serious trouble, but he reached for another cookie instead of coming up with a game plan to thwart said trouble. He closed his eyes and forced himself to chew slowly, savoring the burst of flavors on his tongue and the varied textures in his mouth. Food had never given him a hard-on before, but these cookies might have if not for the robust rounds of sex with—

Don't say his name. Ivan rolled his eyes even though his lids were closed. His thought was just that ridiculous. Did he think saying Rory's name would summon him like Beetlejuice? *Rory! Rory! Rory!*

Loud, energetic whistling followed his silent chant, and Ivan snapped his eyes open, expecting to see Rory headed back toward the homestead. Instead, it was Dylan who sauntered down the driveway. Ivan smiled at the swagger in Dylan's step, but as happy as he was for his friend, Ivan had no intention of sharing the cookies Ro—*he*—had made for him. Ivan was no stranger to hiding his favorite foods from greedy hands. His younger brother, Innes, had the nose of a bloodhound and a stomach with a storage capacity similar to Mary Poppins's carpetbag. He could sniff out a treat anywhere and was a bottomless pit that could hold an entire bag of Chips Ahoy. Ivan had learned early on that he had to trick Innes's brain if he ever wanted to eat treats again. There was nothing his younger brother hated more than raisins, so Ivan had hidden his stashes inside an empty Raisin Bran box in the kitchen cabinet. Innes's inner bloodhound knew a treat was nearby, but his brain wouldn't allow him to touch the box of cereal, let alone open it up.

Ivan deployed the same tactic with Dylan, whose aversion to Cheerios provided a great hiding place. General Mills made boxes big enough to feed a battalion of kids, which suited Ivan just fine. He opened the flap and slid the storage container of cookies right inside the box and placed it back in the cabinet before Dylan reached the back door. Since he'd never shared his technique with anyone, Dylan was none the wiser. Ivan grabbed an empty coffee mug and filled it to the brim with rich, black coffee. He extended it to his friend when he entered the kitchen.

Dylan accepted the cup with a smile. "Nectar of the gods." He saluted Ivan with the cup, then took a long drink, which gave Ivan ample time to study his friend. What he found made him snort. Dylan's quirked brow made Ivan chuckle. His friend lowered the coffee cup and scowled at him, which pitched Ivan into a deep belly laugh. Dylan set his coffee cup on the counter and placed both hands on his hips. The gesture pulled his sweatshirt tighter, emphasizing the issue. "What's wrong with you?" Dylan glanced down and noticed his shirt was inside out and on backward. "Damn it."

"Add in the wildly mussed hair and the missing sock and it adds up to one hell of a night."

Dylan whipped his sweatshirt off, but not before Ivan witnessed a faint blush and a wicked smile. He'd wiped his expression clean by the time he sorted his shirt. "You're one to talk."

Ivan looked down the front of his body, noting his clothes were on properly, he wore two matching socks, and his boots were on the right feet. "I don't see a problem."

"I wasn't talking about your outfit," Dylan said. He raised his hand and drew circles with his index finger near Ivan's head. "I'm talking about your face."

Ivan ran a hand over his beard and ignored the few cookie crumbs he shook loose. He'd tried the beard oil from Hope's shop and was surprised how much he liked it. The bristles were soft but not greasy.

"I wasn't talking about your chin bush," Dylan said, "though it's looking good. I'm talking about the goofy smile you're wearing."

Ivan snapped his gaze to the toaster and confirmed Dylan wasn't wrong. He relaxed his face so his lips would return to home base, but the smile returned almost as quickly as it faded. *Fuck me.* The Rory Effect.

Dylan laughed, then took another swig of coffee. "Can't wipe that fucker off your face. Ought to make breakfast interesting. Want me to turn my sweatshirt inside out again?"

Ivan forced himself to look away from his reflection. There were far worse things than smiling too much, and he figured he'd sober up when everyone was around. "Nah. I'm good."

"Must be," Dylan replied. "Rory practically floated into the kitchen to report for duty. Pretty sure his feet didn't touch the ground."

"Bullshit," Ivan said, though the idea touched him deeply. "I watched him walk to the ranch house, and I assure you his feet were on the ground." Ivan's cheeks heated when he realized what he'd confessed.

Dylan drained the rest of his coffee, set the mug in the sink, and headed toward the archway. "I'll stop busting your balls and go take a shower."

Instead of heading to the ranch house early, Ivan hung back and waited for Dylan. He wanted to tell his friend how happy he was for him and maybe get some details on the timeline of their relationship. Ivan didn't have to wait long since he and Rory had shared a selfishly long shower not long before Dylan returned. His friend glared at him when he reappeared in the kitchen. He bypassed the second cup of coffee Ivan offered in apology and removed the box of Cheerios from the cabinet. Ivan watched in stunned silence as Dylan pulled the storage container out of the box and helped himself to a cookie.

His friend let out an indecent moan when he bit into the treat, snapping Ivan out of his trance. Ivan snagged the container from Dylan before he could grab a second. "Hands off my cookies."

Dylan rolled his eyes. "I didn't touch the baker, just the baked goods." His friend nearly choked on his next bite, and Ivan nearly applauded. Served him right. Dylan snagged the mug of coffee Ivan still held and took a drink. He cleared his throat a few times, then said, "Settle down. Don't Hulk out on me. I'm madly in love with Harry, so you have nothing to worry about, not that it would matter since Rory only has eyes for you."

Ivan figured he more closely resembled Shrek than the Hulk. And he ignored Dylan's last remark to focus on the love declaration. "Madly, huh? Isn't it a little soon?"

Dylan polished off the rest of the cookie and took another swig of coffee before attempting to speak again. "No," he said calmly. "I've been in love with her since the day we met. It's taken Harry longer to accept her feelings are more than lust."

Ivan quirked a brow. Just how long had they been dating? "How much longer?"

"I stole my first kiss seven months ago."

"Seven months?" Ivan repeated. How had he not known? He and Dylan shared pretty tight quarters to be keeping that kind of secret.

"Yeah," Dylan replied wistfully. "Aspects of our relationship heated up pretty quickly, but others took a while to develop into something deeper…at least for one of us."

"Seven months?"

Dylan set the coffee mug down and scowled at him. "Why do you keep saying that?"

"How'd you keep me in the dark this entire time?"

Dylan snorted. "Dude, you'd sleep through a freight train running through the house."

Ivan arched a brow but couldn't deny his claim. He'd always been a heavy sleeper. How many times had his parents woken him from a dead sleep to get into the storm shelter on their Kansas farm? Tornadoes sounded eerily similar to trains, and Ivan would've slept through them until it was too late if not for his folks. He fought off a hard shiver at the mere thought of a tornado. As much as he loved spring and planting season, Ivan dreaded the tornado-producing storm systems that came with spring and summer. Luckily, tornadoes weren't nearly as common in the foothills of the mountains where the ranch was situated, but Ivan had a hard time convincing his brain of that when the skies turned black and the wind whirled and whistled.

"And we were really careful," Dylan added, completely oblivious to Ivan's inner turmoil. "Harry tried to convince me we were only experiencing lust, and that we didn't have enough in common to form a meaningful bond." A smile tugged at Dylan's lips and a chuckle rumbled in his chest. Then his eyes took on a faraway expression, and Ivan doubted he was even aware of his presence. "I was more stubborn than she was about the subject and was determined Harry would accept our love as real and not just a fling."

Alarm bells should've sounded in Ivan's head, and not little whimsical chimes either. Big-ass air raid sirens that could wake the dead because Harry's initial denial sounded a lot like the bullshit Ivan was feeding himself and Rory. But no bells trilled. No sirens wailed. Just another sappy-ass sigh that snapped his friend back to reality. "Waited her out, did you?" Ivan asked. "Wore her down?"

Dylan blinked the room into focus and scrunched up his brow as if trying to locate the dangling conversation thread. Then he nearly blinded Ivan with a megawatt smile. "I was patient. That was the secret. I showed her unwavering affection even when she got scared and pushed me away."

"Still can't believe I missed the signs. Yeah, I'm a heavy sleeper, but I'm usually more observant."

"At first, you were too busy trying to convince yourself you were jealous of Finley falling for Kieran." Dylan arched a brow when Ivan opened his mouth to dispute…what part, exactly? There was a lot to unpack in that one accusation. "You were never in love with Finley," Dylan said firmly. "You were in love with the idea of him. Finley was the type of guy you thought you needed." Dylan scoffed. "No way. He's too nice. You need someone to stand up to you. Give you hell when you need it."

Ivan thought of the spitfire he'd held in his arms all night long and didn't disagree with Dylan's assessment. Any of it. He had loved Finley, still did, but he'd never been in love with him.

"The way you look at Rory, though…" Dylan let his words trail off and let his smirk do the talking.

Ivan had stomached as much bonding as he could on coffee and carbs. He'd need a belly full of protein if he was going to listen to Dylan dole out relationship advice like Dr. Phil. As if reading his mind, his friend threw up his hands in surrender, then mimed zipping his lips. The silence lasted until they were halfway to the big ranch house.

"Harry and I are talking about getting a place off the ranch, so you might have the old homestead to yourselves soon." Cue the return of the smirk.

Ivan knew damn well he hadn't included Finley in the equation. He was happy as a clam sharing the small cabin with Kieran. All the things Ivan and Rory could get up to alone in that house played in his mind like a naughty montage. "He's not staying," Ivan said. But he wasn't sure which of them he was trying to convince?

Dylan's smartass smirk said he had the same question.

chapter

TWELVE

THE EFFORT, CARE, AND ORGANIZATION HARRY PUT INTO feeding her people wowed Rory. He'd said as much when he'd arrived to find her sitting at the kitchen island, sipping coffee and going over her plans for the morning on her laptop. The previous day, Rory had learned that she kept both paper and digital copies of her recipes. She stored printed versions in binders in her office, which she'd arranged by meal or occasion. He could happily spend hours or days flipping through them. Some she'd found on the internet and tweaked to suit the people she cared for either by volume or ingredient preferences. But most had come from her grandmother. She kept the handwritten versions of those cherished recipes in her safe deposit box at the bank to preserve them for future generations.

"In case Finley or I have kids someday," she'd said wistfully.

Harry and Rory had spent a lot of time sharing stories about their Southern grandmothers while baking and prepping food for poker night. It was great to talk to someone who understood the significance of Eustice Stuart's role in Rory's life, especially during his formative years. While Harry didn't know Rory's grandmother, she'd grown up with her very own version. So their first foray working together in the kitchen had been relaxed and wasn't influenced by a time crunch. Rory expected the vibe to be different when he arrived at the ranch the following morning. Sunday was a day of relaxation for most of the residents, but not for Harry. She outlined her tasks for the week and did as much meal prep as possible. Her dedication to her tasks was evident in the serious expression on her face when he'd entered the room. She'd shut the laptop quickly and forced a smile to her face. Was she upset he'd arrived early and interrupted her quiet time?

"Would you like me to come back?" Rory asked.

Harry stiffened. "What? No. Why would you ask that? I'm so glad you're here. Now that I have an extra set of hands, I want to be a bit more adventurous with the menu."

"You seemed overly serious when I walked in."

"And you were worried I was having second thoughts about you helping?" Harry asked thoughtfully. She eased off her stool and hugged Rory. "Not in the least. If anything, I would like to have you full-time." Harry stood back and smiled at him. "I'm preparing to make some big changes in my life, and I was overthinking things when you walked in. I'm much better now. Ready to get started?"

"Definitely. What did you have in mind?"

Harry winked, then launched into the menu she'd planned. "You have a wonderful flair for flavors. I'd really like to jazz up the fried potatoes and the scrambled eggs."

"Diced onions and peppers in both is probably overkill," Rory said. He took a sip of the coffee Ivan had made for him and considered his options. The perfection of the java sidetracked him and reminded Rory of the kisses they'd exchanged while waiting for the pot to brew. *You're doing it again. Get your shit together.*

Rory brought the room into focus and found Harry smiling at him. "What?"

"I recognize that expression," she said. "I wear it a lot."

Rory made a show of feeling his face, fingers stalling on his lips. Had he ever smiled so broadly? "I can't find anything unusual about my expression," he lied.

Harry snorted. "Uh-huh. You started off trying to decide how to enhance the eggs and potatoes without going overboard, and then your thoughts veered off toward Ivan." She waggled her brows. "You were probably thinking of the spices you could add to breakfast, and the hotter ones reminded you of him."

Her comment hit much closer to home than Rory liked. "Not even close." He sniffed, took another sip, and said, "How about we sprinkle a smoky spice combo on the potatoes as soon as they come out of the fryer? The key ingredient will be paprika to give smokiness without heat. I'm thinking ancho chili, garlic, and onion powder would complement it well."

It was hard to tell if Harry's smile was over the flavor profile he'd suggested or his blatant change of subject. "Brilliant," she replied. "All the guys love peppers, mushrooms, and onions. What about a cheesy egg scramble with those vegetables added in?"

"My mouth is already watering," he replied.

They took stock of the cheeses on hand, and Rory suggested the smoked gouda over the other options.

"I agree," Harry said. "Do you want to handle the eggs and potatoes? I'll take care of the meat, yogurt parfait, and bread options?"

"Absolutely," Rory said, though his voice suggested more bravado than he actually felt. He'd never cooked for so many people nor had he dreamed of a situation where he would. Yet he cracked three dozen eggs into a large bowl, shredded a truckload of cheese, and sliced and diced a mountain of vegetables and potatoes. "Do you have heavy whipping cream?"

"Always," Harry replied. "Thinking about adding some to the eggs?"

"It makes them creamy and fluffy." Rory laughed when it came time to figure out how much heavy cream to add to three dozen eggs. He pulled out the phone Nicky had given him to do the calculation and determined he needed just over a pint.

The commercial grade equipment cooked and fried the food more efficiently, but there was too much to prepare in one go. It still took him a while to figure out the right volume for each batch, but he got there with Harry's suggestions and encouragement. Rory bounced back and forth between the fryer and the stove. Then he transferred the finished food to the massive warmers before starting the next batches. He stirred, shook, seasoned, and stored like a champ. By the time they finished, Rory was sweaty but buzzing with pride over the food he'd prepared. The experience had been so much different from baking cookies with his mom and grandmother or hosting a small dinner party for friends.

"I feel like an iron chef in this moment," he said breathlessly as he assessed the fruits of their labor.

"I'm so proud of you," Harry said, slipping an arm around his waist.

Rory patted her shoulder before easing to the side. "I'm a sweaty mess."

She snorted and waved off his worry. "That's why we have a small bathroom just around the corner. I always freshen up a little before I signal for the fellas to help carry the food into the dining room."

Rory was in awe of her genius. "Ladies first."

"Don't mind if I do," she said before breezing out of the kitchen.

He heard footsteps approaching, but they were heavier than Harry's and coming from the opposite direction she'd gone. Rory's heart hammered in his chest because he recognized the footfalls. But how? Ivan came into view before he analyzed his question.

"Hi," Ivan said, sounding shy.

"Hiya. Hungry?"

Ivan's eyes shone like polished amber stones beneath the bright kitchen lights. "Positively famished."

Rory swallowed hard because Ivan hadn't even looked at the food. The big man kept coming forward and looked as if he would devour Rory right there in the kitchen. If not for Harry's sudden reemergence from the powder room, he thought Ivan might've done just that. Instead, Ivan stopped on the other side of the island and noticed the food for the first time.

"Wow," he said. "This looks and smells incredible."

"Because it is," Rory replied.

"Perfect timing," Harry said cheerfully. She squeezed Ivan's upper arm as she passed by. "Use these big muscles to carry out some food, and then use your leadership skills to recruit help."

Ivan looked down at Harry and grinned. "Normally, you just bellow for us to come help. Why are we standing on ceremony now that Rory is here?"

Harry placed her hands on her hips, and Ivan crossed his thick arms over his chest. They might've looked like gunslingers squaring off if not for the goofy grins on their faces. Rory shook his head and left them to sort it out so he could get cleaned up. The last thing he wanted to do was drip sweat into the food he'd worked so hard to prepare. He washed his hands, then splashed cool water on his face. Rory caught sight of his reflection in the mirror and noticed a new shimmer in his blue eyes. It wasn't lust or anger fueling the spark; it was pride and peace. He dabbed his face with a paper towel and reached for the door. When he walked into the kitchen, Harry was alone. She picked up the platter of sausage links, leaving the bacon for him to carry. Apparently, Ivan had recruited help to carry the rest.

Harry fanned her face with one hand and smirked at him. "I was about to reach for the fire extinguisher when I got back from the bathroom. Ivan gives a whole new meaning to smoldering glances. I thought you were about to go up in flames any minute."

Rory snorted and picked up the platter of bacon. "Whatever."

Harry snickered all the way to the dining room. The gathered men broke into a round of applause when they entered with the last of the food.

"Thank you, thank you," Harry said as she set her bounty down.

Rory placed the bacon between the sausage links and thick slices of ham, then took a bow. His mouth watered at the display of food.

"Grab your plates and fill up," Ivan told Harry and Rory.

Rory was on the verge of refusing until Harry nudged him. "Better do it," she said, spearing a piece of ham. "There will be a stampede."

She wasn't wrong. Ivan gave the rest of the crew the all clear once Harry and Rory finished. The guys practically knocked one another over to form a line. Ivan didn't join them right away. He waited at the table and held out a chair for Rory, who just blinked at him for a few seconds before lowering into the seat.

"Aww," Owen cooed before taking an elbow in the gut from Tyler.

Rory glanced up at Ivan to see if it bothered him, but Ivan seemed fixated on the scrambled eggs on Rory's plate instead of the shenanigans going on at the buffet. Rory offered his fork, and Ivan accepted. He took a small bite of eggs and closed his eyes while he chewed. Rory recognized that rapturous look on Ivan's face and averted his gaze before he blushed and gave his thoughts away.

"Get that line moving and save me some eggs," Ivan demanded before setting Rory's fork down and getting in line.

Rueben was smiling when he sat across from Rory. "Surprised the big guy didn't pull rank and advance to the front of the line."

"Why the hell didn't I think of that?" Ivan groused.

Owen raised his hand. "I know! I know! Because you—" This time the jab came from Kieran.

"Tough crowd," Owen teased, rubbing his belly.

Rory was going to wait for everyone else to sit down before eating, but he noticed Harry had already tucked into her food. She met his gaze and gestured toward his plate with her fork. Rory gave in and was glad he did. Everything was perfect. He was halfway through when Ivan returned to his seat. Rory always thought you could learn a lot about someone by observing their eating habits. Ivan was so tidy about everything from the napkin across his lap to the biscuit he'd split into two equal halves. Rory looked at his biscuit in comparison and couldn't help but smile at his lopsided top and bottom. The top was huge, about three-fourths of the biscuit. The size difference kind of reminded Rory of him and Ivan.

"Would you like some honey?" Ivan asked as he drizzled the liquid over his biscuit.

Rory was usually more of a jam person, but he was eager to taste Ivan's creations. Rory leaned closer and lowered his voice. "Is that the liquid gold you've been telling me about?" he asked.

Ivan briefly met his gaze with a smirk. "The one and only. Best honey you'll ever have."

Was that a euphemism for something else? "Can't wait."

Ivan handed him the pot shaped like a whiskey barrel and the honey dipper. Rory skipped the butter and drizzled a generous amount of honey onto his biscuit. He noticed the bee and mountain logo on the handle when he replaced it in the pot. He rotated the barrel and saw the same logo on the opposite side.

"Is this how you package your honey for retail?" Rory asked. Ivan had shoveled food into his mouth, so he nodded. "Genius marketing."

"Ivan designed and made the prototype, which is the one you just used," Harry said.

"You're good with wood too?" Rory asked, then realized how that sounded.

Ivan made a slightly choked noise but smiled as he chewed.

"Power and manual tools," Rueben said. "He can create such pretty art from a block of wood."

"You whittle?" Rory asked.

Ivan took a drink of orange juice and nodded. "My grandfather taught me when I was a kid."

Rory smiled. "My grandfather whittled too, but he couldn't convince my grandmother I was ready to learn."

Ivan held up his hand and pointed to the scars on his thumb. "The ladies in my life weren't thrilled with the number of stitches I required until I learned better control and skill."

"I learned how to play the guitar, though," Rory said, realizing it sounded like they were on a date.

He looked around the table and noticed all eyes were on them. Ivan didn't seem remotely concerned about anything but his breakfast, so Rory followed his lead. He was doing well until he bit into the biscuit and tasted Ivan's honey for the first time. It was sweet and rich, coating his tongue and going down smoothly. Rory didn't mean to emit a hum that sounded like a moan. Utensils clattered to plates, and Rory jerked his eyes open. He wasn't conscious of even closing them. The expressions around the table ranged from amused to slightly embarrassed for him.

Ivan's hand settled on Rory's leg, just above his knee. Ivan gently squeezed, and Rory wasn't sure what kind of reaction he was having to the moan. Was he trying to quiet Rory or turn him on? He glanced over at Ivan and relaxed when he saw the smug grin on his face.

"Best you ever had, right?" Ivan asked.

"Without question."

"Are they still talking about the honey?" Owen mock whispered.

Tyler sighed. "I'm concerned that you have to ask."

Rory forced his gaze away from Ivan before he did something truly indecent and concentrated on eating. Ivan didn't remove his hand until they finished their food. Everyone carried their dishes to the kitchen to rinse and stack in the dishwashers, but the crew was on a rotating schedule to do a deeper clean after each meal. They had to wash big items by hand, stow all the condiments in their proper places, and wipe down the surfaces. It took two of them twenty minutes or less to do the whole thing. It was Ivan and Dylan's turn to clean, but Rory nudged Dylan out of the way and shooed him away with his hands.

Ivan smiled at him when they were all alone in the kitchen. "The best you've ever had, huh?"

Rory understood it was a loaded question, and he replied with an unequivocal and emphatic, "Yes."

Ivan closed the small distance between them and searched Rory's gaze. He released a shaky breath and said, "I think you mean it."

Reminded of Harry's phrase, Rory realized what a comfort it was to believe every word that came out of someone's mouth. He didn't want to bullshit Ivan or sell him anything; he wanted Ivan to believe the words that rolled off his tongue, no matter where they were or what they were doing. "I damn well do." Ivan was not only the best lover he'd ever had, but that honey was in a class of its own.

"Would you like to come to my office and meet my new queen bee? You said you wanted to learn about my operation. We can do some more interview prep before Roberto arrives this afternoon."

Rory tilted his head slightly. "You realize what you're actually inviting me there for, right?"

Ivan smiled wickedly. "Absolutely."

"In that case, I will gladly come over and check out the inner workings of your honey pot."

Ivan snorted and turned to the sink, shoving his hands into the soapy water. "It was this or pull you in for a kiss. I'm desperate to taste my honey on your tongue." Ivan stared at Rory's lips so intently it felt like a caress.

Rory sighed. Nothing had ever sounded sexier to him. He dipped his hand into the same soapy water and caressed Ivan's forearm while pretending to search for other items to wash. "I'll be over as soon as I finish my tasks." With incentive like that, he figured it would cut his work time in half.

chapter
THIRTEEN

THE MORNING SEEMED TO STRETCH ON FOREVER, AND IVAN found himself watching the clock. He tried his best not to act like a petulant child denied his favorite treat, but that's exactly how he felt. Ivan was too mature to act in such a way, and Rory deserved more consideration from him. Rory didn't exist solely to bring him pleasure, though the look in his eyes earlier said otherwise. Ivan propped his feet on his desk and leaned his chair back, lacing his hands behind his head.

"I'm desperate to taste my honey on your tongue." Had he really said that? Yes, and he'd meant it—and not just the golden liquid his bees made. Ever since he'd uttered the words, Ivan couldn't stop picturing Rory on his knees with his seed smeared across his lips. His office door locked, and they could make the fantasy a reality. Rory had been jealous of Ivan's first, but this would be one they could experience together. Hell, there were several firsts Ivan wanted to share with Rory. He closed his eyes and let the rest of his office blow job fantasy play out.

"Well," Rory said from the doorway. Ivan had been so engrossed he hadn't heard him arrive. "Someone is working hard."

Ivan lowered his feet and spun his chair around to face the door.

He lowered his legs, parted them, and cupped the semi erection through his jeans. "I'm getting there." He crooked his finger for Rory to enter his office. "And shut the door."

Rory did as he was told, but he didn't head straight for Ivan. He detoured over to where Ivan's research data, honey production charts, and weather reports hung.

"Welcome to my office," he said, gesturing around.

Rory stepped farther into the room but didn't shut the door. "More like a mad scientist's laboratory."

The remark made Ivan smile, but it also reminded him of what was at stake. Everything on the wall represented the dream he'd been building for five years. Today was an opportunity to take the business to the next level as long as he didn't fuck it up.

"Ivan," Rory said softly as he came to stand in front of him. "Is everything okay? I meant the mad scientist remark as a compliment. Maybe I should've used a better quantifier. Sexy scientist?" Rory was worried he'd said something that had offended Ivan or hurt his feelings.

"Mad scientist is probably more fitting," Ivan replied. He patted his lap and Rory sauntered across the small room and straddled his thighs.

Ivan cupped the back of his neck and pulled him down for a hot, hungry kiss. When they broke apart, Ivan reached into his top desk drawer and pulled out a small tin of lip balm. He removed the lid and ran the pad of his forefinger over the smooth, gold surface. "I would love nothing more than to drizzle the actual honey over your lips and tongue and suck it off, but it would make a horrible mess. I'm already a nervous wreck. Perhaps lip balm made from my beeswax will be a good substitute until we can disappear behind locked doors." Ivan rubbed the balm over Rory's lips, and he pursed his mouth into a cute pout.

"And here I thought you were going to drizzle *your* honey on my lips."

Ivan released a hungry growl before capturing his mouth in another kiss. "We'll do that too, but first I need to get through my interview." He checked the clock. "Roberto will be here in two hours."

Rory stood up, and Ivan clenched his fists to keep from reaching for him. "Assume he'll arrive earlier than that. Is that what you want to wear?"

Ivan glanced down at his flannel shirt, jeans, and boots. "Yes, unless you think I need to dress nicer."

"This is perfect. The orange and navy in your shirt make your amber eyes pop. You'd make a burlap sack look hot, though." Rory leaned forward and kissed him. "You're going to do great. Let's run through some tips on posture and posing. I assume he will want to take pictures."

Ivan nodded. "I'm not taking him to my beehives, though. Not willing to give away my trade secrets."

Rory spent the next twenty minutes demonstrating what Ivan's posture should look like when he was sitting down or standing. They tried a few different angles to see what looked best before he decided that Ivan looked good in all of them.

"I don't think that's an objective opinion," Ivan said.

Rory waved him off and suggested they practice answering questions again. After two or three, he dusted off his hands and said, "I believe my work here is done."

Ivan tugged him back onto his lap and they made out for a little while, making sure not to take anything too far.

Rory rested his forehead against Ivan's. "You make me forget my name."

"Rory," Ivan said.

The gorgeous man shook his head. "That's just a nickname."

"What's your first name?"

"What do you want it to be?" Rory teased, giving Ivan a glimpse of the minx who'd first arrived on the ranch. "Seriously, what's your name?" Ivan could look it up in a heartbeat, but he wanted Rory to tell him.

"Maybe I'll save that for one of our confessions."

Ivan thought of the whispered words they'd shared in his bed and realized he liked the idea. "What if one of us offers something deep and meaningful and the other only imparts a trivial tidbit?"

Rory tipped his head to the side and considered the question. After a few moments, he straightened up and pinned Ivan with the most serious expression he'd seen yet. "Nothing you tell me would be too great or too small. I'll give everything equal weight, and your confessions will always stay between us."

Ivan realized he was right. Nothing he learned about Rory would feel trivial or small. "Deal."

Harry sent Ivan a text to let him know that Roberto had checked in at the gate, and she'd let him in. The editor would be there in moments. His anxiety started to spike again when he read the message out loud to Rory.

"You've got this. I'll be here the entire time to cheer you on."

Ivan opened his office door, then turned to look at Rory. "Wait, you said Roberto knows you. Maybe you should head back to the ranch or old homestead. I don't want to take a chance on your location getting leaked, even by accident. I'll be fine by myself. You prepared me thoroughly." He could tell Rory wasn't convinced so he pressed a quick kiss to his lips. "I won't show Roberto my beehives, but I'll take you there after he leaves."

Rory looked smug as hell as he headed toward the door. "I'm going to check out the library. I might lie on the couch and read a book while I wait for you to finish."

Ivan suddenly imagined Rory stretched out on the sofa with his nose tucked in a book and his feet on Ivan's lap. Ivan would have a book in one hand and would massage Rory's feet with the other. All three cats would be cuddled around them, and a fire would crackle in the fireplace, casting a warm glow in the small room. Foot rubs would lead to calf rubs, then up to the thighs and beyond. Books would get tossed, clothes would fly, and cats would scatter. Ivan would take Rory in front of the fireplace so he could watch the play of light on his skin as he sank into him. The scene was pure domestic bliss—something Ivan didn't expect to have for himself, yet it seemed wholly attainable when Rory was nearby.

"I'll join you as soon as I can." Ivan's voice sounded rough and gritty, and Rory responded with a wide smile.

"I don't know where your mind went just now, but I like it." Rory stood on his tiptoes and pressed a quick kiss to Ivan's lips before heading out. "Good luck, not that you're going to need it. I know you're going to be great."

Ivan heard a car pull up not long after Rory left and took steadying breaths to settle his nerves. He forced a smile to his lips and headed outside to greet Roberto, who would act as the interviewer and photographer. The editor had black hair, an olive complexion, and twinkling brown eyes.

"Ivan, thank you so much for meeting with me. Especially on such short notice. Cash said interviews aren't normally your thing, and that makes me even more grateful you agreed to this one. Your honey is superb, and I can't wait for my readers to learn more about you and your operation." His warm demeanor put Ivan at ease right away and that held throughout the interview. Ivan wasn't sure if it was because Rory really had prepared him well or if it was just knowing that Rory would be waiting for him after everything was done, but the interview wasn't as horrible as Ivan had anticipated. Roberto was kind and genuinely interested in what Ivan had to say. The experience was nothing like Ivan's previous encounters with the press when it had always felt like the reporters were trying to catch him out and trip him up so he'd look like the asshole they wanted him to be.

Cash arrived near the end and greeted Roberto with a backslapping hug. They took a few minutes to catch up, and Roberto pivoted to questions they both could answer. At no point did he employ gotcha tactics, and Ivan felt silly for being nervous at all. Then they transitioned to photographs. Roberto snapped pictures of Ivan and Cash individually and together, but he spent most of his attention on the little barrel of honey. Harry arrived with a basket of baked goodies and another barrel of honey just as they walked Roberto to his car. The man was delighted with the treats and helped himself to a muffin as he was buckling his seat belt. Roberto drove off with a honk and a wave.

Ivan turned to Cash once he left. "How'd the meeting go with the FBI about Salvation Anew?"

Something dark washed over Cash's features, but it was gone before Ivan could place the emotion. It wasn't anger or fear. More like annoyance. "It was probably a waste of time, through no fault of Nick's.

The agent I met with, Joplin, didn't seem too motivated to dig into their background. There have been no violent acts or laws broken. They're just a nuisance right now."

"What did he suggest if anything?" Ivan asked.

Cash quirked a brow. "Joplin said I needed to counter their recent bullshit targeting the ranch with positive deeds the community will rally behind. He suggested hiring a PR person."

"Sounds like a job for Rory," Ivan said. "He worked wonders preparing me for my interview."

"I can see that." A knowing smile crept across Cash's face. "I'll talk to him about it tomorrow. I'm sure Rory has better things to do than to talk marketing strategies on a Sunday afternoon." He slapped Ivan on the shoulder and said, "And I won't keep you either."

"Yeah, I have some laundry to catch up on."

Cash snorted as he headed to the ranch house. "Sure you do."

Ivan couldn't wait to tell Rory all about the interview but kept his gait slow and steady in case anyone was watching. He found Rory lying on the couch beneath a blanket with three cats piled on top of him, a book in his hand, and a fire crackling in the fireplace. The scene was almost an exact replica of his recent fantasy. The only thing missing was him, and Ivan planned to rectify that immediately.

chapter

FOURTEEN

S CRUFFY RAISED HIS HEAD AT A NOISE RORY COULDN'T HEAR or movement he couldn't see, yet he felt Ivan's nearness just the same. Awareness brushed over his spine like the big man's callused fingers when they cuddled naked in bed. Warmth spread throughout his body, and Rory would've curled his toes if Candy wasn't sleeping soundly on them. The littlest feline, Tux, had pressed his little body right up against Scruffy's. Rory could practically feel Ivan's intentions crackling in the air and taste them on his tongue. Even thinking the word *taste* made Rory think of their private conversation in the kitchen that morning. Only a few hours had passed, but Rory's body hadn't stopped buzzing like Ivan's beloved bees since their parting words.

I'm desperate to taste my honey on your tongue.

Ivan's approach was silent and might've caught Rory off guard if not for all three cats running across Rory's chest to get to their master. There was a whisper of rustling fabric as Ivan lowered himself next to the armrest behind Rory's head. He would've arched his neck to look at Ivan, but the only thing he'd see was fluffy cat belly or butt. A cacophony of meows greeted Ivan, and rumbling laughter followed Rory's attempts to get out from under his cats.

"Kids, kids, kids," Ivan said as he scooped them off Rory's chest one by one. "Daddy missed you too."

Free of furry beasts, Rory arched his neck to look up at Ivan. The cats were clamoring over one another to get his full attention. Scruffy was headbutting his chin, Tux was batting at his earlobe, and Candy crooned to him in the squeakiest little voice he'd ever heard. Adele she was not, but Candy made up for it with her precious adoration. Ivan split his attention between the trio of felines the best he could.

"For someone who doesn't want to be called Daddy, you sure refer to yourself that way with your cats."

Ivan met his gaze and smiled. "That's because I'm their father." Ivan carefully set the cats on the back of the couch and leaned over until his lips hovered over Rory's. "The things I want to do to you aren't fatherly."

"You don't want to feed me?" Rory asked.

Ivan licked Rory's bottom lip. "Does my cock count?"

Rory recalled the feel of Ivan's erection in his mouth, taking it down inch by glorious inch, and nodded. "I think you also want to pet me and make me purr."

"Very much," Ivan said. He stood back up, and Rory got an eyeful of the semierection pressing against Ivan's jeans. "Did you do all this?"

All this? Rory blinked to get his thoughts off the ways he could make Ivan go from semi to fully erect. "The fire? No. Dylan started it for us." Recalling the conversation he'd had with Ivan's best friend before he left made Rory smile. "He made it very, very clear that he would be gone for several hours and we'd have the place to ourselves." Harry had eventually confessed that their afternoon house hunting was the reason for her distractedness when he'd first arrived. "If I were the blushing sort, my cheeks would've been red with Dylan's unspoken insinuations about what the two of us could get up to while he was away."

Ivan cupped Rory's face and gently swiped his thumb over his mouth. "Not the blushing sort, huh?" He leaned forward and kissed him hard. "Sounds like a challenge to me. Want to continue this conversation up in my room?"

"And miss out on the fire?" Rory asked. He reached under the cushion and removed the lube and condoms he'd stashed there once Dylan left. Then he shoved the blanket down his body to reveal he wasn't wearing pants. The only thing separating Rory's dick from Ivan was a skimpy pair of dark red briefs. "I believe someone promised me honey kisses."

A sexy little growl rumbled from Ivan's chest as he whisked his shirt over his head and dropped it to the floor. He shucked off his pants and underwear with enough force to make his thick, gorgeous erection slap against his lower belly. The three cats scampered from the room as if embarrassed by their father's brazen behavior. *Damn, you are one sexy son of a bitch.*

Ivan's gaze grew tender. "Thank you."

Rory's eyes went wide and his cheeks turned pink with the thing Rory claimed he didn't do. Ivan chuckled but didn't point out the obvious. "Did I say that out loud?"

Shaking his head, Ivan said, "Your expression said it all." Ivan came around to the front of the couch and knelt before him. "But you can speak the words out loud if you wish."

Rory parted his legs to make room for him, but Ivan cupped his thighs to keep him in place. Ivan shifted both hands to his right leg and slid them slowly over his knee and calf. Warm palms smoothed over his ankle and heel, eliciting tiny sparks in his core which burst into flames when Ivan pressed his thumbs into the curved arch. "Damn, you are one sexy son of a bitch." Rory let out an indecent moan when Ivan pressed a little deeper as he worked his thumbs toward the ball of his foot. "I—" His breath hitched, and he needed a minute. Could a man come from a foot rub? If it were possible, Ivan could make it happen. "I take it back," he said breathlessly.

Ivan arched a brow. "You don't think I'm sexy?" he asked as he pinched lightly and pulled on Rory's big toe.

Rory's eyes threatened to roll back in his head. No one had ever rubbed his feet before, so he didn't know it could feel so good. "So fucking sexy," Rory moaned. "I just take back the insult to your mama."

Ivan chuckled, lifted Rory's foot, and placed a kiss on the tingling arch. "I appreciate that." Then he did the gentle pinch-pull on all the toes, making Rory's dick jerk each time.

He wanted to close his eyes and tilt his head back, but he couldn't tear his gaze away from Ivan. The firelight glowed against his skin and shone in his eyes. The flames danced and flickered, matching the ones warming up Rory's insides. Ivan's gaze was downright incendiary, but Rory wanted to see if he could make it burn even hotter. He rested his left foot on Ivan's hairy thigh, then slowly inched it upward. The angle of Ivan's body put most of his lower abdomen in shadow, but Rory had become very familiar with his gorgeous body in a brief span of time. Rory angled his foot down at the perfect moment to brush over Ivan's inner thighs and caress his balls. Tucking his toes under the taut sac, Rory zeroed in on Ivan's taint with unerring accuracy.

Ivan sucked in a sharp breath and his big body tensed. "I'm supposed to be seducing you." If he'd wanted to sound convincing, he should've put more oomph into his voice and maybe not spread his thighs farther.

Rory didn't retract his foot. He rotated his ankle to massage and press a little deeper into the erogenous zone. Ivan's head tipped back, his lips parted on a sigh, and his thumbs found a spot between the arch and ball of Rory's foot that made him jerk upright. The motion sent Rory's curious foot deeper between Ivan's legs and his toe grazed over Ivan's pucker. The big man jolted, and his fingers tensed around Rory's foot before he continued the massage. It was impossible to tell if Ivan's reaction was good or bad, so Rory retreated to massage Ivan's taint and the underside of his balls. Then he waited a few seconds and slowly eased his toe back toward Ivan's pucker, giving him plenty of time to object, but Ivan only spread his legs wider. The tentative action made Rory think Ivan might be an anal virgin—a curious one at that. "Have you ever…" He let the unfinished question float in the air.

With his head still tipped back and eyes closed, Ivan said, "No."

Rory pressed his toe harder against his anus, and the big man shivered. "Not even a finger?"

"No."

This was something Rory could give Ivan that his hookups and first love hadn't…if he was interested. Judging by the moans coming from his throat when Rory circled his puckered rim, Ivan was very, very interested. But he wanted to hear the words. "Do you want—"

"Yes," Ivan said eagerly.

Rory chuckled. "How curious are you?"

Ivan lowered his head and looked at him. Amber eyes burned with the intensity of the fire. "I want it all with you. There are many firsts I can give you."

Rory's heart galloped in his chest. He had to remind himself that Ivan wanting it all with him was about sex; it wasn't a declaration of love. Rory retracted his foot a little to massage his taut sac, bouncing it a little with his toes. "So my finger?" Rory asked.

"Mmmhmm."

Rory eased his foot back to where Ivan seemed to want it most, but he stopped at his taint once more. "My dick?" Ivan's swallow was audible over the crackling fire and blood rushing through Rory's veins. "My tongue?"

The responding gasp was a mixture of surprise and curiosity. Ivan pinned him with a stare so hungry it flayed Rory to the bone. "Do you?"

"Do I what? Are you asking if I like the feel of a wet, hot tongue circling my rim and pushing inside my ass? Or do you want to know if I enjoy returning the pleasure?"

"Yes," Ivan replied.

"I don't know," Rory answered honestly. "I've never reached the level of intimacy with another man that would allow the act, at least for me." *Until now.*

The unspoken words hung in the air for several seconds while Rory worked up his courage to make more than his body vulnerable to Ivan. He pulled his foot free from Ivan's hand and retracted the other from between Ivan's legs. Rory sat up and cupped the back of Ivan's neck, but he didn't need to pull his conqueror down for a kiss because Ivan was reaching for him too. Before their lips touched and Rory lost his train of thought, he placed his hand over Ivan's heart and stilled his descent.

"I'm coming to realize that anything and everything is on the table where you're concerned," Rory said. "There isn't a spot on your body I don't want to explore intimately." There wasn't a part of the man Rory didn't want to know, but that admission might not be as welcome.

Ivan palmed the back of Rory's head and tangled his fingers in Rory's hair. "You make me want so damn much."

"Then take it."

Their lips met in a hungry meld of tongues, teeth, and shared breaths. Hands roamed, exploring planes and valleys. Ivan didn't break the kiss to remove Rory's shirt, he just shoved it up to his armpits. Their lips remained fused while they removed Rory's underwear, repositioned his legs, and aligned their cocks—flesh to flesh—and nothing had ever felt so good. Rory moaned, and Ivan swallowed it. As hot as they were for one another, neither seemed in a hurry to advance to the next phase. Rory slid his fingers into Ivan's armpits and smiled through their kiss when the big man shivered. His lust tasted better than any dessert Rory had ever sampled, and he was dying to explore the parts Ivan had kept to himself.

He hadn't meant to push the issue, but his hands had a mind of their own. Rory slid them around to fondle Ivan's ass and learn the curve of the taut globes, but his curious fingers got sidetracked in his ass crack, bisecting the cheeks instead. Ivan's dick, already slick with precum, jerked against Rory's as Ivan thrust his hips forward in short bursts. If that little caress cranked his gears, then pegging his prostate would turn him into a rutting beast. There was suddenly nothing Rory wanted more, but this position wouldn't allow it. He wanted Ivan at his mercy, but he didn't want to push him too far too fast.

Rory finally broke their kiss to look up at him. Ivan's lips were red and swollen, his cheeks flushed with desire. "Do you trust me?"

Ivan swallowed hard. "More than is probably wise."

Rory smiled and pressed a quick kiss to his lips because he understood. What had started out as a simple agreement between two horny men suddenly felt more…profound. So Rory eased out from under Ivan and slid over to the next cushion. He patted the one he'd vacated, and Ivan claimed the spot without hesitation. Rory swung his legs over to straddle his thick thighs, and Ivan's hands immediately went to his ass, gripping and separating the cheeks. The movement stimulated his own pucker, making Rory hungry for the drooling cock pressed against his own. The position was temporary, though. Rory just wanted more kisses before working his way south. He kept his hips still because frotting would generate friction that would end their fun too soon. When Ivan fully relaxed against the cushions, Rory began a slow descent down his body, taking time to kiss, lick, and nuzzle his face in Ivan's tummy hair. He couldn't and wouldn't ignore the eager beast jutting from a thatch of trimmed auburn curls. Rory kneeled between Ivan's thighs and swirled his tongue around the crown, capturing his essence on his tongue. Then he leaned up and reclaimed Ivan's mouth. The big man growled and gripped Rory's head in a firm hold and deepened the kiss to taste his *honey* on Rory's lips and tongue.

When Rory pulled back, he grabbed the lube off the sofa cushion. While he didn't brandish it like a game show host, he took his time opening the cap to give Ivan time to object, but he only parted his thighs wider. Instead of going knuckle deep right away, Rory relied on seduction and finesse. He focused his attention on Ivan's dick first, licking and sucking the crown into his mouth, slowly working toward the base. Ivan slid a hand into Rory's hair but didn't guide his head up or down. He seemed to be holding on for the ride or possibly anchoring himself to the earth. Rory would've grinned if not for the mouthful of cock. *Baby, we're just getting started.*

When Rory's lips stretched around Ivan's thick base, he circled Ivan's puckered rim with a slick fingertip. Ivan sucked air between his teeth, and his cock jerked in Rory's mouth. In case Ivan's lusty moan wasn't enough to encourage Rory to be bolder, he lifted a leg up and propped his heel on the edge of the couch. The position exposed his hole to Rory's hungry gaze and curious touch, but he still didn't push in. Rory continued sucking Ivan off while teasing his crinkled entrance until the hand in his hair became more urgent. Only then did he push a slick digit beyond the tight ring of muscle.

"Fuck," Ivan groaned.

Rory angled his head to glance up at Ivan's sexy body. He'd thrown his head back against the couch, arching his neck. Firelight flickered against his skin, revealing a thin sheen of sweat. Rory pushed his finger in farther, sucked Ivan's dick deeper, and reveled in the way his Adam's apple bobbed with his hard swallows. Ivan slung one arm over the back of the couch and kept the other hand fisted in Rory's hair. He was the epitome of a man lost in pleasure, and Rory had never been prouder of himself or more turned on than he was in that moment. To have Ivan, someone so private and borderline repressed, freely give himself and his pleasure over to Rory was…dizzying and addictive. Rory wanted more moans, surrender, and…more everything. He slowly bobbed up and down on Ivan's dick, keeping the suction light but his dick sloppy wet. He took his time introducing Ivan to anal penetration, easing the slick finger in and out in shallow strokes. Rory tasted his arousal and felt it thrumming through Ivan's powerful body like an electrical current. And to think he hadn't even gotten to the best part yet. On the next gentle surge forward, Rory bent his finger and pressed against Ivan's prostate.

"Fuck!" Ivan roared. Rory fought the urge to wriggle in triumph as Ivan tightened his fist in Rory's hair and thrust deeper into Rory's mouth. "Christ, baby…" Ivan panted. "Do that again."

So Rory did, again and again, adding a second finger and stronger suction until Ivan had both feet propped on the edge of the couch. He'd slung both arms over the top of the sofa, opening himself fully and completely to anything and everything Rory wanted. And what he wanted—*needed*—was to claim that virgin ass for his own. Rory had never cared about that kind of thing until he met Ivan. But he fucking cared now. Too damn much.

Rory eased his fingers free and let Ivan's dick slip from his mouth. Their eyes locked and held while Rory slid on a condom and slicked it with more lube. "You can say no at any point, and I promise to stop," Rory said.

"I won't."

Rory grabbed one of the back cushions from the couch and tucked it under his knees to give him a little more height, then he lined his dick up with Ivan's primed hole. He leaned forward to capture Ivan's mouth in a torrid kiss and slid all the way inside him. So much tight heat. Ivan groaned low and slow but relaxed into Rory's penetration instead of fighting it. Rory expected Ivan to grab onto him, but he kept his arms on the back of the couch and his feet and legs splayed. But Ivan wrapped his lips around Rory's tongue, sucking on it the way his tight pucker clenched Rory's dick. He'd wanted to go slow, to draw out their pleasure, but Ivan's complete submission was his undoing. Rory snapped his hips forward and reached between their bodies to stroke Ivan's dick with slick fingers. Ivan ground his hips to meet each thrust, and they rutted and groaned like animals as they chased their climax together. Rory came first, filling the condom with breathless thrusts until he felt dizzy. His hand on Ivan's dick briefly faltered, but he renewed his rhythm and leaned forward to capture a hard nipple with his lips.

Ivan's entire body tensed and his cock jerked in Rory's hand. Hot cum splattered between them, and Ivan grunted in equally short bursts. The hot clench of his ass tightened around Rory's sensitive dick, but he didn't pull free yet. Rory leaned forward and swiped his tongue through the mess Ivan had made all over his chest. Ivan growled hungrily and met him halfway, capturing his mouth and sharing the taste of his release. When the kiss broke, Rory collapsed on Ivan's chest. Strong arms and legs folded around him, holding him in place, not that Rory could've moved if he wanted to. Ivan ran his fingers through Rory's hair and kissed his temple, his cheek, and finally, his lips again. Ivan said so much with the tender kisses he gave Rory and in the way he couldn't seem to let go.

Rory eased his dick free after a few minutes and rested his head against Ivan's pounding chest. "I know," Rory whispered in response to Ivan's unspoken thoughts. Neither of them had worked the other out of their system. Their intensity gathered steam each time they came together instead of dissipating like they'd expected. "Give it time," Rory whispered, then placed a kiss against Ivan's sternum. "You'll be sick of me in no time, and I'll be out of your hair."

Ivan said nothing, but his tightening grip on Rory revealed everything. *Dare I hope?*

chapter
FIFTEEN

RORY STRETCHED AND MURMURED SOMETHING INAUDIBLE, BUT it was enough to jostle Ivan awake. He lay there, blinking to bring the room and his brain into focus. It took him a few moments to realize there wasn't anything wrong with his vision. The fuzzy brown landscape was the back of the sofa in the living room, and Ivan's memories stirred to life. All of them—delicious, sexy, and heartwarming.

They'd cleaned up and returned to the couch buck-ass naked with only the throw blanket to provide a modicum of modesty. Instead of worrying about who could show up and find them, Ivan drifted off to sleep and forgot about the things that had bothered him prior to his death by orgasm. Maybe that's why he didn't care when he woke up to find Rory had ended up with seventy-five percent of the blanket and his bare ass was hanging out in the wind. The fire had died down, casting the room mostly in shadows since someone had drawn the living room curtains. Ivan's money was on Dylan. His best friend was head over heels in love and wanted everyone else to be that way too. *He's not staying.* After what Ivan had shared with Rory, it felt like a good time to remind himself.

"How do you feel?" Rory asked from the vicinity of Ivan's armpit.

That was a loaded question if ever Ivan heard one. "Wrecked." It was the simplest answer to the tumultuous emotions spinning through his brain faster than a sidewinder.

"What?" Rory jerked up and bumped the top of his head against the underside of Ivan's jaw.

Thank goodness for quick reflexes or the collision could've hit Ivan like an uppercut and taken him down for the count. He worked his jaw to the left and right to assess the damage while Rory winced. Ivan couldn't tell if it was in shame or pain, and he didn't like either option. "Did you hurt yourself?"

Rory worked his bottom lip as he shook his head, and Ivan reached up and gently freed the plump flesh. "But I heard your teeth rattle."

Ivan grinned and suspected that was an exaggeration. He'd taken plenty of hits to rattle his teeth during football, and this collision wasn't close to that. "I'm fine. You just caught me by surprise."

"Same," Rory said breathlessly. "Are you sore? Did I hurt you?"

Then Ivan realized how Rory had interpreted the answer to his question. He thought Ivan meant he was physically wrecked and Rory had been too rough for his first time. Ivan shook his head, cupped Rory's face, and pulled him forward for a slow kiss. "You were perfect," he whispered against Rory's lips after several moments. "I have never felt anything so good, and I'm looking forward to feeling you inside me again."

Rory's tension dissipated, and he practically melted against Ivan's chest. "Thank goodness." Then he jerked his head up again, but Ivan was quicker the second time, and Rory's head missed his jaw by a few inches. "What did you mean when you said I wrecked you, then?"

Ivan brushed the back of his fingers over Rory's cheek and his short beard. "Parts of me are smarting because I'm not very flexible. My thighs are demanding to know what the hell I was thinking." Ivan smiled and whispered, "Spoiler alert: I wasn't because I was too busy feeling." He inhaled slowly and considered his next words and the wisdom of being so open with Rory. Then he recalled the way he'd opened other parts of himself and decided not to hold back. "Something about you entices me to make myself vulnerable in ways I've never done with others, and I don't just mean sexually. I want to tell you things and share experiences with you—good and bad. I just don't get it."

Ivan thought Rory had beautiful eyes in the sunlight, but he wasn't prepared for how mesmerizing they were in dim firelight. The various shades of blue formed a sea of emotion and seemed to shift and move with the flames, though he knew that was only a trick of the light. Still, Ivan felt like he could fall into the bottomless blue depths. The water would be perfect, a shifting temperature based on his body's needs. Ivan could just swim there, his safe place, and not care about resurfacing. But the warmth of Rory's smile lured him like the sun, and he swam toward it.

"Where'd you go just now?" Rory teased.

"I was right here with you."

Rory smirked and shook his head slightly. "Maybe physically, but your thoughts were a million miles away."

"I wasn't that far."

"I don't want you to do anything that makes you feel uncomfortable," Rory told him. "That's not what we're about."

Ivan considered that for a moment. While it was true they'd agreed to a no-strings affair—a better term evaded him at the moment—they'd acted in the exact opposite way. They didn't just fuck and go their separate ways. They shared a bed and meals and found little ways to stay connected, even if it was a parting comment about the next time they'd be together. Rory hadn't left Ivan's thoughts since he'd arrived on the ranch. Ivan opened parts of his body and soul to him, and instead of regretting the vulnerability, he was looking forward to doing it again. *Would now be too soon?*

A sudden bout of anxiousness gripped him, but Ivan breathed through it. He hadn't spoken of the incidents leading up to his arrest or his history with the press in a very long time. Ivan probably should've worked with a counselor afterward. He'd thrown himself into learning beekeeping in jail, and the process had become a therapy of sorts before it became a business. He still turned to his hive whenever he needed a healthy outlet for stress. Maybe that's why the ranch hives were not only productive but a picturesque little fairyland for bees. The urge to share his Honeyland, as Harry called it, and his past trauma with Rory, gripped Ivan with surprising intensity.

"You make me very uncomfortable," Ivan said. Rory's eyes widened, and Ivan hastened to clarify his remark. "But in the best ways. I think it's called growth. You make me want to tear things down and build them back up again just so I can become the vision of me that you see." *Even if Rory wasn't around to witness it.* That thought put a damper on his mood, so he shoved it into the back of his brain's closet where he kept other thoughts best left alone.

"Fuck, you really are a poet," Rory whispered. His eyes shimmered with moisture, and he looked on the verge of tears.

"Not normally," Ivan said. "That's another thing you bring out in me. I feel things deeply, but to say the things I've said to you... It's a first. I feel like a different person when you're around. Not better. Not worse. Different." *Whole.*

Rory swallowed hard and inhaled a shaky breath. "But we've only known each other for ten days. How is this possible?"

"It just is," Ivan replied.

"I feel the same level of comfort and challenge when I'm with you like maybe I might like me because you do."

"Let the world see how amazing you are, and you'll attract the kind of people who deserve your devotion," Ivan said. Those assholes who blabbed his personal business to the press sure as hell didn't deserve it.

Rory's smile faltered, and Ivan wished he could kick himself in the ass for bringing up painful things. Maybe he would've tried it if not for still feeling the effects of their lovemaking. Damn, he used to be so fit and limber. Hope was always trying to recruit him to yoga classes and meditation, and maybe he should take her up on the offer. Ivan couldn't take the words back, which was probably for the best. At least one of them needed to keep their footing on solid ground. Rory wasn't staying. Pretending otherwise would lead to heartache neither of them needed, which reminded Ivan of the confession he'd wanted to make to Rory. Waiting until nighttime no longer sounded appealing. Ivan wanted to air out his laundry in the sunshine with Rory as his witness. And he knew just the right setting.

"Would you like a proper tour of my beehives and the ranch?" Ivan asked.

Rory rose up on his elbow and kissed him. "I'd love to see this beautiful place through your eyes."

Who's the poet now?

They tidied up the living room to make sure they didn't leave behind traces of their passionate exchange. Ivan cut off oxygen to the fire, reducing the small flames to smoldering embers before they parted ways to dress. Most of Rory's belongings were still in his room, so he headed there while Ivan went upstairs to change. When he returned, Rory wore the same outfit as when he'd arrived at the ranch. The flannel shirt was a fleecy material but wouldn't be enough to ward off the chill in the dwindling sunlight. Don't get him started on the distressed jeans with holes.

"We need to make a quick stop at the general store," Ivan said on their way out of the house.

"In town?"

"No, that's what we call the supply room here on the ranch," Ivan replied. "Cash keeps a variety of work clothes here for the crew. Proper attire is important, and most new members of the crew don't have the means to buy their own upon release, so Cash makes work clothes part of our benefits."

"Wow," Rory said. "That's one hell of a perk." His reaction grew even stronger when he stepped inside the store. Ivan had already learned that a wowed Rory was a quiet one. He turned in a slow circle, taking it all in with his hands on his hips.

Ivan glanced around, remembering the first time Cash had shown the space to him. Being able to wear garments other than prison scrubs was a big deal. Being able to call them his was even bigger. A person had so much stripped away when they were incarcerated, and little things like wearing clothes you owned felt huge. New clothes, even ones for work, felt as luxurious as owning a yacht after incarceration.

Rory stilled and met Ivan's gaze. "I didn't think people like Cash Sweeney existed anymore." He tilted his head and added, "I might be in the presence of a veritable saint. Coming up with ways to beef up the ranch's reputation in the community is going to be a cinch." So Rory had spoken with Cash about the project. Ivan hadn't asked because his mind had been elsewhere when he saw Rory on the couch.

Ivan snorted. "Don't let Cash hear you call him a saint. He gets angry that his way is an exception and not a rule."

Rory pursed his lips and glanced around the room again. "That's what I'd expect a saint to say." He met Ivan's gaze. "I can't imagine what it would feel like to stand here after getting released from lockup and have the freedom to choose whatever you wanted. It would be like winning a shopping spree."

"Without the cart and timer," Ivan said, recalling the sense of overwhelm he'd experienced as he'd taken it all in.

Rory reached for his hands and stepped closer to him. "How long were you in jail?"

"Three years." Ivan's voice sounded flatter than he'd intended, and he wasn't sure if that was the reason Rory raised a brow or if the length of the sentence surprised him. A little voice, unbidden but persistent, urged Ivan to push himself harder. "Unlike Kieran, I committed the crime I went to jail for, and I'm not sorry about any of it, not the act itself or a single second I spent behind bars. If given the same set of circumstances, I'd probably do it again."

Rory's nostrils flared, and he swallowed hard, but he didn't step back. "You're testing me."

"Am I?"

He nodded. "You are. But why? Because I've gotten too close and you think I'll bolt when I learn the truth?"

"I've always known you're going to leave," Ivan reminded him.

"Knowing it here"—Rory tapped his temple—"and knowing it here"—he tapped his heart—"aren't the same thing." Instead of pulling away, Rory stepped closer and placed his hand over Ivan's heart. "Whatever you did, it was to protect someone you cared about or loved."

Ivan had thought he loved Curt Washington, and maybe he had, but it was hard to judge the veracity of his feelings. Curt had been his first…everything, and their ill-fated romance had ended publicly and nearly tragically. Ivan's best method of stress relief had been stripped away from him when his college football coach suspended him after his sexual orientation was exposed. O'Reilly hadn't come right out and said that of course. He'd claimed the action was for Ivan's benefit, to give him space and time to recover from the scandal and to get a break from the attention it had drawn. What he'd really meant was that no one wanted him in the locker room or weight room. Ivan's shame, hurt, and anger built into a tsunami without a healthy outlet to release the pressure. He'd kept his head down and shifted his focus to preparing for final exams since he was only months away from graduation. Ivan thought he had everything under control until—

"Ivan." Rory's soft voice yanked him from his trip down memory lane. "Am I right? Did you get in trouble for protecting someone you cared about?"

Ivan looked around the room, reminding himself of his entire journey with a single glance. It might've agitated some, but Ivan found it centering. He would not shy away from who he was or what he'd done. Cash Sweeney had taught him that. "Yes." The love he'd felt for Curt might not have lasted a lifetime, but it had been real and was strong enough to spark a tempest that had irrevocably changed Ivan's life.

Instead of looking nervous about being alone with an unrepentant convict, Rory looked smug. "You can tell me if you want to, but it won't change a damn thing. I'm still going to want to climb you like Mount Viking as soon as you'll let me."

It was on the verge of Ivan's tongue to ask if Rory had enjoyed what they'd shared as much as he had, but it was a diversion neither of them needed. Besides, he already knew the answer. He'd witnessed the blissed-out expression on his face and felt the intensity of Rory's orgasm. Ivan had resented the barrier between them and wanted to feel Rory's hot release in his channel. He couldn't think of anything more intimate than sex in the raw, but that wasn't a wise move for their no-strings agreement. Ivan knew he could distract them both with talk of their shared orgasm, but that wasn't the need riding him hard. He wouldn't say he wanted to confess to Rory or even unburden his soul. It just felt suddenly important for Rory to really know him—both who he was then and the man who stood before him now. And Ivan wanted to do that in the place that represented him best.

"Good to know." Ivan leaned forward and kissed Rory, quick and hard, then said, "You're going to need warmer outerwear and jeans for our tour. You can leave your clothes here and we'll swing by and grab them on our way back." He picked out a sherpa-lined jacket and a pair of Wranglers in sizes that looked right. He grinned when they fit Rory perfectly. Ivan took a few seconds to jot down what they'd taken on the inventory sheet Cash used for taxes, then they made the quick trip to an equipment barn. Ivan opened the passenger door of the side-by-side ATV and gestured for Rory to get in.

"Such a gentleman," Rory said with a wink as he climbed inside.

"Not always."

Ivan hit the gas and launched the vehicle forward. The wind carried off whatever Rory had been about to say. Delighted laughter burst from him instead as Ivan accelerated over the terrain. He'd start the tour in his beloved place and end with meeting the horses and dogs on their way back to the main ranch for dinner.

"I'm glad you insisted on a warmer jacket," Rory yelled.

Ivan glanced over and saw that he'd ducked his chin into the open collar. He should've given him a hat and offered to go back, but Rory declined.

"Show me your special place."

That unbidden and persistent voice made itself known again, telling Ivan that Rory's heart could be the most special place of all. Fuck. He really was turning into a poet. Ivan let off the gas when they neared Honeyland and slowed to a crawl just outside the gated entrance.

"I don't freaking believe it," Rory said in awe. "You're not playing around, are you?"

Ivan assessed the large section of meadow Cash had sanctioned for honey production. The spring wildflowers were just blooming, but within weeks, the place would be awash with vivid color. Ivan and Cash were the owners, but the rest of the ranch was represented in the cluster of hives spread throughout the space. "Not just me," he said. "Rueben made the wrought iron fence and arched gate, and Kieran helped me

paint each hive to look like a house, so the clusters became honeyhoods."
The play on neighborhood had been Cash's idea. And no two honeyhoods were the same. Some looked like farmhouses, and others resembled urban dwellings like brownstones and high-rise apartments. "Tyler's
family owns a plant nursery in Texas. He knew a lot about which plants,
flowers, and shrubs attract bees and aid in pollination. We have blooming plants from spring to fall. Harry found old bird baths at yard sales
and filled the bottom with various sized stones and marbles to give the
bees a safe place to perch while hydrating. Owen laid the pavers to create the pretty walking paths throughout the honeyhoods. Dylan placed
various gnome, mushroom, and wildlife lawn ornaments throughout
the area. I think it makes the space look like an amusement park for the
bees." Pride and community swelled inside his chest. "This might be my
passion project, but they all made it theirs too."

"It's beautiful," Rory said. "Can we go inside, or will we disturb
the bees?"

"It's okay to go in." Ivan glanced over at him. "The bees are pretty
lethargic and confined to the hives until it gets warmer. If we do encounter one, it's likely to be aggressive and sting. Are you allergic?"

Rory shook his head. "I got stung plenty of times on my grandparents' farm in Oklahoma. My grandmother used to warn me constantly
not to go out barefoot, but I didn't listen. I loved the feel of grass under
my feet."

Ivan climbed out of the side-by-side. When Rory joined him, Ivan
reached out for his hand. He hadn't planned to do it and hadn't con-
sciously thought about the gesture. He just saw Rory and wanted to
touch him. If he was surprised, Rory didn't show it. He laced his fingers
through Ivan's and walked beside him. Ivan unlatched the gate with his
free hand and gestured for Rory to precede him. Ivan wasn't sure where
he wanted to begin his story. Did he start with the event that landed
him in jail, where he'd learned to keep bees, or did he work backward?

"You don't have to say anything," Rory said. It didn't surprise Ivan
that he'd picked up on his uncertainty. They were oddly in tune with
each other. "I know everything I need to about you, Ivan. Your character is on display in everything you do." He gestured to the surrounding

hives. "Honeyland is a testament to how much everyone adores you on this ranch, and you don't cultivate those types of relationships by being a bad person. Your past can stay just that…your past."

Somewhere in the recesses of his mind, Ivan probably recognized how much his found family loved him, but he really felt their love at that moment with Rory. Pointing out everyone's contributions validated what he'd felt in his soul, and he finally knew where and how he wanted to start his story.

"I didn't like myself for a long time. In fact, I spent much of my life hating myself," Ivan said. Rory's fingers tightened around his, but he said nothing. "I suspected I was different from the other boys around age eleven and was certain of it by thirteen." Ivan didn't laugh because the memories weren't funny. Eighteen years had passed since his first boy-induced boner and the shameful crying that had ensued afterward. It still hurt to remember how lonely and scared he'd been. Ivan didn't push away the memories; he embraced them the way he wished he could hug that confused kid. If only he could somehow go back in time and whisper in young Ivan's ear that everything would turn out okay.

Rory must've mistaken Ivan's silence as hesitance or regret because he stopped and tugged Ivan's hand so he'd do the same. Turbulent blue eyes stared up at him, and Ivan desperately wanted to soothe the rough waters. He pulled Rory into his arms and kissed him right there in the middle of Honeyland. Ivan's heartbeat sped up as it always did when Rory was nearby, and the pounding seemed to knock something loose in his chest. A chink in his armor, perhaps, making him feel lighter and more open. He palmed Rory's head and deepened the kiss, and he could practically hear his inner thirteen-year-old weeping with joy instead of shame and fear. Tears of relief stung the back of Ivan's eyes, but they didn't spill down his cheeks when he broke the kiss and met Rory's worried gaze.

"I want to do this," Ivan assured him. But he needed to burn off some excess energy, so he continued the walk among the hive clusters, hand in hand with Rory. "We attended a very strict church where sins-of-the-flesh sermons were a weekly thing. The pastor made his views on homosexuality very clear, so I silently hated myself while worrying that people could read the shame on my face. My parents never spoke about homosexuality—for or against it—so I assumed they agreed with the pastor's views. I thought my parents would hate me and cast me out of the family like the pastor preached, so I fluctuated between ignoring who I was and pretending it wasn't real. Schoolwork, farm chores, and football became my existence. I didn't date, but my parents would simply remark that I was too focused on building a future when asked why I didn't have a girlfriend." Ivan leaned toward Rory. "It also helped that I was an awkward, red-headed giant. The girls weren't exactly beating a path to get to me."

"They were fools. Luckily for you, I wasn't around," Rory said. "I would've charmed your parents in their living room, then coaxed you out of your overalls in your bedroom."

Ivan snorted. "I didn't wear overalls."

"Pity," Rory said with a sigh. "Are there any back in the store?"

"If not, I know where to get my hands on some."

"Yessss," Rory hissed. "Now get on with the trauma so I can kiss it all better." His tone was matter of fact, not flippant. Rory believed he could make Ivan's pain better, and the hell of it was, Ivan believed he could too.

"I had high expectations for college," Ivan told him. "After earning a full-ride scholarship to play football, I majored in agricultural studies. I thought I'd meet the girl who would fix the parts of me that were broken, and I expected my classes would reinforce what I knew about farming."

"That didn't happen?"

Ivan chuckled. "I met a boy who made me think being broken wasn't so bad, and I discovered alternate ways of farming. The term sustainable agriculture is pretty common now, but it wasn't as well known back then nor was it welcomed by my father. We butted heads over it during phone calls and visits home, and a chasm grew between me and my folks. I can see now that I was bracing myself for their rejection when they found out I was gay."

"You pushed them away before they could cast you out?" Rory asked.

"Yeah, I think that's fair to say." Ivan took a deep breath. "It never occurred to me to give my parents the benefit of the doubt. My phone calls and trips home became fewer and fewer as my infatuation with Curt Shepherd grew." Rory stiffened, and Ivan used their connection to tug him closer. Ivan released Rory's hand to wrap an arm around his waist. "Don't get jealous. I'm here with you."

Rory sighed heavily. "Sorry."

"I'm not. I like that you care." Ivan pressed a kiss to the top of his head, then kept the conversation going before they got sidetracked. "Curt and I were very careful because neither of us were out to our families. His folks aren't as rich as yours, but they're well off and very connected at the university. Anyway, we attended a party at a house off campus a few months before graduation. We both had a little too much to drink, got careless, and forgot to lock the door of the bedroom we stumbled into upstairs. You know how quickly people whip out their phones to take pictures or videos, even drunk or high."

"No, no, no," Rory whispered. He stopped and turned into Ivan's body, hugging him tight. "I'm so sorry."

Bile churned in Ivan's stomach, but he'd come this far, and Rory's embrace helped ease the hurt the memories caused. "The fallout was a nightmare. The football team shunned me. One asshole was so offended that he made sure every person on campus saw the pictures or brief video of Curt on his knees with my dick in his mouth." Ivan puffed up his cheeks and exhaled slowly, bracing himself to get through the worst part. "I got harassed some, but my size kept most reactions to silent sneers or passing jeers. But Curt..." Ivan shook his head as awful images flooded his mind. He reminded himself that he'd just seen the man. He was happy, healthy, and had a family. "No one tracked down my parents in Kansas to tell them I was queer, but Curt's family found out right away through their connections at the college. They were very upset and said hurtful things to Curt, and he..."

"Oh no," Rory said, his handsome face stricken with worry for a person he didn't even know. Tears of sorrow filled his eyes for a man he'd been jealous of just moments prior.

"He survived," Ivan rushed to assure him. "Curt had stopped taking my calls right after the incident, but I got a sick feeling in my gut when he stopped going to classes too. I checked on him and found he'd intentionally overdosed on something he'd scored on campus. He was still alive but barely. The paramedics arrived and took him to the hospital, but his folks wouldn't let me see him during any phase of his recovery, and he never came back to school. I hadn't seen him until I ran into him on the street Friday night."

"I'm so sorry, Ivan." If Rory hugged him any tighter, he'd strangle the breath right out of him.

"His husband hugged me so tight and thanked me over and over for saving his life. Curt didn't bring up the incident, but I saw what I needed to in his eyes. Maybe getting this out in the open will help me heal and move past it." Ivan took another deep breath for courage. "This asshole on campus, Danny, ran his mouth around school about how the world nearly had one less…" Ivan let his words trail off. He wouldn't allow himself to think about the slur, let alone speak it.

"I get the drift," Rory said. "You don't have to repeat it."

"Some people say words are just words, a formation of letters that don't hold any kind of power."

"Bullshit." Rory could pack a fuckton of vehemence into two syllables.

"Anyway, Danny was stupid enough to say that shit in front of me. His bullying had taken something precious from me, and I wanted to return the favor. So I took a baseball bat to Danny's brand-new Mustang in a fit of righteous rage. His parents had bought it for him as an early graduation present, and the smug fucker thought he was the big man on campus. When I finished, it was a mangled heap of blue metal. Several people caught everything on their phones, but I wasn't the least bit sorry about it. I provided a running commentary for the gathered audience, letting Danny, the school, and God know what I thought about them."

"And you got arrested," Rory said.

Ivan nodded. "For criminal mischief. The value of the totaled car made it a third-degree felony. I plead guilty because it was the right thing to do. The prosecutor played the video before sentencing. I looked like a raving lunatic in the footage, and the judge agreed. I was wholly unrepentant and so fucking bitter, and he gave me the maximum sentence."

"Which was?"

"Thirty-six months, and it felt like an eternity." Ivan's chest felt tight as he remembered the fallout during that time. "I humiliated my family. The church community they loved so much rejected them. My behavior shocked them and broke their hearts. My folks didn't recognize the angry man from the video. They feared him." Ivan swallowed hard and released a shaky breath. "The media coverage was brutal both for me after my arrest and during the trial and for my family back home. It turned their lives upside down. They didn't visit me in jail or offer any financial or emotional support during the trial. My mom and brother came around quicker. We reestablished a relationship through correspondence when I was in jail. It took years for me to regain any ground with my dad. In fact, we didn't make real peace until a few months before his death. Losing that precious time with my family is the only thing I regret about my actions. I'm not sorry about what I did just about the hurt it caused the people I love."

Ivan looked around the hive clusters, seeing the signs of his found family everywhere. "But my mistake also brought Cash into my life. He gave me opportunities to put the information about sustainable farming practices that had intrigued me into practice. He gave me a ragtag group I love and call my family. Cash supported and encouraged my beehive business, and I won't let him down. Which is why I agreed to do the interview with Roberto, even though I've been dragged through the mud by the press before and it was hard for me to say yes. I owe Cash everything."

Rory stood on his tiptoes and kissed him. "I'm so proud of you, Ivan."

Ivan's heart swelled. "That means more to me than you know." He took a deep breath and released it slowly. "As much as the people on this ranch love me, I have this weird feeling that only you really see me." *And I'll miss you so fucking much when you're gone.*

"I feel the same way about you," Rory replied. "I've spent so much time trying to be what my dad wanted me to be or the exact opposite of that to gain his attention after my mom died. And I've lost myself in the process. I second-guess every instinct I have or decision I make."

Rory met Ivan's gaze with a serious expression. "Except you, Ivan. You're just for me."

Ivan swooped down and captured Rory's mouth in a fierce kiss that grew hotter even as the air cooled around them. "Let's finish the ranch tour and continue getting to know each other back at the homestead."

Ivan showed Rory the breathtaking land while there was still daylight, then took him to see the animals. It didn't surprise Ivan in the least when the dogs and horses greeted Rory enthusiastically, even the most skittish ones.

"How does anyone get work done around here?" Rory asked. "I'd want to love on the animals all day long."

"Part of the love comes in caring for them properly to ensure their health and happiness."

Ivan looped his arm around Rory's shoulders as they headed toward the old homestead to get cleaned up for dinner. But once there, priorities shifted and so did their roles from their earlier sex session. Ivan put Rory on his hands and knees facing the dresser mirror across from his bed and gave him a little of the dominant treatment he'd teased Ivan about when they'd met. By the time they finished, they were too tired to slink over to the ranch, so they finished the rest of Ivan's cookies for dinner. Dylan took pity on them and brought home leftover spaghetti and meatballs, then Ivan and Rory promptly locked themselves in Ivan's room for the rest of the night.

"My first name is Riordan," Rory whispered in the dark.

"A beautiful name for a beautiful man."

"My dad picked it out," Rory said, pressing his face into Ivan's neck. His voice strained with the effort to hold back his sorrow, much like stretching an elastic bandage over a hole in the Hoover Dam. It was a losing battle, and Ivan preferred for Rory's emotions to spill out when he was wrapped up tightly in his arms.

"I know things probably feel impossible between you right now, but I know they're going to get better. You're holding in a lot of emotion, and it's not healthy. I don't want you to explode like I did. Get it all out here. You're safe with me. I can't imagine how hard it is for you to trust after what's happened to you, but I promise I'd never betray your confidence."

Rory pressed a quick kiss to Ivan's neck. "I know." He sniffled once before the levy broke, releasing a torrent of tears.

Ivan held him close, rubbing his hands up and down Rory's back and pressing kisses into his hair. He hoped his whispered words of encouragement helped, but he wasn't sure until Rory finally started to talk.

"Dad and I used to be two peas in a pod. To be honest, one reason we butt heads is because we're too much alike, even though we sometimes find ourselves on opposing sides of an issue. We both approach a subject with the same passion and intensity, and our intentions don't always align. When my mother—" Rory's voice broke, and he cleared his throat. "When my mother was living, she was this amazing mediator when we were on opposing sides. She knew the perfect way to soften my dad's edges and could communicate things in a way that didn't trigger my stubborn streak." Rory chuckled before continuing. "She could literally repeat his words verbatim and get a completely different reaction from me. It drove my father nuts, and as an adult, I can understand why. As for my dad, my mother translated my sullen teenager angst into something he could understand, even if he didn't relate to it. I'm pretty sure Charles Snyder skipped the sullen teenage phase. I think he was born an old soul. He didn't do the rebellious stuff because he was smarter than that. But I'm also my mother's son, and she was a real hell-raiser at times. She learned to challenge the status quo in thoughtful, nonthreatening ways. I wish she was still around to teach me those lessons and remind me that all relationships require compromise, compassion, and empathy."

Rory swallowed hard and exhaled a shaky breath. "Dinah Snyder was our universe, and when she died thirteen years ago, she took pieces of us with her. Dad and I had completely different coping mechanisms that put us at odds more than ever. We've struggled to find our way back to each other since she died, and I'm terrified we'll revert to being cold strangers again. And I hate that our dirty laundry getting aired because I confided in the wrong person could cost my dad his dream of becoming governor."

"Your dad getting elected is completely out of your hands," Ivan said. "But you can take steps to repair your relationship. What's one thing that would make you feel better about the situation?"

"I want to hear his voice and not just in a video clip where someone is shoving a microphone in his face and asking him to explain my past behavior and asking why he didn't do things differently as a father."

"Call him tomorrow," Ivan said.

"He might refuse my call. The chasm between us feels so wide that he couldn't even hear the echoes of my regrets."

"But he might answer," Ivan countered. "And if he doesn't, call him back the next day and the next."

"Maybe." He wrapped his arms around Ivan's waist and squeezed. "I do feel better. Thank you."

"You're welcome."

When Ivan had just about drifted to sleep, Rory whispered, "I could quit you if I wanted to."

Ivan chuckled and held Rory tighter. *We'll just see about that.*

chapter
SIXTEEN

"REMEMBER TO BREATHE THROUGH YOUR NOSE," HOPE said two weeks later. Her voice was soothing and encouraging, even as Rory's muscles screamed in protest. He thought he was in excellent shape, but the sweat dripping from his face onto the pale purple mat during the standing forward bend said otherwise. What the hell had he been thinking when he'd agreed to this torture? He'd come to town with Harry for pedicures on a Saturday afternoon. He'd been too wound up with tension to worry if someone recognized him. But somehow he'd ended up contorting his body into the twelve positions Hope had called sun salutations.

"Let's swing by my mother's studio and say hello," Harry had said.

"Oh, Rory, you look tense," Hope had said after laying eyes on him. "Maybe you should stick around for my morning class. It's just about to start."

Hope's energy had drawn him in, and sun salutations sounded so…peaceful. "I don't have anything to wear."

Hope's smile grew even brighter as she patted his cheek

affectionately. "Leave that to me." She'd produced a pair of black shorts and a tee sporting the studio's logo.

"That's pretty tame," Harry remarked when he'd returned from the changing rooms a few moments later. "Where are the shirts with the risqué slogans?"

"Sold out." Hope's smug smile was adorable.

It wasn't until Rory hit the cobra pose that he realized the silent exchange between mother and daughter during Harry's departure was downright suspicious. Had they set him up? Maybe Rory wasn't as adept at hiding his tension as he'd believed. The conversations he'd had with Ivan in Honeyland and their nighttime confessions had triggered a lot of introspection. Ivan's story had touched him on so many levels, but his grief over losing his father hit Rory the hardest. His mother often visited Rory in his sleep. She'd plead with him to make amends with his dad and remind Rory that tomorrows are never guaranteed. Often those dreams turned into nightmares where Rory waited too long and never got a chance to make things right with his father. Rory would wake up determined to connect with Charles until he checked the daily headlines. The scandal wasn't going away. It must've been one dull news cycle, which was hard to believe considering the state of the world.

Today's headline read: Sleeping with the Enemy. Beneath it was a picture of Rory kissing Seth Miller, the youngest son of Charles's opponent in the party primary. They were shirtless and sweaty with colorful confetti sticking to their skin. Rory remembered the moment clearly because he'd been clean and sober. It was taken at a Pride event five years before either of their fathers had made a bid for public office. There was nothing salacious about the photo, but the media was acting like the photograph was taken five days ago, not five years. Clearly the leaks weren't coming from the Miller camp. Dolan Miller wouldn't throw his own son under the bus and draw that kind of scrutiny on his family. Or would he if he was tired of Charles getting so much press? The polls still showed them neck and neck.

"Inhale," Hope gently said, "now root your feet on the mat to rise, bringing your hands back over your head."

Rory had stopped counting positions somewhere around the

equestrian pose, but he thought they were on the second to last position in the sequence. Hope guided them to the prayer pose and then the mountain. *Off by one.* Rory sighed his relief that it was over.

"And now we go through the poses once more, leading with the opposite foot."

He'd meant to stifle his groan, truly, but it slipped out of his mouth anyway. A smattering of giggles sounded around him, and the older woman on his right held up her fist for him to bump.

"I hear ya," she said when their knuckles touched. The woman's dark hair was damp with sweat, but her skin looked dewy and luminescent. Flushed cheeks gave her skin a natural blush money couldn't buy. Rory imagined he looked the exact opposite—sweaty as a gym rat with a blotchy red face.

"Everyone, take a moment to hydrate before we continue," Hope said.

Rory picked up the reusable bottle Hope had provided with the clothes. The water was ice cold and mildly flavored with fresh fruit.

"I'm Abigail," the woman with the dewy glow said.

"James," he replied, using his middle name just in case. "Been at this long?"

"Just a few months. The movements have come easier, but I still fight turning off my brain and tuning in to my body. I still cycle through a to-do list occasionally. Mindfulness is the ultimate goal," Abigail told him. A blissful expression crossed over her face as if she were discussing a dream vacation in a tropical paradise.

And maybe the concept of being completely in tune with her body and living solely in that specific moment was the ultimate destination for her. Rory tipped his head to the side as he considered it. No past. No future. No ruminating on what happened or what could've been. No anxiety about what was yet to come. Just the splendor of the present moment. That kind of thinking wasn't sustainable all the time, but it could provide a healthy break from reality.

"Okay, everyone," Hope said. "Let's take three cleansing breaths, and then we'll begin once more in the mountain pose."

This time through, Rory shoved aside any thoughts that didn't relate to the way his body felt as he moved from one position to the next. He still wobbled on certain poses, but he turned his attention to how his muscles felt sleek and strong. He focused on the flow of air in and out of his lungs, and the power that came from letting go. They ended the session with corpse pose, which felt apropos.

"You did good, James," Abigail said.

Sitting up, he looked over at her and smiled. "Thanks. Your comment about checking out and tuning in helped a lot." His body hummed with soft pleasure, kind of similar to the afterglow Ivan's orgasms gave him just on a much smaller scale. When Rory stood up, his legs felt like limp noodles, and that also reminded him of sex with Ivan.

The group exchanged pleasantries while some people sterilized and returned their borrowed mats. Others rolled and stowed ones they'd brought from home. Hope meandered through the group, speaking to each person individually. She thanked them for their time, congratulated them on a great session, and wished them peace and joy. By the time Rory changed back into his clothes, there were only a few stragglers left. Hope made eye contact with him and winked before returning her full attention to the lady speaking to her. Rory debated heading over to the nail spa to see if he could still get an appointment, but he got distracted by a display of candles, lotions, and lip balms on the retail side of the studio. The sign on the table identified the products as a joint offering between Rocky Mountain Liquid Gold and New Hope Wellness Center.

Rory crossed into the shop for a closer inspection. As much as he loved lotions and potions, his eyes were drawn to the pastel candles made from beeswax. Rory had spent a lot of time working with Ivan in Honeyland over the past seven days as he prepared the hives for spring. Ivan had produced protective gear for him, and together they placed pollen patties inside each of the cute little beehives. Rory had learned the patties were bee food that would boost brood production. Ivan had lapsed into a lengthy chat about the bees needing protein and fat besides carbohydrates. He'd broken off midconversation to make sure he wasn't boring Rory. If not for the nets protecting their faces, he would've kissed Ivan silly.

His zest and passion for his bees and honey was so damn endearing. Ivan had stressed the importance of using as much of the hive as possible. The bees worked too hard not to practice sustainable beekeeping wherever they could. Ivan told Rory he used the beeswax to condition his wood carvings, though he hadn't shown Rory any of his art yet. The products for sale in Hope's store were additional proof of Ivan's principles and business acumen. Rory really loved when the conversation veered into how bees impacted the ecosystem. Ivan even let him record segments for future episodes on his channel.

Thinking about Ivan made Rory smile and his heart yearn for more time with his conqueror, even if he was covered head to toe in protective gear. He thought back to his casual comment about quitting Ivan at any time and nearly laughed out loud. They'd spent every night together since their first shared orgasm, and their chemistry seemed to burn hotter each day instead of waning.

Rory might've worried about it if he wasn't so busy enjoying each moment they had together.

They lived like they were on borrowed time. Kissing, touching, and fucking like each encounter might be the last—desperate and needy. And wasn't that mindfulness in practice? When they were alone, Rory didn't worry about his past or future just the present moment with Ivan. And he found more peace in the collective joy of stolen minutes than he'd experienced in his lifetime. The bliss he found in Ivan's bed could probably span several lifetimes, and Rory wasn't ready for it to end. A part of him wondered if he would ever be ready, but he choked off that little asshole's oxygen before hope could take root.

"Have time for lunch with an old lady?" Hope asked softly from behind him.

Startled, Rory flinched but didn't drop the candle he held in his hand. Strange how he didn't recall picking it up. So much for mindfulness. He made a big show of looking around the store. "Old lady? Where?"

Hope swatted his arm playfully. "Charmer." She stood up on her tiptoes so she could kiss his cheek, and Rory leaned toward her to make it easier. "Do you have time for lunch?"

Rory quirked a brow. "Why don't you tell me since my presence in the yoga studio is something you and Harry cooked up together. Am I right?"

Hope batted her eyes innocently, but her impish grin ruined the effort. "Busted," she admitted when it became clear Rory wasn't falling for that act either. "Did you benefit from the class, though?"

He thought of the overall experience and her instruction. The studio was bright and airy. There were groupings of plants and flowers throughout the space. The wall mirrors allowed her students to check their form as they moved through the poses while making the room look bigger. Hope had lit tranquil-smelling candles prior to class and softly played waves crashing against a shore during the lesson. Rory had closed his eyes a few times and imagined himself doing the poses on the beach until he lost his footing and reality intruded. As for Hope's instruction, she was fantastic. Her voice was low and melodic without being monotone or somniferous, and she displayed both her patience and sense of humor throughout the lesson. Rory enjoyed the moments he'd spent in tune with his body and his sense of pride upon completing the session.

"I absolutely loved it," he admitted. "I'm really grateful Harry conned me into coming to your class."

Hope clapped her hands. "I'm so happy to hear that. Can I please treat you to lunch?"

"I don't suppose you'd let me do the treating?" Rory asked.

"No way," Hope said. "My kids are head over heels in love, and I don't get to spoil them much anymore. Please let me have this little, tiny thing." She held up her hand to show her thumb and forefinger an inch apart.

Rory released a heavy sigh. "Playing the mom card, huh? Fine. You can treat me to lunch this time. I'll pick up the tab next time." Rory set the candle down when he noticed the name of the product line on the promotional sign. "The Fuck All, huh?"

Hope laughed and picked up a pale pink candle. "Let's just say I was feeling a certain way when I came up with the names for the candles."

Smiling, he checked the name of the lilac-colored candle in his hand. "Zen as Fuck. What exactly does that even smell like?"

"One way to find out," Hope suggested.

Rory pulled the silver lid off the top and lifted it to his nose. "Vanilla with a hint of lavender. Even I know lavender is a calming aroma." He smelled it again. "I would've named it Calm the Fuck Down."

"I'm making a mental note in case Zen doesn't sell. Sometimes a simple rebranding can take something from no profit to a best seller."

"So I've heard." Rory replaced the lid and set the candle down to look at the pastel orange candle next to it called Positive as Fuck. He opened the lid and inhaled. "Oh, this smells like happiness in a jar. What's in here?"

"Jasmine and orange blossom," Hope said. She handed him the pale pink candle she'd named Focused as Fuck. "Peppermint."

Rory sniffed the candle, impressed with the quality. Too much peppermint smelled like toothpaste, but this one was refreshing. He could see how it would inspire clarity and focus. There was one last candle. It was ivory, and he expected something serene. Rory read the name and jerked his gaze up to meet her mischievous gaze. "Really?" She'd named the candle Ready to Fuck.

"It's my favorite."

"Fragrance?" Rory pressed.

One corner of Hope's mouth curved up. "If you say so."

Rory chuckled, pulled the lid off, and got a good whiff. "I recognize vanilla and sandalwood, but the third note is new to me."

"Ylang ylang," Hope replied. "Isn't it dreamy?"

"Gorgeous." He wasn't sure what Ivan thought about candles, but he was about to find out. Rory replaced the lid and extended the candle to Hope. "I'm going to buy this one." He could tell she was going to protest, but he cut her off. "I insist."

"Fine. We'll do the transaction after lunch."

They locked up the shop and headed toward the diner. He noticed that religious sect had picked up two more reporting crews at their protests. He kept his head down as they walked past and refused to let their presence ruin his bliss. Rory expected Harry to magically appear

182

out of thin air now that the yoga session was over, but she still hadn't joined them by the time they sat down. They'd fixed a large breakfast for the crew, and he didn't imagine he'd be hungry again until dinner, but his stomach growled as he read over the menu.

"I know damn well you eat good on the ranch."

Rory laughed. "Too good. Another week and I'll need to go up a pants size." He expected Hope to laugh or comment. When she didn't, Rory looked up to find her watching him. Was she like him and wondering if he'd still be there in another week? "What?"

Hope reached across the table, covered both Rory's hands, and said, "I can tell something is bothering you, though you conceal it well behind that pretty smile. You don't know me well enough to trust me yet, but you will. And I'm a damn good listener if you ever want to talk."

"You're wrong," Rory said.

Hope rolled her eyes. "Don't listen to whatever my husband said about my alleged selective hearing. Tuning out one another's nonsense is how we've stayed happily married. I compare it to picking my battles and using a filter before I speak." Hope waggled her finger and said, "Yes, I have a filter. I just don't use it as often as I should."

Rory laughed and shook his head. "I wasn't referring to either of those things. You're wrong about me not knowing you. I've spent enough time around your kids to know the person you are."

Hope patted his hands and smiled. "That's very sweet of you to say. Everything we discuss stays between you and me," Hope told him.

Rory looked out the window while considering his options. He could continue rehashing the same thoughts in his head over and over or he could talk to an intelligent, objective woman with incredible insight. When framed like that, it was a simple decision. Over lunch, he opened up to Hope in ways he never had before, not even with Ivan. Something about Hope reminded him of his mother, even though they were nothing alike. It was the way she leaned into the conversation and gave him her undivided attention.

She reached over and squeezed his hand. "Fear is a powerful thing, Rory. You'll know the right time to have a conversation with your dad. I hope he's open to listening when you do approach him. If not, that's his problem and you should make peace with that." She released him to take a bite of banana pudding, and Rory did the same with his chocolate cream pie. "I've got a spare bedroom with your name on it if you ever decide to move on from the ranch and need a place to stay."

"I appreciate you saying that, and I can't thank you enough for letting me vent." She waved him off with her fork before digging back into her dessert.

Rory forked up another bite of pie. It was rich, silky perfection with the perfect balance of chocolate and cream. He knew a certain conqueror who'd love to sink his fork into it. "Do they sell whole pies here?"

"They do," Hope said with a smile.

They lingered over a second cup of coffee after the waitress took away their dirty dishes and Rory secured a pie for Ivan. Harry was waiting for them back at the shop when they returned. Hope lived up to her agreement and allowed Rory to buy the candle. When she told him the amount due, he looked at her with narrowed eyes. Twelve dollars? Had she slashed the price because he'd insisted on paying?

"Too much?" Hope asked.

"Too little," Rory replied. "Three-wick candles like these sell for a lot more."

"Told ya, Mama," Harry chimed in.

Hope rolled her eyes at them. "I'm not trying to get rich. I just want to help people."

She was another person Rory had found almost too good to be true. He'd never been so glad to be wrong. He hugged her tightly when they parted and promised to attend her next Saturday class too. As soon as he and Harry cleared her shop, Rory hooked his arm through Harry's and said, "Thanks for setting me up. It was exactly what I needed."

"I didn't intend it when I suggested the pedicures," Hope replied. "I could just tell you had a lot going on and could use a reset. My mama's classes are excellent for that. I would've stayed too, but I wanted you to have some alone time with her. Hope has a way of seeing to the heart of an issue."

"Yes, she does." Rory glanced over and saw a display of suncatchers hanging in a shop window. One caught his eye and made him stop in his tracks. It reminded him of someone special, and he wanted to buy it for him. "Do you mind if I make a quick stop in there?"

Harry followed his line of sight and smiled when she saw the honeycomb suncatcher made from multiple shades of amber glass. "He'll love it."

By the time they arrived back at the ranch, it was almost time for poker night. Ivan had volunteered to order food at breakfast, which had resulted in a round of boos. Apparently, his menu lacked creativity. Finley had spoiled the guys away from the standard fare Ivan provided. Harry and Rory had taken the baton from Finley the previous week and had driven the expectations even higher. Cash took pity on everyone and said he'd arrange the food and would host poker night at the big ranch since it was getting pretty crowded at the old homestead.

"See you guys tonight," Harry called out after they parked and exited her zippy red car.

"Whatcha got in that pie box, Rory?" Owen asked.

Hell-bent on getting to Ivan, Rory hadn't even seen Owen and Tyler standing near the barn. "Nothing for you to worry about," he quipped.

"Poker night is at the big ranch house," Tyler called out when Rory continued toward the old homestead.

"I know."

"Must be something incredible if he's making a beeline straight for Ivan," Owen said.

"Beeline," Tyler replied. "I like what you did there."

"I think we should get him," Owen added.

Rory picked up the pace, even though there was no real threat in Owen's voice. Gravel crunched under rapidly approaching boots, and Rory broke into a run toward the old homestead.

"What's going on?" Rueben asked, though Rory wasn't sure where he'd come from.

"Rory bought a special dessert for Ivan," Tyler said. "Pretty sure I smell chocolate."

"I want some," Rue called out moments before another pair of boots joined the stampede.

Rory dug deep and churned his legs faster but worried they'd fail him after his yoga session.

"Ivan!" Rory shouted like a madman. "Help!"

The back door flew open moments later, and Ivan stepped out onto the porch. Relief washed over him, though Rory doubted very much that any of them would've stolen their foreman's pie.

"What the hell is going on?" Ivan bellowed.

Rory didn't spend any time trying to explain; he just kept his legs pumping. He didn't take an easy breath until he darted up the porch steps and ran into Ivan's open arms. "They're trying to get your pie," he managed between jagged pants. Fuck, he was really out of shape.

"What kind of pie?"

"Chocolate cream from the diner," Rory panted out.

Ivan narrowed his eyes and took the box from Rory's outstretched hand. He flipped the lid open and hoisted the pie out of the box. He didn't quite strike the proud daddy lion pose from *The Lion King*, but it was very close. The three men that had been chasing Rory like it was the last pie on earth skidded to a halt at the bottom of the stairs.

Owen placed a hand on the porch railing and panted. "You wouldn't."

Ivan quirked a brow. "Wouldn't I?" He lowered his head to the pie and licked a stripe through the mound of cream while the three ruffians groaned in defeat. "Licked it, so it's mine." Ivan looked at Rory with a wicked gleam in his eyes that made Rory's heart race harder than it had during his mad sprint. Ivan hooked his free arm around Rory's waist and pulled him close. Then he lowered his head and licked a path up Rory's neck with a possessive growl that made his knees weak.

"Gross," Owen teased. "You guys should stay home tonight and skip poker."

Ivan looked from the pie to Rory and grinned wickedly. "Good idea." He backed Rory through the door and tossed a, "Good night, fellas," over his shoulder before closing it behind them.

chapter
SEVENTEEN

Rory presented Ivan with three things upon entering the house—a candle inviting him to fuck, a chocolate pie, and a honeycomb suncatcher. He wasn't used to people buying him gifts for no reason, and the gesture touched him deeply.

"Thank you," Ivan said, suddenly feeling shy.

Rory pressed his lips to Ivan's quickly but came back for a lingering kiss that stole Ivan's breath. "You're welcome. The question is, in what order would you like to enjoy them?"

"I'm a multitasker," Ivan replied. He picked up the candle in one hand and the pie in the other. "Bring the suncatcher. I know the perfect place to hang it."

Rory tilted his head to the side. "Not the kitchen window?"

"Nope. You'll see."

Up in Ivan's bedroom, he placed the pie and candle on the dresser, then used the little suction cup to secure the suncatcher to the window next to his bed. The genius of Rory's gift and Ivan's chosen spot to hang it became obvious when sunshine filtered through the stained glass. It cast various shades of amber and gold over the bed. He turned to tell

Rory to strip down, but he was already moving. His shoes, socks, and shirt were already off, and he was working his belt open.

He didn't have matches or a lighter, but the candle's scent was strong enough without them. Removing the lid was enough to fill the room with an enticing aroma, but that wasn't what made Ivan's dick hard or filled him with a sense of urgency. It was Rory, stretched out naked on his bed and lazily caressing his chest. Ivan kicked off his shoes and pulled off his socks all while feasting his eyes on the beautiful sight before him. Amber and gold shimmered against Rory's skin as if someone had drizzled honey over his body. An idea for another day perhaps. Each slow, downward slide took Rory's hand closer to the place Ivan wanted to kiss and touch the most. Ivan's attempts to remove his shirt failed when Rory's fingertips brushed the head of his cock on the next pass. Rory let out a little gasp, and a shiver rippled through his abdomen.

"Christ, you should be illegal in all fifty states," Ivan growled.

"What about the US territories?" Rory asked.

Ivan stripped his shirt off and reached for his belt before answering. "Those too." He shoved his pants and underwear down his legs and stepped free. Instead of climbing onto the bed, Ivan just stood there and watched wicked fingers trail up and down Rory's shimmering torso. "You're so beautiful."

Rory's fingertips brushed over his cockhead and kept sliding south over his erection. Rory's mouth fell open, but no sound escaped. His eyelids lowered to half-mast and goose bumps popped up all over his flesh. "Have you ever done this before?" Rory whispered.

"Jerked off? I'm a pro."

One corner of Rory's mouth tipped up in a seductive smirk Ivan wanted to kiss. "I meant, have you ever done it in front of someone else either individually or simultaneously?"

Ivan's skin heated at just the thought of deliberately stroking himself in Rory's presence. "No."

Rory quirked a brow. "You mean until now?"

Ivan glanced down and was surprised to find his hand slowly

working up and down his shaft. He was too caught up in watching Rory to be conscious of his own movements. "Until now."

Rory's smile was blinding and brilliant. "Another first for both of us." He crooked the forefinger of his idle hand, and Ivan immediately complied. Rory rolled onto his side, and Ivan lay beside him, facing the man who'd rocked his world in big and small ways. Each quake tore away more of his armor, freeing Ivan from harmful, imprinted notions and ideas that what he needed was wrong.

"Are there any rules?" Ivan asked.

"Just kiss me. Please."

Ivan leaned in to kiss Rory but didn't linger too long because he didn't want to miss watching Rory pleasure himself. It was hard to say what turned Ivan on more, having Rory's eyes on him while he stroked his dick or watching pleasure spread throughout Rory in a full body blush. Their bodies were close enough that their knuckles brushed occasionally, but that was the only source of connection between them. Ivan craved Rory's hands and mouth on his body, but that only amplified the mounting pleasure. They eventually found the same rhythm, both in their breathing and their strokes. It was one of the most intimate things Ivan had ever experienced, even though they weren't touching aside from their knuckles. Ivan kept his gaze locked on Rory's as his orgasm built. He fell over the cliff first, his release coating both their hands. Rory released a sexy little growl. Then he rolled Ivan onto his back, straddled his hips, and rutted against his slick dick with the fiercest expression Ivan had ever seen. Rory's body stiffened, and he came loudly and lustily before he collapsed onto Ivan's chest in a boneless heap.

"I'll move in a minute," Rory said, even as he snuggled closer, tucking his head under Ivan's chin. He was so close that his exhales ghosted over Ivan's neck, and he felt the rhythm go from nearly panting to a soft, sleepy pace just before he drifted to sleep. "Or thirty," Rory murmured. Ivan's skin muffled his voice, and the words came out sluggishly.

Ivan tightened his hold around Rory and decided they could rest a little before cleaning up. Ninety minutes later, the pair stood in the shower washing off what remained after their ill-advised nap. Rory brushed his finger over the bald spot on Ivan's lower abdomen and worked his bottom lip between his teeth. The patch was red and angry, but Ivan was more concerned about the self-recrimination in Rory's gaze.

"It'll grow back in a few days."

Rory raised a skeptical gaze. "A few days."

Ivan pointed to his beard and nodded. "I can shave this in the morning and a new beard will take its place by dinner."

Rory laughed and rolled his eyes. "Be serious."

"Okay, it might take longer than a day, but you'll see firsthand just how fast it grows…if you don't quit me." He'd meant the last part to be a teasing reminder of Rory's past comment.

Instead of a typical snarky comeback, Rory leaned into him and rested his head against Ivan's chest. There'd been an undercurrent of frenetic energy coursing beneath Rory's skin lately. Ivan sensed he was going through something. He'd waffled between trying to get Rory to open up and letting him be, and he'd chosen the latter. Ivan hoped it wasn't the wrong path.

"Just try to shake me loose," Rory murmured.

And maybe they were better than okay. Inspiration struck Ivan like a thunderbolt. In fact, it struck him so hard and fast he could almost smell the ozone burning. Or maybe that was the smell of his brain cells regrouping after sex. "Let's go out to dinner."

Rory jerked his head up, but Ivan was on to him and leaned out of harm's way. "Sorry. Snuggling this close to someone is still new."

"I enjoy being your first something." Rory had traveled the world and rubbed elbows with some of the richest men in the world. That didn't make those guys better than Ivan, but it definitely made them more interesting. They could give Rory things he couldn't. But Ivan recalled the version of Rory that had arrived on the ranch and reconsidered. What Rory had received from others thus far was a busload of cow manure.

"You're the only guy who's wanted me for me and not what my connections could do for him," Rory told him. "You're the best *first* I've ever had." Rory tilted his head to the side. "Were you serious about dinner?"

"Extremely."

"Like a date?" Rory pressed.

"Yes. Is that o—"

Rory cut him off with a hard kiss. Ivan wasn't sure what spurred him to move quicker—the shower, Rory's energized prodding, or the water tank's warning that they were almost out of hot water.

The Feisty Bull, a favorite among the ranching locals, was slamming on a Saturday night, but they only had to wait thirty minutes for a table. The restaurant didn't look like much from the outside. It was a long, white clapboard building with a red roof in the middle of nowhere, but it served the best steaks and seafood Ivan had ever tasted. The interior was a tad outdated too, with gleaming wood as far as the eye could see only broken up by red leather chairs or booths and white tablecloths. A long bar was at one end of the building and a massive fireplace constructed from local stone was the focal point at the opposite end. They'd scored a table near the fireplace, which pleased Ivan since it would be quieter there. The locals gathered at the bar for loud discussions, ranging from sports to politics and everything in between. Someone there could recognize Rory, and that would put a damper on their first real date.

The Feisty Bull was considered casual dining, so they hadn't needed to dress up. Ivan had still spent a ridiculous amount of time on his hair while Rory experimented with more of Hope's skincare line for men. A candle flickered in a mason jar in the center of the table, casting a warm glow on their table. Rory's skin looked luminescent, proving his effort was worth it. He looked around the restaurant with a smile on his face. "I like the atmosphere here."

"This is one of my favorite places away from the ranch, and I wanted to share it with you."

The building and decor were understated, but the service and food were exceptional. Ivan and Rory couldn't decide what to eat. They were both torn between one of the seafood pastas or the pricey steaks, so they ordered both to split. Rory chose shrimp and scallops in a lemony garlic sauce over linguine, and Ivan went with a porterhouse steak, parmesan mashed potatoes, and broccolini. They started with a crusty loaf of French bread and a variety of butter spreads. There was one with maraschino cherries in it that Rory had been determined to hate but adored on first bite.

"I don't like maraschino cherries," he said after his second piece of bread with a quarter inch of cherry butter on it. "But I can't get enough."

"I bet it's the other ingredient you're drawn to," Ivan said.

Rory narrowed his eyes. "Is your liquid gold in this butter?" The question came out louder and a tad more lurid than Ivan would've liked. "Your honey, I mean."

Ivan bit back a laugh. "The Feisty Bull was my first contract."

"Makes this place even better." He took another bite of bread and did a little shimmy in his chair. Rory seemed to recall where he was and stiffened.

Ivan imagined those kinds of displays wouldn't be welcome in the Snyder home, especially in public, where people judged their every word and move. That was no way to grow up. There were years when his family's farm had performed so poorly that Ivan's mama had to make their clothes or buy them from the Goodwill in a neighboring town. He still wouldn't trade his parents or his humble beginnings. "Don't stifle your joy. I love how you find it in the smallest things."

"And the biggest," Rory said.

Ivan was on to him, and his deflection wouldn't work. "Like the butterfly that landed on your arm this morning in Honeyland."

Rory, who claimed not to blush, did just that. "It's hard to imagine something so pretty started out as a caterpillar." He got a faraway look in his eyes before refocusing on Ivan. "Its wings felt like velvet and seemed so delicate, yet they hold up in the strongest winds."

"Reminds me of you," Ivan said. "You're coming into your own, just like the butterfly, and you're stronger and more resilient than you realize."

Rory's smile was the brightest thing in the dimly lit restaurant. "Today has been eye-opening."

Ivan took a sip of water. They'd both passed on alcohol, though Rory had chosen sparkling water to Ivan's still. "How so?"

"Well, first, Harry and Hope tricked me into taking a yoga class at the center."

Ivan grimaced. "Did you have to wear one of her bawdy graphic tees?"

Rory laughed. "No. Hope said she'd sold out of them when Harry asked. How bad are they?"

Ivan rattled off the few he could remember, and Rory threw his head back and laughed. "She changes them up all the time. How did you like yoga?"

"I actually loved it," he said with a sheepish grin. He repeated the conversation he'd had with Abigail about checking out and tuning in to his body and his breathing. "It was harder than I expected, but I felt like I had accomplished something when it was over, and I felt much calmer. Ivan?"

"Hmm?" He set his butter knife and the slice of bread he'd been buttering on his plate.

"I want to treat your inner thirteen-year-old Ivan to something he wishes he could've done."

That's how they ended up making out in a dark corner of a movie theater. They'd chosen an obscure foreign film with subtitles that few people would choose on a Saturday night. Stale popcorn, chocolate-covered peanuts, and two hand jobs later, Ivan's inner teenager was happier than he'd ever been in his life. Thirty-one-year-old Ivan was feeling pretty damn good too.

Over the next month, he expected those feelings to fade. Ivan expected to wake up one morning and not be excited to find Rory sleeping on the pillow beside him. He expected they'd run out of confessions. That never happened, though, so Ivan braced himself for the day Rory woke up and announced he was ready to leave. But that never happened either.

Rory stopped bragging about how he could quit Ivan at a

moment's notice. Ivan stopped caring about where they were and who was around when the urge to kiss Rory hit him. Standing in line in the dining room to fill their plates at breakfast? No problem. He tapped Rory on the shoulder and planted one on him. At the skating rink while living out more of teenage Ivan's fantasies by holding hands during the slow skate? Bam! Right on the mouth. Ivan couldn't say what song had been playing, but he'd remember the look of pure happiness in Rory's eyes for as long as he lived.

chapter
EIGHTEEN

"**S**oooooo," Harry said to Rory as soon as she turned out of the ranch's drive onto the main road. "How was the drive-in last night?" She punched the gas, rocketing the little car toward Last Chance Creek or sudden death.

Rory had ridden with her enough that he should've been used to it, but he still gripped the armrest like it was the first time. "Why don't they put oh-shit handles in zippy little cars like this?"

Harry's responding laugh was worthy of a Disney villainess. "Quit deflecting and give me the deets on your date with Ivan."

He didn't bother to correct her terminology because they had been dating over the past month. They'd admitted it privately and to each other, but what exactly did that mean? Rory softened his gaze, and the world around him blurred as his eyes lost focus.

The sex was still off the charts but not as frantic as it had been when they'd first stopped fighting their mutual attraction for one another. They took their time, making sure every kiss and caress counted and savoring each embrace like it could be the last. The expiration date on their romance had once been a source of comfort, but now it felt like a curse. At least it did for Rory, and he was pretty sure Ivan felt the same way, but that was something neither of them had brought up. It wasn't as if they didn't talk. They spent most of their evenings chatting about everything and nothing at the same time. Ivan often whittled away at a block of wood, turning it into a piece of art. It might shock some people that Ivan's enormous hands could craft such intricate designs, but it didn't surprise Rory. Those same fingers skillfully brought him the most pleasure and comfort he'd ever known. As for Rory, he was relearning how to play his grandfather's guitar thanks to some YouTube videos he'd discovered. He'd play chords throughout his day and even in his dreams. More than once, he'd practiced on Ivan's bare skin, and Ivan's reaction each time had tugged on Rory's heartstrings. They'd acknowledged early on, even jokingly, that they were headed toward trouble, and Rory couldn't shake the feeling that the reckoning was closer than he liked. And fuck, he wasn't ready for it.

"Rory." Harry's voice nudged him from his thoughts.

He glanced over and studied her profile. Harry's brow was furrowed and her lips pinched instead of curving into her perpetual smile. "Sorry. I tuned out there for a second. What did you say?"

"I wanted to know how your date went at the drive-in since I haven't been to one of those in ages. Hell, I didn't even know there were any around here."

It wasn't exactly close, but that hadn't been the point of Rory's online search for a drive-in. Ivan's friends had gotten to take their dates to one in Kansas when he was in high school, but he never had. He'd always been the awkward third wheel who didn't know what to do when everyone around him started making out. Rory thought about cuddling with Ivan while the movie played out on the big screen. He'd learned Ivan was terrified of tornadoes but not until after they'd bought their tickets for a double screening of disaster movies. And, of course, *Twister* was the first film. Rory had always loved the movie, but Ivan had never seen it. Tornadoes and the devastation they caused hit differently when you grew up in Kansas.

"You're not in Kansas anymore," Rory had teased to lighten the mood. It had worked until the movie opened with a tornado that sucked a farmer out of the cellar in front of his family. He'd suggested they leave, but Ivan insisted they stay. Rory deployed distraction techniques later in the movie that involved a different type of sucking. Damn, he loved turning the prowling lion of a man into a purring, spoiled house cat. He could still see Ivan's eyes glittering with lust and feel his fingers digging into his scalp. *Swoon.* His next exhale came out as a long sigh.

"Wow," Harry teased. "That good, huh?"

"Scary good." And he hadn't meant the hand job Ivan had given him after he'd tucked his spent dick away.

"Why scary?"

"Well," Rory said, "this thing with Ivan is so damn good."

"You're right. That is awful."

Rory snorted. "It can't be real."

"Why not?" Harry asked.

"Just can't."

Harry snorted. "I call BS. What else do you have?"

Rory chuckled. "I need more reasons?"

She glanced over at him with a quirked brow. "So many more."

Rory practiced the breathing techniques he'd learned from Hope during his weekly session. He now attended her classes faithfully, but this Saturday would be an exception. It was all hands on deck at the Redemption Ridge dog adoption day at the feed mill. The ranch hosted the event once a month at various venues in Last Chance Creek, but this time they'd deployed Rory's new community outreach tactics. The crew would serve free burgers and hot dogs and give demonstrations on pet grooming and obedience training. Rory wanted it to be a smashing success, and he honestly could've used a little yoga before the event. They'd made multiple trips over with food and other items someone had forgotten. The last journey back to the ranch was to get cleaned up.

Once he felt calmer, Rory said, "Ivan is the first thing on my mind each morning. My eyes open, and I immediately start thinking of ways to make him smile and loosen up."

"You've almost dislodged the stick."

Rory chuckled and fought off a blush. He was intimately familiar with Ivan's ass, and he knew the big man didn't have a stick lodged up there, though Rory had thought that was the case when he'd arrived. "I've never really thought about anyone but myself before meeting Ivan. And…it's downright scary how much he's come to mean to me."

Harry reached over and placed her hand over Rory's. "Have you told Ivan any of this?"

Rory shook his head. "No way." The thought alone terrified him. "That isn't what he's looking for with me. We agreed to no strings." Rory sighed again. "This isn't what I was looking for either."

"Maybe what you wanted isn't what you needed. Ever consider the universe has bigger plans for you than you realize?"

Rory narrowed his eyes suspiciously. "Since when do you believe?" Hope frequently lamented her children's lack of spirituality.

"I'm more spiritual than I let on. I just like to irk Mama," Harry said. "Sometimes it's hard to recognize those miracles for yourself because you're too close to the situation. I've seen it with others—first with Kieran and Finley and now with you and Ivan." She glanced over at Rory and placed a finger over her lips. "Don't tell Mama. She'll never stop hounding me about it."

"Your secret is safe with me…as long as you promise not to hoodwink me into yoga or anything else again."

She extended her pinky toward him. "I promise."

Rory hooked his pinky around hers, and they shook on it. Harry returned her hand to the steering wheel, which only made him feel moderately safer because her lead foot was the real problem.

"Just think about what I said," Harry told Rory as she searched for a parking spot close to the feed store.

"I will." He'd shot himself in the foot plenty of times in the past and wasn't looking to repeat those mistakes with Ivan.

They ended up having to park two blocks away, but Rory could still hear the music thumping from the speakers and smell the sizzling meat on the grill. His stomach growled. A hundred or more people milled around the parking lot area sectioned off for the event.

"This is a great turnout," Harry said.

Rory had no idea what the previous adoption days had looked like, but he knew Harry wouldn't blow smoke up his ass.

Dylan and the crew had set up obstacle courses in the grassy areas for the dogs. They wanted to provide plenty of opportunities for people to interact with the ranch's permanent canine residents. That's where Patsy showed off her skills. There was also a mobile grooming van off to one side with a long line of customers and their pooches. The guys had pitched several tents for designated areas. The tent on the left provided shelter from the midday sun so the pups could meet prospective adopters. They'd designated the center tent as their information center. People could learn more about Redemption Ridge Rescues and complete an application to adopt a dog. The final tent on the right was where the aroma of delicious food was coming from. Hamburgers, hot dogs, and all the fixings took up one table. They'd loaded down two others next to it with every side dish and dessert a person could want. Rows of long rectangular folding tables and chairs provided a shaded place for people to sit and eat. The grill was a safe distance away from the tent, and that's where Dylan was, splitting his attention between cooking and answering questions about adoptions. He winked at Harry when he noticed them approaching.

"My man," Harry said proudly.

Rory thought the same thing when his gaze landed on Ivan. He was squatting in front of a toddler who was rocking pink overall shorts. Her blonde pigtails bounced every time she reached a chubby hand out to pet the young beagle Ivan cradled in his arms. The pup licked her arm, and the little girl squealed, giggled, and clapped her hands. Ivan's smile was so big and bright Rory tripped and nearly went face-first to the ground.

Harry laughed and hooked her arm through Rory's once he steadied himself. "Let's go say hello."

Ivan looked up as they approached, and his smile was even bigger and brighter as if someone had turned a dial up to eleven.

Harry leaned into Rory and said, "That smile isn't just for you. It exists because of you." *The Rory Effect.* That's what Ivan called it. "No matter what happens, I want you to remember this moment. Promise?"

Rory nodded because he was incapable of forming words. Harry led them toward the food tent. Whatever token protest Rory would've offered died when his stomach growled again. He loaded his plate with a cheeseburger and the trifecta of salads—potato, pasta, and macaroni. Perhaps macaroni was a pasta salad since elbow macaroni was technically a noodle. Rory followed Harry to an empty table at the far corner of the tent, and they dug in. "You're going to have to roll me back to the car," Rory said several minutes later.

Harry turned to him, and a tiny burp escaped instead of words. Her eyes went wide, and she slammed a hand over her mouth. Rory's breath hitched in his chest for a few seconds before he erupted in laughter. Harry narrowed her eyes and launched a potato chip at him.

"Sorry," Rory said, waving both hands. "I just…" He started a second peal of laughter. Harry was so petite and feminine that he just never expected that kind of noise to come from her.

Dylan sauntered over with a broad smile. Rory looked to see who'd taken his place and was surprised to see Cash there with a spatula in one hand and a spray bottle in the other. Dylan kissed the top of her head and bounced a curious look between Harry and Rory. "What's so funny over here?"

Rory pointed at Harry and said, "She—" His words died when he caught her mutinous expression.

"Absolutely nothing," Harry said.

The more indignant she became the funnier Rory found the entire situation. He doubled over, held his stomach, and tried his best to rein himself in. What was he? Twelve?

"Oh, for crying out loud," Harry hissed. "I opened my mouth to say something but a tiny burp escaped instead thanks to the cola."

"Was it tiny?" Dylan asked Rory.

Rory nodded. "Yeah, it was just so unlike her."

"She's let loose a few that rattled the roof," Dylan said.

Harry set her sandwich down and slowly turned to look up at her boyfriend. It wasn't quite an *Exorcist* moment because her head didn't rotate completely around, but it was damn close. Dylan's smile melted, and he swallowed hard.

"Oops," he mumbled. "This is where my inexperience shows."

"Are you making a joke about our age gap?"

Dylan's eyes widened comically. "No way. It took me two years to overcome said age gap. Months to get you to move in with me. I wouldn't blow it in one moment with a stupid remark like that." He cocked his head to the side. "Not intentionally at least." He reached over and brushed a red curl out of her face.

Harry let out a tiny snort that turned into a giggle. "I'm just messing with you." She smiled at Rory and said, "I belch and curse like a sailor sometimes."

Dylan cupped his mouth and leaned toward Rory. "And she farts in her sleep."

Harry's outraged gasp sounded genuine enough. She jumped up from her seat, and Dylan bolted, though Rory wasn't sure where the hell he planned to hide from her. Rory shook his head and watched their antics play out, but Dylan turned at the tent farthest away from Rory's seat, and Harry's pursuit took her out of sight too.

Rory tucked back into his food until he felt a shift in the air. When he looked up, Ivan was headed his way with a look of determination on his face that made Rory's insides quake.

"Wanna get out of here?" Ivan asked.

Figuring he should play a little hard to get, Rory said, "I just got here, and I'm hungry."

"I'll drive, you eat. Every person on the farm is here. We could really get up to some mischief."

Before Rory could probe further, a not-so-subtle groan caught his attention. Hushed murmurs that made him uneasy quickly followed. He turned his head to see the source of the disturbance and locked eyes on a large group from Salvation Anew marching on them like a thundercloud of doom. It disheartened Rory to see they'd brought their little kids with them. His mood plummeted even more when he saw that five reporters and their camera crews followed behind. They called out questions and filmed the entire thing.

"Oh no," Rory said.

Ivan whipped his head around and murmured, "Son of a bitch."

"Exactly," said the man at the next table.

Ivan apologized when he looked over and saw small children at his table.

"You've just expressed how most of us feel," the man said. "Now we can't adopt dogs and eat burgers without getting harassed."

Rory couldn't help wondering why the locals didn't do something about it if they were so unhappy. He didn't have time to bring it up because the army of stupid and their entourage of journalists had arrived, filling the tent and sucking out the oxygen and joy. Ivan removed his ball cap and placed it on Rory's head. Rory pulled it lower and lifted his head enough to see what was going on around them. The Salvation Anew members either looked vacuous and sedated or frenzied and high, though he suspected hate was their drug of choice.

"The time has come for the town of Last Chance Creek to cast out the miscreants living among them," said a white-haired man. He thought either his first or last name started with Samuel.

"Starting with you, old man," someone answered from the back of the tent. "Go back to where you came from."

A female follower gasped and clutched her throat as if she expected to find a strand of pearls there. Maybe they once graced her neck before she'd sold her soul to this devil. Harry and Rory had recently listened to a podcast about cult behaviors, and it was common for the followers to sell off their assets and give the proceeds to the leader. This lady was definitely missing her pearls, even if they were only figurative.

"I can tell you where you're headed if you don't stop associating with convicts and perverts. Listen to me, young man," the Samuel guy told the heckler. The old man's eyes glittered with malice as he launched into Bible verses, but a familiar female voice quickly cut him off.

"I find your selective preaching very offensive," Hope said. Rory turned in his chair and watched her progress as she walked toward the *church* leader. Several of the members huddled closer together and began murmuring as they kept a wary eye on Hope.

"That's the witch," one of the women said.

"The Bible contains many passages about love and acceptance. 'Dear friends, let us love one another, for love comes from God,'" Hope said. "Are you familiar with that passage?"

"Of course," the Samuel guy snapped. "I don't need to be lectured about the word of God from the likes of you."

"That's just what I'm talking about," Hope said. "You're not better than me. You're no more deserving of love, acceptance, and grace than anyone under this tent. These men that you disparage are worth a thousand of you."

The man vibrated with fury as he glared at Hope. Before he could respond, a startled cry rang out from under the tent, and Rory braced himself for some kind of attack. Moments later, a small, curly-haired dog came running through the crowd, dragging a pink leash. It wasn't one of the current Redemption Ridge Rescue dogs, but Ivan had told him that previous adopters liked to bring former program pooches back for a visit. One of the little girls from the fellowship squealed in delight and reached toward the dog, and the pup headed straight for her. The dour-faced man beside the little girl scrunched up his face in rage and stepped forward. Rory was out of the chair and launching himself toward the dog as the guy brought his leg back to kick the innocent animal. Rory managed to grip the pup's harness and lift her out of harm's way, but he wasn't fast enough to avoid the booted foot when it swung outward. Since Rory had been leaning down, the blow glanced off the side of his forehead, barely missing his temple.

He rose to his feet and staggered back as black dots swam in his vision. Rory was aware of shouting and lots of bodies surging around him, but he was too stunned to comprehend what was going on. He just cradled the little dog against his chest as he tried to regain his equilibrium.

"Rory! Rory! Rory!" His name was repeated over and over, but the voices were different. Some he deciphered quickly like those belonging to Hope and Harry, but others took a moment longer. Their voices changed from concerned to full-on panic.

"Rory! Ivan needs you!" Cash's voice cut through the chaos.

Rory whirled back around so fast it made him dizzy. He blinked to focus on the melee happening all around them. People were shoving one another and fists were flying, though no one from the ranch joined in the fray. Cash hollered again, and Rory turned toward his voice. Dylan, Rueben, and Cash were trying to restrain Ivan to keep him from going after the man who'd kicked Rory. The reporters and their cameramen were capturing every second of the struggle, and Rory knew this wouldn't go well.

Handing the trembling dog to Harry, Rory pushed through the crowd without a care for his safety. He dodged fists and bodies, throwing elbows when needed to get to his guy. Rory placed himself between Ivan and the man who'd kicked him. The guy from Salvation Anew taunted Ivan and tried to provoke him into attacking. Ivan's tense body strained against the tenuous hold his friends had on him. His muscles bulged, and his amber eyes glowed with the fierce loyalty he felt for Rory. He wouldn't be the reason Ivan's carefully reconstructed life went to hell.

"Ivan," Rory said calmly. He wasn't sure Ivan heard him over the shouting and whatever emotions were churning through his mind. He moved closer, placing his hands on Ivan's chest until he dropped his gaze to Rory. "There's my guy," he said with a smile. "I'm okay. Let's just leave."

"He can't get away with kicking you in the head," Ivan snapped. "He has to pay."

"And he will, but you won't be the one to mete out the punishment. That isn't who you are. Look at me," Rory said more firmly when Ivan shifted his gaze back to Rory's assailant. He placed a hand on Ivan's cheek and implored him to listen. "If you hit him, you'll play right into their hands. Don't give them the satisfaction." Rory called up every ounce of the sass he'd displayed during his first days on the ranch. "Take me home and give me satisfaction instead."

The glow in Ivan's eyes shifted from rage to passion, and he relaxed in his friends' grips. "I'm okay now," he told them. "You can let go." The guys' relief was palpable when they dropped their hands and Ivan only pulled Rory into his arms for a hug. "Let's give them something to pray about," he whispered in Rory's ear.

That was the only warning Rory got before Ivan cupped his head and planted a kiss on his lips. Apparently, a smooch between two men was the antidote for religious fanaticism. The fellowship grabbed their members and scampered from the tent. Everyone else cheered for their exit.

"And don't come back," said the man who'd spoken to Ivan and Rory before the fight broke out.

"Rory, do you want to press charges?" Cash asked.

The guy was already long gone, and they wouldn't have any luck getting his name out of the leader. "Nah, I'm not hurt."

"Let Rueben check you out. He has EMT training."

"Really?" Rory asked.

"From a previous life," Rue said with a sheepish grin.

Maybe that's how the guys thought of things—life before and after the ranch. Or maybe it was before and after jail. "You're all so interesting."

"Rory!" Harry came rushing over. "I returned the little dog to her owner. They're so grateful you intervened, but they feel awful you got hurt."

"It's no one's fault but the jerk who kicked me."

"Hold still," Rueben said and began his examination. "This reminds me of the time Finley nearly knocked himself out the day he met Kieran."

"Jesus, not this story again," Finley said from somewhere on Rory's right. He tried to look at him, but Rueben cradled his head in place.

"Struck by my beauty," Kieran said. "Then he got struck by a muck rake when he stepped on its tines. BAM! A direct hit to the forehead."

"Ouch," Rory said. "I don't feel so bad. Mine was a glancing blow at least."

"Excuse me, Mr. Snyder," said an unfamiliar female voice. Rory bit back a groan. He may not know who the woman was, but he knew what she wanted from him. His hat had gotten knocked off when the kick landed. Not that it was much of a disguise. With a sinking feeling in the pit of his stomach, he turned and faced a pretty brunette with a microphone in her hand. "I'm Kristin Rogers from Fox Fifteen. I'd like to ask you a few questions if you have a minute."

Fuck my life. "No comment."

chapter
NINETEEN

IVAN LACED HIS FINGERS THROUGH RORY'S AND TUGGED HIM AWAY from the encroaching reporters. Rory's method of soothing his rage had prevented Ivan from noticing the reporters moving on them like vultures on roadkill. *There's my guy.* That's what Rory had said. Had he meant it?

"Rory!" A different woman cried out. "I'm Anita from CBS Ten. I just have a few questions." Did she expect Rory to change his mind about an interview because she reported for a different affiliate?

"And I have no comment for you either," Rory called over his shoulder.

Ivan and Rory lengthened their strides, hoping to put more distance between themselves and the reporters. "Do you think you can jog? I'm parked behind the feed mill."

"That just makes us look guilty, and don't think for a minute because the reporters are wearing heels that they won't keep up with us. That business is brutal, and they've battled numerous competitors to land their positions. They'll stop at nothing to get their interviews."

Sure enough, the reporters kept pace with them and badgered Rory with questions, each one more intrusive than the last. They asked about his relationship with his father and even inquired about his boyfriend's identity. The reporters wanted to know if he was dating one of the farm felons. Farm felons? Did they think Cash was growing them on the ranch instead of providing the men a safe place to live and employment opportunities?

"They're just trying to provoke us," Rory said so quietly that Ivan barely heard him. "Don't give them anything."

Ivan reached into his pocket with his free hand to unlock the truck with the fob. The headlights flashed, and the horn let out two quick beeps. Ivan squeezed Rory's fingers and silently encouraged him to move even faster. "They won't block the truck, will they?"

"Probably."

Something landed with a resounding *splat* near them, and a startled gasp and "Oh shit" quickly followed. A second object exploded close enough to splatter moisture on the back of Ivan's shirt. He was momentarily confused until he caught the reflection of a light blue water balloon sailing through the air in the truck's passenger window. It hit the cameraman following Kristin, and he went down hard.

"Someone's throwing water balloons at us," Anita cried out.

Rory turned mischievous eyes on him just as Ivan wrenched his door open. They both knew who the culprit was. Ivan wasn't sure who'd suggested the water balloon toss for the kids, but he wanted to hug them.

"Get in. Save yourself," Ivan said dramatically before shutting Rory inside. Ivan whirled in time to see a green water balloon arcing toward the reporters, who kept running into one another in their frenzy to get away.

Ivan darted around the truck and climbed into the cab, so he didn't see which of them got pelted. He fired up the engine and pulled away without bothering to put his seat belt on. He maneuvered around the confused journalists and drove toward safety. As they neared the feed store, Ivan rolled down his window and pointed to Hope. She held the tennis ball launcher they used for doggie demonstrations in one hand and a hot pink water balloon with the other. She raised them over her head in victory when she saw the guys drive away from the chaos. Ivan beeped the horn twice to thank her and pulled on his seat belt.

Neither of them said a word until they were well outside Last Chance Creek.

"Pretty sure Hope has a water kink," Rory said.

Ivan laughed so hard he had to pull over. Rory volleyed his attention between the rear window and him.

"They could still pursue us," he said, sounding a little worried. "The big logo on the side of your truck tells them where we're headed."

Ivan sobered up. "We don't have to go back to the ranch. We could head out of town and get a hotel room tonight."

"And my troubles will still be waiting for me when I get back."

"*Our* troubles. You only saved a puppy, but I nearly pounded an allegedly pious man into a pulp. It took three men to hold me back."

"The letter for today is *P*, boys and girls," Rory said, his mouth creeping into a wry smile.

Ivan was happy for the display of humor and leaned forward to kiss him. "You called me your guy."

Rory went to work on his bottom lip. "Did I?"

"You did, and I think you know it." Ivan cupped his cheek. "The question is, did you mean it?"

Rory swallowed hard and darted his eyes to the rear window again. Ivan realized he was truly concerned about the reporters following them, so he merged onto the road. That didn't mean he would table the conversation for even a second. They'd been skirting around their feelings for a while, and it felt like a good time to get everything out in the open between them.

"I did." Rory's tone made it hard to figure out how he'd punctuated his response. It wasn't a period or a question mark.

"I hear an ellipsis followed by a *but*," Ivan said.

Rory snorted. "No, you didn't."

"Yep. I did. Dot, dot, dot *but*. That's exactly what I heard." Ivan was afraid to hear what followed the unspoken but.

"Ivan, I think I need to leave the ranch."

A weight settled in Ivan's chest, making it hard to breathe. He opened his mouth, but no words came out. Ivan forced himself to take a deep, steadying breath, but it barely eased the tension in his chest. Silence and stoicism would not get him what he wanted most in the world, and that was the man sitting beside him. "Leave? No! Why would you say that? How did you go from calling me your guy to telling me you're leaving me?"

"I'm not leaving *you*," Rory said. "I'm leading the reporters away from you and the ranch. They're about to turn your life upside down because of me."

Even though things had gone well during the interview with Roberto, the mere thought of another media intrusion by reporters who were looking for the juiciest details made Ivan queasy, but losing Rory would be so much worse. "No," Ivan pleaded. "There's got to be another way."

"We both knew our time together had an expiration date," Rory said. "It will take those journalists an hour at most to figure out your identity. They will rehash every trauma you've experienced without regard for your feelings or your family's. They will splash the story in every newspaper and highlight it in every broadcast simply because you got tangled up with me. Every good thing you've accomplished since your release will disappear, leaving only the ugly things behind. That's modern journalism for you. They don't care who they hurt as long as they break the story. Ivan, you could lose your clients. The negative press could destroy everything you're trying to build. That's the real Rory Effect." Rory's voice broke, and Ivan's heart fractured with it. But he wouldn't give up.

"No," Ivan said emphatically. "What you said could happen, but you've also taught me there are positive ways to put your message out into the world. We just have to fight harder and smarter than they do."

"What if the reporters don't stop with you? They will start digging to see who else lives on the ranch. Based on the tone of the questions back there, Salvation Anew has already done a good job of casting the ranch in a negative light. We don't know how much time those reporters have spent around that Samuel guy. The media could shine a spotlight on everything they deem a flaw or even newsworthy, whether factual or not. When I look around the ranch, all I see are amazing people who've formed a beautiful family. I couldn't bear to be the one to bring them pain."

Ivan reached over the console to take Rory's hand and was relieved when he rotated his wrist to lace their fingers together instead of pulling away. "You're part of our family, Rory. You don't get to decide what's best for the ranch without giving us a say."

A soft sob echoed in the cab, and Ivan glanced over to see fat tears spilling down Rory's face. Several years had passed since someone's tears cut him as deeply. Ivan had once broken his mother—his entire family—with his selfish acts. He'd never wanted to cause another person that kind of hurt again, so he'd kept people at bay, never letting them get too close. Until Rory. Their insane chemistry drew them together and kept them that way. Rory's willingness to be vulnerable with him is what broke through the barrier because it invited him to do the same. Rory whittled away at Ivan's resistance with every confession in the dark. Those revelations, no matter the size, opened Ivan's mind and heart. It wasn't enough to acknowledge that to himself, though.

"I see you," he said. "The real Rory Snyder."

"Yeah?" Rory asked. "What's he like?"

"Intelligent, curious, and thoughtful," Ivan said. "He's funny and incredibly sexy. He makes me want things I didn't think were possible. He's an amazing friend and a fabulous lover. He gives one hundred percent to every task, even when he isn't confident. He's fiercely protective of the people he loves and loyal to those who deserve his trust. Bakes a mean cookie too."

Rory snorted at the last part, but he tightened his grip on Ivan's hand.

"You make everyone around you better, Rory. My world is a brighter place because you're in it. I don't want an expiration date, and if I'm honest, I don't think I ever wanted one. The concept gave me the freedom to be a version of myself I'd only fantasized about until you arrived. And I want all the time you're willing to give me to explore the places our relationship could go."

"God, I want that too," Rory said. "No ellipsis or buts."

The pressure in Ivan's chest eased a little, even though he knew he wasn't out of the woods yet. "Stay with me. Let's figure this out. We are a family. Let's use your skills to go on the offensive. You've got a large following, and there's no one better to tell your story—our stories—than you."

Rory straightened in his seat. "What are you suggesting?"

Ivan laughed. "Fuck if I know. Brand management is your area of expertise, so manage it."

"Ivan, you're people, not a brand."

"I would think the approach is similar, but we don't need to get too far into the weeds right now. We need to sit down and discuss this with everyone else."

"If they want me to go, I will."

"They won't." Ivan had witnessed firsthand how much everyone cared about Rory.

Rory lifted his hand and kissed it, catching Ivan by surprise. "If they do, it won't be the end of us."

"Hell no, it won't."

They made it back to the ranch without Ivan spotting news vans in the rearview mirror. For all he knew, Hope was still pelting them with water balloons. The memory made Ivan smile, even with so much uncertainty hovering over them like angry storm clouds.

"I want to give my mom a call and warn her about what could come her way. You might want to do the same for Nick and your father."

Rory exhaled a long sigh. "I doubt my dad will take my call, and Nick is going to be pissed. He gave me two simple tasks any idiot should be able to follow—lie low and stay out of trouble. I failed epically."

"Nick won't be mad at you, even if he's annoyed by the circumstance. And as far as your dad goes, all you can do is try. It's his problem if he refuses to hear you out."

Rory squeezed his hand. "You're right."

When they got back to the old homestead, Ivan and Rory parted ways in the living room with a kiss. Rory retreated to his old room, and Ivan went upstairs. Both of them needed some privacy for the conversations they wanted to have.

Mary Gallagher answered on the second ring, her cheerful voice a balm to Ivan's soul. "Hello, Ivan. This is a pleasant surprise."

"Hi, Mama."

"What's wrong?" Just two words from him, and her tone went from cheerful church lady to mama bear.

It eased the tension in Ivan's chest a little and made it easier for him to tell her about recent events. He hated to dredge up reminders of the incident that had driven a wedge between them. Worse, he didn't want to instigate a conversation they should've had years ago when they'd mended their relationship. Instead of getting everything out in the open as he had with Innes, Ivan had taken a bury-it-in-the-past approach with his mother. But nothing stayed buried. Ever. Problems just grew bigger the longer they went ignored and became festering wounds on the soul. Bitterness was always bubbling just beneath the surface, looking for any opening to ooze out and taint even the best moments. The fresh slate Ivan had envisioned wasn't as squeaky clean as he forced himself to believe. He was asking Rory to take a leap of faith and stay with him. That meant Ivan had to be the best version of himself if they were to have a real chance. And he wanted that more than anything.

So Ivan didn't bother denying there was something wrong; he just dove in, starting with the most recent events and working his way backward. The words stumbled off his tongue at first, but then they sprang from his mouth as if his very existence depended on them arriving at their destination. And just maybe it did. Until Rory had arrived, Ivan thought he was doing pretty good. Sure, his love life was nonexistent, but it hadn't seemed to matter until that little spark plug lit up his soul like the Fourth of July.

He talked until his voice grew hoarse, only pausing when his mother said, "Darling, take a breath. I'm not going anywhere." Ivan took a few deep breaths. Then he continued his cleansing, not stopping until he reached thirteen-year-old Ivan, who'd bawled his eyes out in the shower and begged God to change him. By then, both of them were crying. Ivan knew it would be hard for his mom to hear how much he'd hated himself. It seemed necessary to make her understand how his shame and self-hatred had been brewing and festering until it exploded.

"I took that bat to my figurative self just as much as I did to that bully's car after he'd made my life and Curt's a living hell," Ivan said.

A broken sob came through their phone connection, and Ivan closed his eyes as he waited for his mother to say something more than encouragement to breathe. The only sounds he heard for several moments were her sniffling attempts to pull herself together. The pain was more than he could bear, and it drove Ivan to his feet where he paced the length of his bedroom.

"I'm sorry," they said at the same time.

Ivan jerked to a stop, his heart pounding in his chest. "Why are you sorry, Mama?"

"I should've realized that our silence about the things Pastor Vance said came across as acceptance or even approval. Your father and I never felt that way about homosexuality. We didn't understand it, but hate and fear didn't consume our hearts and minds. I didn't realize you were gay, Ivan. It just never occurred to me. I didn't know anyone who was gay, or at least I wasn't aware if I did. I just thought you were studious, dedicated to football and farming, and maybe a little…"

"Ugly?"

Mary gasped. "No. You've never been ugly a single day in your life. You were a tad uncomfortable in your own skin, but I just thought that was typical teenage angst. I didn't know that you hated something about yourself that neither you nor God could, or even should, change. No one should ever feel that way, and I'm so sorry I wasn't smarter. At a minimum, your father and I should've countered what the pastor said with messages of acceptance. But really, we should've left the church altogether. Not all congregations act that way. My new church hangs a Pride flag outside all year long. I regret not leaving Pastor Vance's church sooner, especially considering how they treated Innes, your father, and myself after it came out that you were gay. I've forgiven the ignorant things people have said to me, but you best believe I haven't forgotten a single word. If reporters want to harass me, they'll get the sound bites I should've given them years ago. I'll tell them where they can shove my Pride flag. Once they realize there's no drama to capture on film, they'll leave me alone. And if I can find a sympathetic journalist,

I might just grant them an interview. Maybe another parent can learn from my mistakes."

"Wow," Ivan said, unsure of what else to say. Then he realized it was an excellent opportunity to express his apologies too. "I'm sorry too because I regret not telling you and Dad that I was gay. You shouldn't have found out that way. I hate how the community treated you afterward. I'm sorry for the hurt I caused you."

"You have nothing to apologize for," Mary said.

"That's not true, Mama. Relationships are a two-way street. Everyone puts unrealistic expectations on themselves. What was it Dad always said? Hindsight is twenty-twenty."

Mary chuckled. "That was one of his favorites."

"But it's true. I think we need to forgive ourselves just as much as we need to forgive each other."

"Deal," Mary said. "I'm so proud of you."

"Thank you, Mama. That means a lot to me, and I'm proud of you too." Ivan took his first easy breath since she'd answered his call. Tears of joy filled his eyes. "I feel so much better."

"Oh, honey, I'm not done. I've saved the biggest apology for last. Are you ready?"

Ivan chuckled, and it sent the tears careening down his cheeks. He scrubbed a hand over his face to wipe them away, then glanced up to see Rory standing in the doorway, wearing a look of concern. Ivan waved him into the room and tucked Rory against his chest when he sat on the bed beside Ivan.

"I'm most sorry you couldn't trust me with your truth, and I'm beside myself with regret that you thought I wouldn't love the real you." Mary took a shaky breath. "Shame and regret over our own actions drove the wedge between us. I know your dad tried to explain this to you before he got sick, but I want to make sure you hear me and believe me."

"I'm listening, Mama."

"Of course we were shocked when you beat that car until it looked like a crushed Matchbox toy, but we internalized all the anger at ourselves. We had done so wrong by you, and I think a part of us believed you were better off without us. I failed you, Ivan, and instead of writing you a letter right away or visiting you in jail, I let my silence confirm the worst things you believed about yourself. Even after we reconnected, we never discussed what went wrong. I failed you there too. It was up to me to extend the olive branch, but I was just so scared to rock the fragile foundation we'd built."

"Me too," Ivan admitted. "I just buried my thoughts and feelings deep and built a wall to keep them contained." He tightened his arm around Rory and relished his warmth. "It took someone special to tear down my defenses and disrupt the soil of despair."

Rory sighed and nestled his head against Ivan's chest. "Such a poet."

"When are you going to bring Rory home to meet your family?" Mary asked.

Ivan stiffened in surprise. "How did—"

"Come on, Ivan. You talk more about him during our phone conversations than you do anyone else or your precious bees. So when do we get to meet this wall breaker and soil disrupter?"

"I'll bring him home to meet all of you whenever he's ready," Ivan replied.

Rory sat up and looked at Ivan. He pointed at himself and mouthed, "Me?"

Ivan nodded and smiled at his slack-jawed reaction, then he tucked Rory against his heart again. He continued talking to his mother for another fifteen minutes about the usual things they normally discussed. She caught him up on everything happening around the farm and updated him on baby Claire. She'd apparently discovered her feet and wanted to put everything in her mouth, including her chubby toes. They disconnected with heartfelt expressions of love and forgiveness, but the emotional gauntlet had exhausted Ivan.

Rory looked just as wrecked when he lifted his head from Ivan's chest.

"Any luck getting in touch with Nick or your father?"

"Nicky took my call but couldn't talk long. It sounded like he was in the middle of something important. He said I've done nothing wrong and anyone with a modicum of sense would see that. He offered to come get me." Ivan stiffened and held his breath while he waited for Rory to continue. "I told him I wasn't going anywhere and briefly shared your idea." Rory smiled impishly. "He said you're a genius, and I should listen to you."

"The genius part is debatable, but I appreciate the compliment," Ivan said. "What about your dad?"

Rory shook his head. "Got his voicemail and left a long message. I considered calling his campaign manager, but that guy is a dumbass. They should spin the fuck out of this in the best way, but that moron wants to ignore everything and hope it goes away." Rory sighed heavily. "I've decided how I want to handle the situation with my dad. It will be my peace offering and hopefully will invite further discussion between us like you've had with your mom." Rory sighed. "She sounds wonderful."

"She is. Maybe your dad will surprise you too."

"I hope so, and I truly mean it. Being here on the ranch has given me a lot of time to put things into perspective. There have been many instances that reminded me of the happier times I shared with my father, and I realize I haven't been completely fair. He handled his grief in the best way he knew how, and I need to forgive him whether or not he wants it."

Ivan pressed his lips against Rory's, tentatively at first but with growing fervor each second that passed. It would be so easy to close the door on the chaos and just enjoy the cocoon of happiness they'd created in Ivan's bedroom. That wasn't what they needed. Ivan allowed himself to bask in Rory's affection and enjoy his lush mouth and curious fingers until they reached the point of no return. Rory thought Ivan was reaching into his nightstand to retrieve the lube and groaned when he pulled out a notebook and pen instead.

"We have work to do first. Battle plan now. Get plowed by your farm felon later."

Rory snorted and slapped his arm. "Don't you ever belittle yourself like that again."

"You're right. I'm the felon foreman around these parts."

Rory groaned and sat up. He accepted the notebook and pen before pushing to his feet. "Come on. I need coffee for this. Maybe a cold shower first."

"Can I watch?" Ivan asked, waggling his brows to imitate Rory.

Catching on, Rory screwed his expression into the fiercest scowl. "No."

"Ah, come on," Ivan pleaded as he rose to his feet. "I could stand outside the door and you could narrate the activity."

Rory groaned and shook his head. "God, I was such a brat."

"You were, but I adored every second."

chapter

TWENTY

RORY STOOD AT THE HEAD OF THE DINING ROOM TABLE A FEW hours later and scanned the faces watching him with rapt attention. He'd made pitches to Snyder Global Industries' marketing execs several times before he left the company, but none of those presentations meant as much to him as this one did. He might share a name with the conglomerate's CEO, but the people on the ranch were his family just the same.

"For the first time since its inception, there will be no poker night on the ranch," Rory said. Tyler and Owen shared a confused look before giving him their attention again. "That's because we're facing a situation with much higher stakes than five-card stud." He let the words settle before he continued. "Salvation Anew's reign of terror stops today."

"Hell yeah," Dylan called out while a few others clapped.

Cash smiled encouragingly. "I'm excited to hear your new ideas."

"I admit I was ready to tuck tail and run as soon as we got back to the ranch. My instincts were to pull the media's focus away from all of you like a decoy. I still think I can pull it off and save you guys from a bunch of undeserved scrutiny." The vultures were already circling near the gates when the last of the crew had returned from the adoption day festivities.

"Boooo," Kieran called out. "We want what's behind door number two."

Rory snickered and shook his head. "Seriously, just give me a moment to be real with you and explain what we can expect if I stick around."

They quietly listened as Rory repeated what he'd said during the truck ride home. The guys had a right to know that the journalists would dig up their history and air it out to anyone watching the news or reading online. As for Ivan, he crossed his arms over his chest and glared from one person to the next, making his position crystal clear.

"If you want me to go, I'll go," Rory told them when he finished. "I will set myself up someplace accessible and pull their attention away from the ranch while we implement a second phase." Several people glanced over to take Ivan's measure but said nothing. "This decision isn't up to Ivan," Rory said. "Everyone gets a vote."

"All in favor of keeping Rory right here with us while we stick it to Salvation Anew say aye," Ivan said, sounding every bit the conqueror.

A raucous chorus of ayes echoed around the dining room, and every hand went up. Their support meant the world to Rory, and he felt the telltale sting in the back of his nose that warned of tears if he didn't get a grip on his emotions.

"Okay, then," Rory said. "The ayes have it." After another round of cheers, Rory strategically laid out his plan. "The only way to get rid of Salvation Anew is for the citizens of Last Chance Creek to run them out of here. Cut the head off the snake and the rest of it dies. The best way to do that is to take away that Samuel guy's power. If we can steal his thunder and expose the group's true character, he'll pull up stakes and seek attention elsewhere. We saw evidence that the community has grown tired of the group's nonsense, and we need to keep striking while the momentum is with us. People love a redemption story, so let's give it to them."

"Do you suggest more community events?" Cash asked.

"You could, but this kind of story has the potential to gain national attention. I say we take a broader approach." Encouraged by several nods from the group, Rory continued. "It's not enough to just tell people about our mission. We need to show them too. We start with an overhaul to the ranch's website. Then we could upload weekly webisodes or vlog posts or even create a YouTube channel and upload them there. I have a lot of experience doing this, so we can handle filming, editing, and content management in-house. The YouTube option is a way to monetize the videos, which would bring in additional funds for the ranch. You could even set up a nonprofit foundation to help the surrounding community with a portion of the proceeds."

"I like that idea a lot," Cash said.

Harry's eyes looked suspiciously moist as she smiled at him. "I think this is going to be fabulous."

"I'm glad you think so because you'd make a darling star in many of the vlog posts," Rory replied.

Harry placed her hand on her chest. "Me?"

"Absolutely. You could provide tips on gardening, composting, cooking, and cleaning. You could share recipes or advice for setting up a household schedule."

"You'd kill it," Rueben told her.

Harry reached over and squeezed his arm. "I'm flattered, and I'll do anything I can to help my guys."

"You're not the only one who is both easy on the eyes and brimming with talent. And the emphasis of these webisodes should be on the guys, their redemption stories, and the ranch's primary mission. You guys are the ones Salvation Anew is attacking, and you're the ones who will need to fight back." He went around the room and listed all the things he'd observed and admired from everyone around the table. The crew all downplayed their talents, but it didn't sway Rory. "We'll have videos on working with horses, dogs, and bees. You raise your own eggs, vegetables, and fruits. Rueben is wickedly talented with metalwork. And that's just scratching the surface. A wise man said it's time to go on the offense and stop letting Salvation Anew dictate the conversation about us."

Murmurs of agreement echoed around the table.

"I don't need everyone to commit right now. It's fine if you want to hang back and see how things go. I have a few videos of Ivan in Honeyland I could start with, and Harry and I could record some content in no time at all. I want to be clear that no one should feel pressured to do something that makes them uncomfortable. We want this to be fun and natural. Something forced will be seen as fake, and we don't want that. I'm only looking for volunteers. Who is interested, and what's the topic you'd like to cover for your first video?"

Every hand went up, and they all started talking at once. Ivan crooked his finger, and Rory leaned toward him. "You're about to get very, very busy."

"I'll never be too busy for you," Rory said and pressed a quick kiss to his lips. He straightened up, put pen to paper, then went around the room taking notes on everyone's vlog ideas. When he finished, there were at least twenty content suggestions and his pen was smoking. "We can put out videos less frequently in the beginning to gauge the response. Maybe we can include blooper reels during the busiest times on the ranch when shooting videos, even short ones, isn't convenient for everyone."

Rory opened the floor to questions and was relieved when they were the silly variety. Owen wanted to know who was in charge of hair and makeup, and he looked a little doubtful when Rory replied he was good at getting people ready for the camera. "I did my hair and makeup for my videos."

"I'll help with all the design elements wherever I can," Kieran said.

"Perfect," Rory said cheerfully. "I have some concepts I'd like to run by Cash for feedback. I'm leaning toward illustration-type marketing material for the web series. I know you're great at drawing realistic images and cartoony caricatures, but I'm thinking something a little in the middle. Just the right amount of realism in the drawings." He snapped his fingers. "Illustrations would make excellent graphics to put on mugs, tees, and stickers if we decide to have an online merch store."

"Oh, wow," Cash said. "I love the concept you've come up with and would love to see some sketches. How long have you been thinking about all this?"

Rory checked the time on his phone. "Two hours."

Cash gaped at him. "Two hours? I've had PR and marketing firms present less content when they've had weeks to work on their pitches."

"I had a lot of help," Rory said, gesturing to Ivan.

"By help, he means I made coffee, rubbed his shoulders, and listened to his ideas." Ivan grinned at Rory. "It's amazing to see his mind at work."

Rory fanned his face and said, "Stop, I'm blushing."

He fielded a few more questions and laughed when the comments turned to bets about whose videos would get more views. Rueben was the unanimous choice.

"Me?" he asked, sounding shocked.

"You're beautiful inside and out," Harry told him. "The camera will love your dark eyes and dimples."

"We'll have an entirely different swarm outside the gates," Owen added.

Rueben's cheeks turned pink. "My abuela will get a kick out of seeing me in videos." His family was due for a visit in a few months, and Rory was happy he'd get to meet the grandmother he spoke about all the time.

Rory called the meeting to a close when everyone's attention started to wane, but he and Kieran continued to work a little longer, bouncing ideas off each other. Rory could tell they were going to make a great team. He found Ivan reading in his favorite chair in the living room when he returned to the old homestead. He had one cat on each armrest and the third was sitting behind his head. All of them looked up when Rory came through the front door. Ivan set his book aside, stood up, and crossed the room to hug him.

"You looked exhausted."

Rory nodded and leaned into his embrace. "But exhilarated too." He pulled back and looked up at Ivan. "I want to do one more important thing before I tap out for the night. Will you help me?"

"Of course."

Rory smiled. "You don't even know what I want to do."

"Doesn't matter. If you need me, I'm there. How can I help?"

"Careful what you ask for. My presence on the ranch started out as a favor between Nick and Cash," Rory reminded him.

"You're not a favor, Rory. You're a gift."

Rory inhaled a shaky breath. "You keep talking like that, and I'll fail in my objective."

Ivan tilted his head to the side. "Would that be such a bad thing?"

"Waiting longer will lessen the impact. It might look more like damage control than the olive branch I intend it to be."

Awareness dawned in Ivan's eyes. "We best get to it then."

Rory had left all his major recording equipment and specialty makeup behind, but he wasn't worried about how he looked. He took a few minutes to tidy his hair and put some moisturizer on his skin to improve his complexion. He decided to film the most important video of his life in Ivan's comfy chair in the living room. The cozy fabric would feel like one of his hugs. The cats were still where Ivan left them, and he offered to shoo them away, but Rory declined. Their purring presence was relaxing. Tux crawled into his lap as if he knew Rory was anxious, and Rory stroked his sleek back a few times, then met Ivan's steady gaze and nodded.

"You'll count me down from five, then press Record," Rory told him.

Ivan sat on the matching ottoman and studied Rory's image on the phone. He scooted the foot stool back a few inches and reassessed. "That's better," he said. "I press Record on one or after one?"

"After one."

"So on zero," Ivan said, the earnest expression on his face endearing.

"Yeah, that works. Thanks for being my cameraman."

"At least I don't have to duck water balloons," Ivan replied. "Or run in high heels."

They shared a laugh, and it eased Rory's nerves. "Ready?" Rory asked him.

"I am. Are you?"

Rory nodded, and Ivan counted him down. He closed his eyes and took deep breaths to settle his racing heart and ease the tightness in his chest. When Ivan hit one, Rory opened his eyes and found himself in the perfect headspace. "Hey everyone, Rory here," he began. "I know

I've been absent for a few months. There's a ton of speculation floating around about me, and I've decided to clear the air the only way I know how. And that's to look you in the eye and speak my truth." He looked into the phone Ivan held steadily and bared his heart, speaking of loss, regrets, and redemption. Rory closed with his usual farewell, then sighed when Ivan stopped the recording. "What did you think?"

Ivan set the phone down and tugged Rory onto his lap. Wrapping his arm around his waist to hold Rory firmly in place, Ivan leaned in for a kiss. "I think you were wonderful," he said once they broke apart. "Honest and sincere. I want to believe your message will move your dad."

"That makes two of us," Rory said. "I don't expect it to fix all our problems, and certainly not overnight, but I hope it opens an honest dialogue between us." He inhaled deeply and exhaled slowly. "If not, I feel like I've put myself out there and attempted to set things right. I can't do this all by myself."

"No, you can't." Ivan kissed him again. "What's next?"

"I need to edit and upload the video to my site, then schedule the release for the morning. I'm going to send a copy to my dad first so he doesn't feel ambushed. It will give his campaign manager time to muster whatever damage control he thinks is necessary."

Rory hadn't been online all evening, but it was likely scenes from the pet adoption fiasco were already floating around. He'd have his work cut out for him. Rory yawned and leaned his forehead against Ivan's shoulder. It had been a very long day, and it wasn't over for him. He allowed himself a few minutes to bask in Ivan's warmth and affection before pushing himself to his feet.

"Can I borrow your laptop?"

"Of course," Ivan said.

Rory curled up on the couch and went to work on his edits while Ivan whittled in his chair with his snoozing cats. He typically loved the editing process, but he kept getting distracted by his yummy guy. It occurred to him that he'd declared his intentions earlier in the day, but Ivan hadn't reciprocated beyond insisting Rory stay at the ranch.

"Am I your guy?" Rory asked, breaking the silence.

Four heads snapped up and turned in his direction. The cats looked sleepy and curious while Ivan looked confused. A slow smile spread across his face, and he said, "I guess I didn't respond, huh?"

"Nope."

Ivan nodded toward the laptop. "Finish your editing, and I'll show you properly." The look in Ivan's eyes made it very clear the method he planned to use to deliver his message. Talk about incentive.

A little shiver of anticipation snaked its way down Rory's spine, and his commitment to finishing his project increased tenfold. When he finished, Rory slipped on Ivan's headphones and played the video from the beginning. He wasn't one hundred percent confident it would land the way he hoped, but it was worth a try. Rory emailed the video to his dad with a heartfelt message, knowing Charles wouldn't see it until the morning. There was no guarantee he'd even open it, especially if the pet adoption footage made Rory and the RR crew look bad.

He closed the laptop and turned his full attention to Ivan. "I'm ready for that demonstration."

Hand in hand, they went upstairs to their little haven where Ivan showed Rory where he belonged with every kiss, caress, and whispered endearment. As they lay tangled up in one another, Ivan pressed his lips to Rory's ear. "You are absolutely my guy."

The day had been one revelation and confession after another, but Rory wanted Ivan to know something else about him. He lay his head on Ivan's chest, listening to the comforting sound of Ivan's heartbeat.

"Confession," Rory said. "Snyder men are notoriously bad at showing their affection. I don't think I ever heard my father tell my mother he loved her."

"Yet you knew he was crazy about her," Ivan said.

"Head over heels. He lit up when she walked into the room." Rory sighed. "I see what you did there."

"Maybe your father saved the words for when they were alone. Maybe he showed the depth of his devotion in other ways. I don't think there's one way to love someone or accept love."

Rory sighed and rubbed his cheek against Ivan's chest hair. "My poet."

"You bring out the best in me."

Rory pressed a kiss to Ivan's chest and sighed happily. "We bring out the best in each other." He closed his eyes and drew a lazy heart on Ivan's sternum as sleep loomed ever so close.

"Rory," Ivan said.

"Hmmmm."

"I know you're going to be massively busy with this new project, but do you think you could schedule some time off in August? I would really like to take you home to meet my mama."

Tears filled Rory's eyes and stung the back of his nose. He was grateful for the dark that hid his reaction, but when he blinked, the tears spilled onto Ivan's chest. Strong but oh-so-gentle fingers eased into Rory's hair to rub his scalp. "Another first," Rory whispered.

"For me too."

"The beauty of my work is that I can film extra segments in advance and schedule their release. I would love to go to Kansas to meet your family."

They celebrated their plans with a kiss, and the kiss led to wandering hands, which led to lazy sex that took them late into the night. When Rory woke, the sun was high in the sky. He panicked until he saw a note on Ivan's empty pillow.

You worked late last night, and I thought you deserved to sleep in. I'll bring breakfast back to you. He'd drawn a heart before scrawling his name under it.

Rory went to the bathroom and brushed his teeth before returning to bed. Scruffy had sprawled in Ivan's spot during his absence, and the tabby cracked open one eye as if to warn Rory that it was too early for petting or cuddling. Fools would not be suffered lightly if they dared to touch the belly. Rory barely resisted the urge but reached for his phone instead.

His heart was in his throat when he checked his email to see if his father had responded. The same heart fell to his stomach when Rory only saw junk mail in his inbox. He blew out a harsh breath and set his phone down. One book he'd purchased from Hope's store talked about the benefits of a gratitude practice. No matter how difficult the situation a person found themselves in, there was always a reason to be grateful. Focusing on the positive helped shape a person's approach to the negative things that cropped up during each day.

"Today feels like a good day to start a gratitude practice," Rory said. Scruffy let out a *mrrrt* sound that sounded like a feline version of a derisive snort. "Okay, I'll say them to myself." Though he rolled over and sank his hand into the cat's soft fur. *I'm grateful for Ivan. I'm grateful for Ivan's cats. I'm grate—*

His borrowed phone rang before he could finish his third acknowledgment. This was the first call he'd received since Nick had handed it to him. Since his brother was the only contact programmed into it, just the phone number showed on the caller ID. Rory still recognized it.

With a slight shake in his voice, Rory said, "Hello."

"Hi, Rory, it's Dad. I got your email and video this morning. Is now an okay time to talk?"

"Now is perfect."

There was a slight pause then, Charles said, "I'm sorry I haven't called or texted you. I let Fossy convince me that no contact would be best for us until the frenzy died down." Fossy was Gene Foster, Charles's campaign manager. The man had managed several successful campaigns in the late eighties and nineties, but his approach was as outdated as his wardrobe. Rory had been skeptical of the man from the start, and the feeling had been mutual. It didn't surprise him at all that Fossy suggested radio silence where Rory was concerned. "But I don't want to go back to the way things used to be right after your mom died. You needed me, and I was too suffocated by my own grief to notice you were slipping away from me. After I saw your video, I realized the only way to attack this is together. And…I realized you were right about other things. I fired Fossy this morning, and I'm presently looking for a new campaign manager. Know anyone up for the job?" Charles didn't bother hiding the hopefulness in his voice.

Rory's chest swelled with love and pride for his father, but he had zero desire to assume campaign manager duties. He broke the news to his dad, but softened the rejection with, "I would be happy to interview some candidates with you and offer the odd piece of advice here and there." In fact, he already had someone in mind to manage Charles's campaign. He'd known several political science majors but only one was actively trying to gain a foothold in the uber competitive field. Rory passed the name on to his dad and promised to get his contact information after they hung up.

"You've got yourself a deal," Charles said. "Hey, Rory."

"Yeah?"

"Would you rather have an endless supply of ice cream or a plane ticket to anywhere in the world?"

Would You Rather was the game his mother had always played with him when tucking Rory into bed. He smiled because he knew they were going to be all right. "Is it my favorite flavor of ice cream or just ice cream in general?"

Charles laughed. "Your mama's influence is powerful. She never took my proposals at face value, always probing."

"You and Mom played this game?"

"Who do you think she learned it from?" Charles countered. "She was gun-shy after her failed marriage to Nick's father, and I had to take things slow. She assumed I was just another corporate asshole who wanted to sleep with the sexy new secretary. And lord, she was beautiful. Did you know I ran headfirst into a closed elevator door the first time I saw her?"

Rory laughed. "No, she never told me that. What happened after?"

"She just shook her head and walked away. It took me three more days to work up the courage to approach her at her desk. My dad had hired her to replace his secretary after she retired. Your grandfather opened up his office door and shooed me away like I was a fox in the henhouse. The only thing missing was a broom. Apparently, every single man—and probably some married ones too—had stopped by her desk during those first few days. They were interfering with her ability to work, and my dad wasn't having it. Your mama smiled up at me, albeit shyly, and I knew I couldn't give up." Rory heard the smile in his voice when he paused.

"I instituted Would You Rather as a way for her to ask me anything she wanted. Before email, we exchanged questions through interoffice mail. You don't know how much I looked forward to receiving her questions and answers. When it was my turn to ask questions, she always sent the slip of paper back with quantifying questions, just like you asked. Pretty sure I fell in love with her that first week. I never knew what I was missing in my life until your mama showed up. There were plenty of beautiful women in my inner circle, but not a single one of them ever baked me cookies just because."

Rory thought of the look on Ivan's face when he'd baked the kitchen sink cookies. Had that been the beginning of something more for them too?

"And it seems to me you might have met someone special on the ranch," Charles said. "Your video isn't the only one I've seen. Who's the big handsome fella that was going to tear that dog-kicking asshole limb from limb?"

Rory bit back a groan. He didn't want an internet search to ruin the mood he was in. "That's Ivan, Dad. Ivan Gallagher. You're probably going to read and see some things about him that concern you, but I promise you he's the most wonderful guy I've ever known."

"Believe it or not, I know how to cut through the crap and see to the heart of a man. I'm fully aware of Cash Sweeney's mission for Redemption Ridge, and I know he's not harboring dangerous people. Nicky wouldn't have dropped you off there if he was at all concerned about your safety. I promise not to read any of the nonsense written about Ivan, and I will go into meeting him with an open mind."

"You want to meet him?"

"He's an important part of your life now. Of course I want to meet him." Charles chuckled at Rory's silence. "Listen, I know what happens when a Snyder falls in love. I recognize that expression on your face when you looked into his eyes. Then there was that sweet 'There's my guy' comment."

"Do you think Mom knew how much we loved her?"

"I promise you she did. And I love you, Rory. I'm sorry I haven't reached out to you. I thought you were angry at me for disrupting your life with this campaign."

"And I've been too mortified that my past behaviors have caused you so much trouble."

"Rory, the only person who should be sorry is the one behind these personal attacks. And we're going to trap a rat and expose them to the world. Then we're going to pivot the conversation to the things our constituents really care about."

"Sounds like a good plan to me."

They continued talking for a long time. Ivan stopped by with breakfast at some point, then backed out of the room with the food. Rory didn't mind reheating it later. Talking to his dad was more important. Before they hung up, they agreed to play Would You Rather every morning, no matter where they were or what they had going on. Rory was already planning his first question for the following day. Rory and Charles had built a bridge back to one another that had been ravaged by grief, and while things weren't perfect between them, they had a path back to one another. For the first time since his mom died, Rory had hope he could have his family back. Well, his family by blood. He had found a different but equally important family at Redemption Ridge and in Ivan. And Rory would do everything he could to protect both of his families.

He found Ivan in the living room when he went downstairs. Instead of heading into the kitchen for something to eat, Rory plopped onto his lap like one of his cats. He rested his head on Ivan's shoulder, but neither man spoke for several minutes. There was beauty in the silence, something Rory had never experienced with anyone else. When he was ready, he shared the highlights of the conversation he'd had with his dad.

Afterward, Ivan kissed him tenderly and brushed a finger over his face. The moment felt right for a significant declaration.

"I'm going to keep you," Rory whispered as he stared into the eyes he adored so much.

"Not if I keep you first."

epilogue

VAN RAN HIS NOSE ALONG RORY'S NECK, PRESSING A KISS AGAINST his skin every few inches until he reached Rory's ear. "Do you know what today is?" he whispered.

Rory squirmed on the blanket Ivan had laid out in the center of his high school's football field. They'd been in his hometown for two wonderful weeks, giving his family the chance to fall for Rory the way Ivan had. He'd never brought a boyfriend home to meet them, so he hadn't been sure what to expect. His mama had been smitten with Rory from the start, and Innes, Sarah, and baby Claire were big fans too, but Ivan had to wrestle Rory away from his mother every time he turned around.

"Friday night," Rory finally said. "A few weeks from now, all the lights will be on in this stadium and people will fill the stands. Do you miss playing?"

"I played at the highest level I wanted to achieve," Ivan replied. "The camaraderie on the ranch surpasses the bonds I made playing football." Ivan tugged Rory's earlobe between his teeth and pulled until the flesh popped free. Rory shivered and wiggled closer to Ivan. "That wasn't the correct answer."

"What do I get if I guess correctly?" Rory asked.

"I won't pull out after I come, and you can fall asleep with my dick in your ass."

Rory turned his head in Ivan's direction so fast their foreheads nearly collided. Ivan was used to his reactions and had already eased back. "That's new." Once they stopped pretending their relationship was temporary, they got tested and tossed the condoms.

"A first," Ivan whispered.

The past two weeks had been a sequence of new experiences. To say he'd lived his best life was an understatement. In the quieter moments, Ivan could almost hear the younger version of himself weeping in jubilation at the love he'd found. Adult Ivan got to hold his boyfriend's hand in the center of town, make out with Rory in his old bedroom, and cop a feel under the football bleachers. Those weren't the moments both versions of Ivan loved the most, though. Earlier that morning, Mama had taken Ivan aside while Sarah distracted Rory and handed him a ring box.

"For when you're ready." Mama's voice was thick with tears, but her eyes had radiated joy. "You'll know when the time is right." The box contained his father's wedding band. "Your dad didn't want me to bury it with him. He wanted you to have it for your special someone so you'd know just how much he loved you."

Ivan struggled to find the words to express how much the gesture meant to him. He flipped open the box but only saw a gold blur through his tears. His father had never taken the ring off, even when wearing the band created a potential hazard on the farm. It was too easy to snag on machinery and lose a finger or worse. But the band represented something far more important to him than his safety. After falling in love with Rory, Ivan finally understood his dad's insistence on wearing it. The thing was, Ivan hadn't told Rory he loved him…yet. And since that seemed like the most important first experience, Ivan had brought Rory to this very special place.

Rory pursed his lips and narrowed his eyes in concentration. "August thirty-first."

Ivan kissed his pouty mouth. "Yes, but that wasn't the answer I was looking for."

"Damn it. I really want my prize." Rory chewed on his bottom lip, and Ivan was too charmed by his determination to intervene. "Let's see. It's the last night of our vacation because everyone knows travel days don't count."

They'd have over eight hours on the road, and Ivan couldn't agree more. "Also true, but still no."

"Damn."

Ivan was just as desperate to fall asleep with his dick inside Rory, so he gave him a hint. "An anniversary of sorts."

Rory's eyes widened, and he rolled onto his side to face Ivan. "We met five months ago today."

"Ding, ding, ding." Ivan's game show noise wasn't all that impressive, but Rory's smile was. "And I love you more and more with each new day."

"Damn, you're such a poet." Rory's eyes widened when Ivan's words fully penetrated. Ivan decided he loved those blue eyes in the moonlight best. Rory's mouth opened, shut, opened again, and then spread into a smile that was bright enough to make the moon jealous. "You love me," he whispered.

"I love you." Ivan kissed Rory's trembling lips. "I've never told a guy that before."

"Another first. I've never said it either," Rory said, still sounding dazed. Then he blinked the world back into focus and smiled again. "I love you, Ivan. So damn much." He expelled a long, shaky breath. "God, I've been holding that in for what seems like forever." Rory laughed and pressed a kiss to Ivan's mouth. "We're in love."

"We're in love," Ivan repeated.

Rory abruptly sat up, tilted his head back, and shouted, "We're in love!" The words bounced off the empty bleachers and made dogs in the nearby neighborhood bark.

Ivan snagged his arm, pulled him down, and rolled him onto his back. "We're in love."

The time to give Rory the ring would come later. Ivan had it tucked away in his luggage until he could place the precious symbol in his safe at the old homestead. Right now, he just wanted to give this moment the attention it deserved. They lay beneath the stars for a long time, kissing, touching, and repeating those three sacred words.

"Is your dick going to camp out in my ass right here in the football stadium?" Rory asked.

Ivan snorted. "We'll wait until we get back to my old bedroom."

Rory purred. "Dirty boy."

Ivan snorted. They'd crossed that milestone off the first night in town, albeit more quietly than the shenanigans they got up to at home. With Dylan and Finley officially moved out, they had the old homestead to themselves and took full advantage. "We better get going. We have a long drive tomorrow."

After one last kiss, they folded the blanket and headed for Ivan's truck. His childhood home was dark when they pulled in, but Ivan hadn't expected his mama to wait up. He knew damn well she'd get up early to make them breakfast before they hit the road. They tiptoed up to Ivan's old bedroom and they made sweet, quiet love and Ivan kept his promise. It felt like the next morning arrived as soon as Ivan closed his eyes, but the smells wafting up from the kitchen encouraged them to get up and moving.

The first thing he noticed when he came downstairs was that his mother had clipped his interview and photographs from Roberto's magazine and hung them on the refrigerator. "Where'd you get that?" Ivan asked.

"Rory brought me several copies so I could share them with special people."

Innes, Sarah, and Claire showed up too. His younger brother held up his copy. "I'm special people, and I'm going to hang your photo in the barn to scare the mice away."

Ivan responded to the comment with playful roughhousing that made baby Claire giggle and clap. "I took it easy on you in front of your kid," Ivan said as he straightened his hair.

They lingered over the meal longer than Ivan had planned. He wouldn't regret the extra time with his family, even if it meant they got caught up in heavy traffic during peak times.

"Uncle Ivan loves you so much," he told Claire as he cradled the sleeping baby against his chest. "She's going to have changed so much by the next time I get to see her." He looked up and met Innes's smug smile. Arrogant bastard knew he had the prettiest baby ever. Rory said all parents thought that, but Uncle Ivan's sweet little angel wore the true crown and carried the title. "Why don't you all come to the ranch after harvest? Maybe for Thanksgiving."

"That sounds like a lovely idea," Mama said.

Ivan gave the sleeping baby back to Sarah when he couldn't delay their departure any longer. The long hugs he shared with his family were bittersweet. As much as he hated to say goodbye, the ranch was his home now, and he was excited to get back. Ivan grinned when his mama held on to Rory even longer than her oldest child. He finally had to extricate himself from her clutches. It was the Rory Effect.

They took turns driving the eight hours back to the ranch. They stopped at a huge truck stop before leaving Kansas, and Rory had insisted on buying everyone silly souvenirs. Just before sundown, Ivan noticed a trio of hawks soaring in the air.

"I thought of a conversation thread for you and your dad," he told Rory.

"What's that?"

"Would you rather soar like a hawk or swim like a dolphin?"

"That's a good one," Rory said. He started to debate the merits of each, but Ivan reminded him to save that for his dad. The pair started each morning with a humorous debate, taking turns at posing the question. The change in Rory after reconnecting with his father had been immediate and beautiful. Rory vetted the new manager and had helped a little with Charles's new campaign strategy, and the latest poll numbers for Charles showed he'd made a good choice. As for the leaks, they miraculously stopped when Fossy left the campaign. They couldn't prove he was the source of the information or his motive for the betrayal, and they didn't dwell on it. The conversation had pivoted to the important issues facing Coloradans and that's what mattered most. Ivan hadn't met Charles in person, but they'd chatted over FaceTime a few times. On one occasion, Charles was trying to make one of Dinah's recipes while Rory mitigated the damage from a few hundred miles away.

Rory was a natural problem solver. His talent extended beyond marketing tactics and reading a room. His campaign to thwart Salvation Anew through positive community interaction was a massive undertaking, but so far, it had been a tremendous success. He'd created a softball team and a charitable foundation, and the Redemption Ridge YouTube channel was a smash hit. As they predicted, Rue and his blacksmithing received the thirstiest comments. Salvation Anew stopped making trouble in Last Chance Creek, at least for the time being. They hadn't packed up and moved on yet, so the community wasn't quite out of the woods. The group could be hunkering down while they planned something bigger, but they'd cross that road if they came to it.

They didn't turn the truck onto the ranch's long drive until nearly ten. There had been a terrible accident on the freeway that reduced traffic to a crawl for almost an hour. Rory had dozed off and on since surrendering the wheel to Ivan, but suddenly sat ramrod straight in his seat.

"That's Nick's car parked by Cash's truck," Rory said, pointing to a sleek black sedan. "His personal car. Something must be wrong."

"Or very, very right." Ivan waggled his brows. Rory had confessed he didn't think his brother's feelings for Cash were purely platonic.

Rory shook his head and vaulted out of the truck as soon as Ivan stopped. Ivan scrambled to catch up to him.

"You're just going to crash into the house like the Kool-Aid man?" Ivan asked.

Rory grinned at the reference but kept walking. "Something is wrong. I know it."

"Nick or Cash would've called you," Ivan countered.

"We were on our first vacation together, and I was meeting your family," Rory said. "They would've only called if it was life-threatening."

"All the more reason we should head home and visit in the morning," Ivan suggested.

"I won't be able to sleep until I know he's okay. Something has been off with Nick for a while."

Ivan hadn't seen him since he'd dropped Rory off at the ranch, but he had looked rough then. "Okay, but I'm not busting down Cash's bedroom door. If they're not in one of the gathering rooms or Cash's office, we're heading home and returning in the morning."

"Fine."

The front door wasn't locked, so they stepped into the foyer.

"Should we call out?" Rory asked.

Ivan shrugged. "This is your mission. I'm just along for the ride."

Rory sighed and rolled his eyes. "I don't want to wake them if they're sleeping, so we'll do a quick check in the main rooms."

The dining room, kitchen, and great room were empty, but a light spilled out from the library.

"I'm not sure about this," Ivan whispered.

"I don't hear any grunting, moaning, or other sexy sounds," Rory whispered back.

They eased down the hall and stopped outside the library. Nick lay on the sofa with his head in Cash's lap. His arm was in a sling, and he appeared to be sleeping. Cash must've been lost in thought because he just stared down at Nick while carding his fingers through Nick's hair. It would have been a gorgeous picture of domestic bliss if not for Nick's injury. Ivan expected Rory to rush in and demand to know what happened to his brother, but he eased back from the doorway and reached for Ivan's hand. They exited the house as quietly as they'd entered and walked back to the truck to get their luggage.

"I saw everything I needed to," Rory said with a soft smile.

The cats met them at the door with a chorus of outraged protests over their absence. "Shameless liars," Ivan said. Rueben had been taking care of the cats while they'd been away and had sent many photos and videos of the felines cuddling up to him and eating. Ivan picked Scruffy up and smiled when the old boy headbutted him repeatedly. "You got roasted chicken for lunch today." He glanced over at Rory and caught him staring. He usually reserved those heart eyes for watching Ivan with his niece. "What?"

Rory set Tux on the back of the sofa and said, "Those brawny arms were made to hold the people and things you love."

Ivan flexed a little just to watch Rory's eyes glaze over. Scruffy must've sensed a shift in the air because he jumped down and fled. "You were made for me to love, hold, honor, and cherish."

Rory sighed. "My poet." His eyes rounded slightly as he recognized snippets of the wedding vows Ivan planned to exchange with him someday. Ivan opened his arms, and Rory stepped into his embrace.

"I love you," Rory said.

"Love you too."

Love and a happily ever after were things Ivan never thought he could have, but the Rory Effect made him believe anything was possible.

The End!

I hope you're excited for more from the Redemption Ridge guys. Cash will find his happily ever after in Saints Like Him. You can preorder the book right now!
mybook.to/Saints_Like_Him

Stay tuned and stay connected and find me on all the socials at
linktr.ee/AimeeNicoleWalker

Want to be the first to know about my book releases and have access to extra content? You can sign up for my newsletter here:
eepurl.com/dlhPYj

My favorite place to hang out and chat with my readers is my Facebook group. Would you like to be a member of Aimee's Dye Hards? We'd love to have you! Go here:
www.facebook.com/groups/AimeesDyeHards

other books by
AIMEE NICOLE WALKER

Curl Up and Dye Mysteries
Dyeing to be Loved
Something to Dye For
Dyed and Gone to Heaven
I Do, or Dye Trying
A Dye Hard Holiday
Ride or Dye
Curl Up and Dye Box Set

Road to Blissville Series
Unscripted Love
Someone to Call My Own
Nobody's Prince Charming
This Time Around
Smoke in the Mirror
Inside Out
Prescription for Love

Welcome to Blissville Collection (Both M/M Blissville series)
Volume One
Volume Two

The Lady is Mine Series
The Lady is a Thief
The Lady Stole My Heart

Queen City Rogue Series
Broken Halos
Wicked Games
Beautiful Trauma

Zero Hour Series
Ground Zero
Devil's Hour
Zero Divergence
Zero Hour Box Set

Sawyer and Royce: Matrimony and Mayhem
The Magnolia Murders
Marriage is Murder
Killer Honeymoon

Sinister in Savannah Series
Ride the Lightning
Mr. Perfect
Pretty Poison
Sinister in Savannah Box Set

Savannah Universe Standalone Books
Invisible Strings
Bad at Love
About Last Night
Just Say When

Standalone Novels
Second Wind

Fated Hearts Series
Chasing Mr. Wright
Rhythm of Us
Surrender Your Heart
Perfect Fit

Redemption Ridge Series
Guys Like Him

Coauthored with Nicholas Bella
Undisputed
Circle of Darkness (Genesis Circle, Book 1)
Circle of Trust (Genesis Circle, Book 2)

acknowledgments

Many, many thanks to Susie Selva for her incredibly thorough edits and to Lori Parks for her keen eye during proofreading. These ladies are consummate professionals and are an absolute joy to work with. And much love to Jay Aheer and Wander Aguiar for this gorgeous cover and to Stacey Ryan Blake for her stunning interior designs. All of you make my books sparkle and shine so beautifully—inside and out. I thank my lucky stars that I get to work with such wonderfully talented people.

Sending much love to Melinda James Rueter and Racheal Yunk for bravely reading my rough drafts and providing priceless feedback. And I don't know where I'd be without CC Bell, my amazing personal assistant, who brings organization and so much joy into my life. Love you, ladies!

xoxo
Aimee

about

AIMEE NICOLE WALKER

Ever since she was a little girl, Aimee Nicole Walker entertained herself with stories that popped into her head. Now she gets paid to tell those stories to other people. She wears many titles—wife, mom, and animal lover are just a few of them. Her absolute favorite title is champion of the happily ever after. Love inspires everything she does, music keeps her sane, and coffee is the magic elixir that fuels her day.

She'd love to hear from you.

Want to connect? All her links are in one nifty location. Go here:
linktr.ee/AimeeNicoleWalker